THE BURIED

NO LIGHT

NO CONTACT

NOWHERE TO HIDE

THE BURIED

Author of RATED

MELISSA GREY

Scholastic Press

New York

Library of Congress Cataloging-in-Publication data available

ISBN 978-1-338-62930-9

1 2021

Printed in the U.S.A.   23

First edition, September 2021

Book design by Christopher Stengel

TO THE PEOPLE (AND
CATS) WHO HELPED ME
THROUGH THESE
TRYING TIMES

—M.G.

WE SHALL MEET IN THE PLACE
WHERE THERE IS NO DARKNESS.

—GEORGE ORWELL, *1984*

PROLOGUE

THE BLESSED DARK

"What the light gives . . . the light can also take away."

That was how every morning began in the bunker.

The three families gathered in the common area. It multi-tasked harder than any other room, serving as a play area, relaxation space, and town hall for its populace of twelve. The bunker itself—a massive, labyrinthine affair with twisting corridors that led to nowhere and doors that opened into solid stone walls—provided more than enough square footage for each soul who lived in it to lose themselves. But the common area felt like the safest, sanest space within its confines. The walls were decorated with the artwork of a generation of children, and a large board detailing chores occupied half the far wall. The chore board—such a mundane, quotidian scrap of life—stood at their backs, guarding the spectacle before it with silent detachment.

At the front of the room, on a dais raised a few inches off the ground, stood an almost frighteningly thin woman. The loose crimson gown she wore hung off her slender form. The belt that cinched all that fabric tight at her waist only served to accentuate the protruding shoulder blades and sharp cut of her collarbone. Wiry muscle corded over the jagged edges of her skeleton, sparing her from looking truly malnourished. Her hollow cheeks glowed with conviction, making her strikingly beautiful in that moment.

"It is our most fundamental truth," Dr. Moran said, her deep dark eyes settling on each person in front of her before drifting to the glass dome on the dais's pedestal. "Light gives us life. It nourishes our plants and warms our earth."

One long-fingered hand settled atop the glass dome. Its presence seemed to agitate the dome's occupant, a solitary fat beetle. Where the beetle had come from no one really knew. The good doctor seemed to have creatures of its sort in ample supply, always ready for a demonstration. The beetle's antennae twitched, rubbing against its glass prison as if testing for escape routes.

There were none.

"But we must never forget the danger the light presents to us." Moran's other hand drifted, slowly, gracefully, toward a switch to her left. The tips of her fingers brushed it, and her audience of twelve held its breath.

"The light gives us life . . ."

Her grip on the switch tightened.

"And the light takes it away."

She rotated her hand, cranking the switch counterclockwise.

The sound came first, a mechanical whirring as a series of mirrors rotated into place. Each mirror reflected a stolen ray of sunlight, carrying it down, deep into the earth, beneath layers and layers of soil and stone, until it reached the glass dome.

The beetle twitched at first as the light hit it. Then it writhed as the light intensified into a single, unforgiving beam. Time stretched lugubriously before them as they watched the beetle's final throes. Eventually, the insect stopped moving, its body limp and smoking beneath the glass.

Silence, as deep and impenetrable as the ground bearing down on the bunker, filled the room.

Then, Dr. Moran looked up.

She smiled.

One by one, nearly every member of her audience smiled too, shakily at first, then with relief. They were down here. The sun was all the way up there, where it couldn't hurt them. They were protected. They were safe.

Moran cranked the switch in the opposite direction, sealing off the reflected light. The room lapsed once more into the soft, artificial glow of the light fixtures cleverly nestled in the walls.

"And in this," Moran said, her voice filling that thick silence with a resonance at odds with her frail form, "we are reminded of the mercy of the blessed dark."

CHAPTER 1

SASH

The nightmare was never quite the same.

There were always differences. Sometimes they were small things. A watch on the left hand instead of the right. The color of a shirt. The absence of a necktie. But the meat of the dream—that never changed. It was the same, every night it came to visit.

Sash hovered in that space between sleep and waking. She could feel the weight of the blanket against her legs. It was bunched up around her knees, as it usually was when the nightmare struck. Her grandmother said she kicked in her sleep, rhythmically, like she was trying to run to something. Or away.

It was always away.

Her limbs were heavy. Useless. Whatever residual energy they'd contained when she'd gone to bed had been wasted during the night as she tried to outrun a memory.

It helped if she kept her breathing methodical. In and out. In and out. Each inhalation equal to every exhalation. A nice, even four seconds each way. Her heart rate slowed as her body began to wake.

The dream sloughed off her like mud, clinging to her skin with stubborn refusal to let go. Bits and pieces remained. The sense memory of her arm burning. The sound of an explosion so loud that it blew out the hearing in her left ear. The right one was fine. She'd had that ear pressed to her father's chest when it happened.

It.

That was how she always thought of it. An event that was not to be named. Giving it a name would make it seem even more horrible than it was. She refused to call it what most of the adults down here did. The Cataclysm. That was a stupid name. Sash hated the way it felt in her mouth when she said it, all jagged edges and burnt metal.

Better in her opinion to just refer to it as . . . it. *It* took out the sting. *It* dulled the power. *It* made it seem inconsequential. Small. Just two tiny letters.

Something soft and fuzzy slammed into her face. It was a cushioned, gentle slam, but a slam nonetheless. It was enough to jolt her awake.

Thank God.

The dream had relinquished its hold on her for one more day. It would come back. It always did. But now, at least, she was free.

Opening her eyes, Sash reached for the soft fuzzy thing that had spared her slumbering subconscious mind further torment.

It was a little pig, once a vibrant pink bordering on lavender, now a sad grayish shade of dusty mauve. One of the pig's eyes was missing, replaced with a crosshatched section of black thread. It glared at her like an empty socket.

She had loved that stupid pig. She still did, though she pretended not to. She was too old for little pigs.

"Wake up," said a harsh voice from the doorway.

Sash considered not doing that at all. She could pull the covers over her head and go back to sleep. The nightmare never came back twice in the same night. Or morning, rather.

But Misha didn't like to be kept waiting. Her brother was a stickler for the rules and acted like it was his personal responsibility to make sure Sash followed them as slavishly as he did.

"Go away," she mumbled.

Misha snorted. "If you miss breakfast, don't come crying to me."

"I have never once in my life gone crying to you," Sash muttered, but it was too late. Misha and his unearned sense of superiority had already departed, off to choke down the same sad gruel they ate every day. It was also a bit of a lie, so it was for the best that he wasn't around to hear it. She and Nastia had clung to Misha a lot as children, especially during those first few months in the bunker. But things changed, as things were wont to do. Misha changed. Sash changed. They all did. The bunker, however, remained the same.

Her arm twitched as sensations—real ones, not dream ones—began to flood back to her body. Painful tingling ran down the length of her arm, from her shoulder to the tips of her fingers. She'd slept on it funny. She usually did. The bunks weren't built for comfort. They had been constructed with necessity in mind, not luxury. There were more than enough to fit them all without having to double down—for that much Sash was grateful—but she was still sharing a room with her younger sister, older brother, mother, and grandmother. Unacceptable at the age of seventeen if anyone asked her, which no one ever did. And even if someone did ask, what could she say? What could she do? She wasn't going to move out and go to college and strike off on her own. There was nowhere to go. No colleges left to attend. There was just the bunker and everyone in it.

She sighed into her pillow, moving her arm in teeny-tiny increments to keep the painful tingling to a minimum. If she jolted out of bed too fast, it would only hurt more.

If she kept her eyes closed, she could at least pretend to be somewhere else. Anywhere, really. She wasn't picky. There was an old atlas—dated 1987—in the small, sad stack of books they called a library in the small, sad space they called a classroom. She had pored over that atlas so often she could probably draw every single map from memory. The names and shapes of each place were emblazoned in her mind, but they were about as real to her as Narnia or Atlantis. Fictional realities she would never know. She'd always wondered about Arizona though. That was a fun name. Arizona.

"Alexandra!"

Her mother's voice rang through the room like a reverberating cannon. The walls were metal, riveted together in great big sheets, perfect for bouncing sound around a confined space like a demented pinball.

"I'm coming!" Sash kicked the blanket to the foot of the bed. Pins and needles pricked at her limbs as she stood, dulling the cold sensation of the floor beneath her feet. Misha would have a fit later if she didn't make her bed with military precision. So she didn't make the bed. There wasn't a lot to do in the bunker, and she had to make her own fun where she could.

And besides, the gruel might be boring and sad, but her stomach was rumbling. She would choke it down for one more day. And then another. And another. And another, until they ran out and died of starvation, hiding underground like a pack of terrified rats, huddled together in the comforting darkness, away from the sun.

"And don't call me Alexandra!"

She tugged on her sweats with more force than she should have. They were flimsy things. The holes in the knees had been patched up countless times. The cotton there was a completely different color than the rest.

They hadn't been hers originally. Nothing she wore these days was.

She had grown out of the clothes she'd been wearing the day they entered the bunker within the first year. Maybe less. Now, she wore her mother's old clothing. Her mother wore the clothes they'd found in the bunker, packed away for a family who had never had the chance to wear them.

Sash caught sight of the letters stamped into the metal wall paneling near the floor.

CPM INDUSTRIES

Everything in the bunker was emblazoned with those words.

Sash didn't know what industry—or industries—had been involved in the construction of the bunker, but she knew she hated the sight of those words.

Every day she saw them was another day spent here, trapped

in these walls. Buried, like a forgotten memory. Like a corpse just waiting for death to catch up.

"I told your mother not to pick that name for you," said a gravelly voice from the doorway.

Sash glanced up to find her grandmother standing at the threshold, gray eyes crinkled with mischief. Deep wrinkles were etched into her face from frowning and smiling, two things she managed to do in equal measure, even down here. Not even a world-ending catastrophe would steal the slightest bit from Olga Eremenko's expressive nature. She'd used it to light up the stage of opera houses from Moscow to Paris. Now, all she was lighting up was a tiny corner of space they'd carved out of the earth. A pit of survival.

"From the minute I felt you kick in her belly, I knew you weren't an Alexandra. But she insisted."

"Well, Babulya," Sash said, tugging the sweatpants up as she stood. "I'm a Sash now."

She was the only one who called Olga Babulya. Her siblings would call their grandmother Baba Olya but Babulya was Sash's thing. To the non-Eremenko kids, the eldest of their clan was Grandma Olga. It was nice, having a thing that was theirs and theirs alone. The Russian diminutives were reminders of the world outside—of the world Before—and the cultures that once made it whole.

"Alexandra!" Misha bellowed down the hallway.

"I'm coming! And my name is Sash!" She tightened the drawstring on the pants. They were slightly too loose. Her mother had worn them as warm-ups before ballet class, back when she'd been on tour with the Bolshoi. Those words and the image they painted might as well have been fiction to Sash.

She couldn't picture it. A stage. The sets. A theater packed with hundreds, maybe thousands, of people.

Unthinkable, that was.

Sash went for the door, but Olga stood her ground. "I don't trust that boy as far as I can throw him." She held out her thin arms, nearly skeletal, as if to display what a short distance that would be.

"Trust who? Misha?"

Olga made a low, affirmative noise in the back of her throat. "I have seen his type. All bluster. Wants to feel important. Will sell out his own babulya for a pat on the head from the Kremlin."

"We're not in Russia anymore," Sash said. And then, as a mumbled addendum, "Maybe no one's in Russia anymore."

Olga smirked. "A tyrant is a tyrant, no matter the borders." She patted Sash on the arm. Even beneath the layers of cotton (Sash's T-shirt) and leather (Olga's gloves), the momentary touch sent a thrill through Sash. It was a rare thing. Delightful for its paucity.

Touch, the words replayed in her head, so many times she had heard them, *was a dangerous thing.*

"I'll be fine, Babulya." Sash took her grandmother's arm—oh, how the doctor would hate to see it—and led her out of the room they all shared. "Misha may be a bully, but I can take care of myself."

Olga laughed, low and soft. "Of that, I have no doubt." She winked, sly, conspiratorial. "Sash."

CHAPTER 2
YUNA

Yuna picked up a plate—metal, with a red painted bottom though she preferred the blue-and-white ones. Her mother had told her to stop picking through the stack of tin plates for the blue-and-white ones years ago, because it was both rude and unsanitary. Yuna didn't see why. She wasn't depriving anyone else of plates. The blue-and-white ones just made her happy. They were the only ones with a pattern painted on the underside. Blue and white flowers, like the big porcelain bowl that had sat at the center of the dinner table in their home, back when they had one. Those little flowers reminded her of a time before the bunker and the tin plates and the powdered gruel brought to awful gelatinous life by the application of boiling water.

Gross, whispered a voice at the back of Yuna's head.

I know, she agreed. Quietly. Internally.

She waited patiently as her parents filled their own bowls from the steaming vat resting on the metal table.

Behind her, shuffling feet and a yawn alerted Yuna to Sash's presence before her mumbled "G'morning" could.

Yuna turned to find the other girl stretching, her faded green sweatshirt riding up on her stomach. It wasn't cold enough in the bunker to merit a sweater, but Sash always wore long sleeves. Yuna knew why—the scars. She'd seen them before. Everyone had. There were no secrets in a shared space as small as theirs. There was an unspoken agreement that everyone looked the other way when someone clearly needed a moment of anonymity, even if it was only pretend. So Yuna never asked about them. They were Sash's scars. Sash's story. She'd share it with Yuna, or she wouldn't. Pushing would be rude. And maybe even unsanitary, but in just, like, an emotional way.

"Good morning to you," Yuna said, watching with envy as Sash plucked a blue-and-white plate from the stack.

Sash's hair was up in the kind of loose, wild bun Yuna could never hope to achieve. Her own hair was too straight, too fine to hold such a carefree shape. Yuna's neat, precise bun with nary a hair out of place was the opposite of carefree. It had many cares.

Sash looked at the plate in her hands. Then at the one in Yuna's.

She didn't even say anything. She just reached out and plucked the red plate from Yuna's grasp and offered her the blue-and-white one with the little flowers painted on the bottom.

Yuna smiled at it. It was a stupid thing, but it made her happy. Little flowers. Imagine that. "Thanks."

"Don't mention it," Sash said.

"I *shall* mention it, and you *shan't* stop me."

Sash rolled her eyes, but she was smiling too, and that made Yuna almost as happy as the stupid little flowers on the plate.

Just tell her you like her, that voice said again. It was a soft, cajoling voice. Male. Half-forgotten. But still there. Always there. That voice went with her everywhere. Ever since that day when it was silenced forever. She'd tried to tell her parents, many moons ago, that she still heard him. Junsu. Her brother. But her mother's palm cracking across her face had dissuaded Yuna from ever trying again. No one believed her anyway. But it was fine. Junsu's voice could be her little secret.

"Yuna," her mother snapped. "People are waiting."

With a little start, Yuna turned away from Sash and dutifully spooned a serving of gruel—calling it oatmeal would have been an insult to oats everywhere, if there were any left topside— onto her plate. The plates were curved at the edges, sort of like wide, shallow bowls. Good for multitasking a variety of edible goods, though variety wasn't exactly what their daily cuisine was known for.

Breakfast in the bunker wasn't quite the same every day, but it was close. Their menu was limited:

- Powdered porridge of dubious origin and absolutely no flavor.

- Canned goods until they ran out.

- Greens from the "garden." (Honestly, calling it a garden seemed a bit odd to Yuna considering it was underground, spread out under ultraviolet lights meant to mimic the sun. But no one had asked for her opinion on that particular issue, and so she had never seen fit to provide it.)

- Freshly filtered water, occasionally punched up with fruit juice concentrate. All that was left was pear, which Yuna didn't really like. Orange had been the first to go, maybe six years ago? Seven? Yuna had lost count. Apple was next. Then cranberry. The blueberry had been odd but enjoyable in its own way, but that had run out last week. So now it was pear or nothing. Yuna went for the pear. Plain water first thing in the morning upset her stomach.

- Some kind of potted meat product. That was literally what it said on the tin: potted meat product. When she had asked her father what was in it, he had twisted his mouth into a pained grimace and said, "You don't want to know." She never asked again.

- And sometimes eggs. They had a few chickens that still produced eggs, but those were usually saved for dinner. Moran had ideas about higher protein foods being better digested at night. Yuna had no idea if it was true or not.

"Yuna." Her mother's voice had always been sharp. Nine years, eleven months, and eight days underground had not softened it in the slightest.

With a smile, Yuna cradled her bowl in one hand and waved at Sash with the other. "See you at school."

They'd started saying it as a joke. And then it stuck. The joke was that school would happen in the same place breakfast happened. It was also in the same place family meetings happened and announcements happened and daily prayer happened. Right here, in this room. All that changed was the arrangement of the tables.

Sash snorted, which was about as wordy as she usually was in the mornings. That was fine with Yuna. Some people were morning people. Sash was not one of those people. Though morning was a nebulous thing when you never saw the sun actually rise. Dawn was, at best, metaphorical. The track lighting that ran the length of the bunker did a poor job of imitating it, but beggars and choosers and some such.

Yuna's parents were waiting for her when she took up her normal seat at their end of the table. The tables were metal, like the tin plates, and reminded Yuna vaguely of cafeteria tables in TV shows she used to watch Before. She'd gone to school herself, briefly, but it had been a small building attached to the church in town. It didn't have tables like this. Kids ate on long wooden picnic tables outside if the weather was nice, but inside at their desks if it rained.

But that was a long time ago. Things were different now.

Yuna picked up her spoon and almost dropped it immediately at the death glare her mother shot her.

"We pray first," came the expected hiss.

Her father, meanwhile, ignored them both. He blew on his coffee. Not sipping it, mind. Just blowing on it to cool it down. The tin cups had a habit of keeping it too hot to drink for quite some time.

"I know," Yuna mumbled, laying the spoon down quietly on her napkin. She hadn't planned on eating before they said prayer. She knew better than that. It was just that she liked having the spoon on the other side of the bowl from where it was usually placed by whoever was on table-setting duty that morning—it was Tuesday, so the Correas. Wednesday was the Shin family's turn. Being left-handed wasn't a sin.

But her mother glared at her all the same. Glaring was Lim Hyojin's favorite pastime, and she excelled at it. She could teach a master class on it, just like Sash's mother taught them ballet the way only a former dancer with the Bolshoi possibly could. With expert proficiency. The glare hadn't always been quite so damning. Yuna remembered her mother being—not softer, really, but less brittle. She used to hum songs from the radio under her breath while packing Yuna's lunch box. The finishing touch was always the inclusion of a cute drawing on those yellow sticky notes affixed to the box. Mostly they were animals doing things animals shouldn't, like wearing sweaters or driving cars or baking cakes. There were no sticky notes in the bunker. No packed lunches. No radios. No songs.

She missed that version of her mother. Another thought she kept to herself. Airing it wouldn't accomplish anything.

"Friends." Dr. Moran's voice carried over the soft sounds of people settling in. Tin bowls coming to rest on metal tables. The odd throat clearing. A cough from the perennially asthmatic Gabe. Poor kid. (They were the same age, but Yuna was taller when she stood up straight and had therefore earned the right to call him "kid.") What he and his equally asthmatic younger brother Lucas probably needed more than anything was fresh air, which was the last thing they were ever going to get.

Silence fell over the three families assembled around their respective tables. Lucas, the youngest of them all, fidgeted in his seat, the toe of his worn-out sneaker scuffing against the metal floor. Faces turned to the doctor, who stood at the front of the room. The smile on her face was warm enough, Yuna supposed, but there was something that always seemed a bit off about it. It was the same every day. Not one variation in the crinkles around her eyes or in the slightly off-kilter tilt of her lips. The right corner of her mouth was always just slightly higher than the left. The depth of the fine lines around her smile was always exactly the same.

"Let us begin our day as we always do. In a moment of silent gratitude." She clasped her hands together and bowed her head. Everyone followed suit. Almost everyone.

Yuna bowed her head but kept her eyes open just enough to see Sash sitting ramrod straight at the Eremenkos' table. Her eyes were focused on the doctor, unwavering. Her head inclined not one inch.

Oh, Sash. Yuna knew the other girl would get a talking-to later, but lectures never seemed to deter her. If anything, they seemed to fuel her minor rebellions.

Moran had to have seen. Nothing escaped her notice. But she gave no hint that she was the slightest bit perturbed by Sash's reticence. She carried on with her routine the same way she did every morning.

"We bow our heads in humble thanks for the food we are about to eat. For the walls that saved us from the storm." Dr. Moran looked up and caught Yuna's eyes.

Yuna dropped her gaze, but it was too late. Eye contact had been made.

"And most important, for the darkness that shelters us. For this, we are blessed."

Twelve voices spoke as one, repeating the doctor's words with dutiful synchronicity. "For this, we are blessed."

Yuna glanced at Sash. The other girl's lips were pressed together in a hard, firm line. Silent and stubborn. Some things never changed. Breakfast in the bunker. Moran's beatific smile. And Sash. And for the latter, Yuna felt oddly blessed.

CHAPTER 3

GABE

The hall lights flickered in and out overhead. They were always on, and power surges were common. Gabe was used to it at this point. It was always a little unnerving, but if he jumped out of his skin every time something weird happened in the bunker, he wouldn't know one single moment of peace.

Understanding why the electricity was spotty helped. It was fed from a generator that ran on an underground water source that Gabe had never actually seen. He'd helped his father repair the generator on more than one occasion, so he had no reason to doubt its existence. They had electricity, and that was all that mattered. Well, they had it most of the time. Sometimes it had better things to do than illuminate their sad little lives underground.

His father swore as something in the wall panel sparked. Another common occurrence. Most of the time it felt like their lives were held together with duct tape and a prayer.

For this, we are blessed.

"Hand me the wrench."

Gabe went fishing in the toolbox for said wrench. The box was a battered old thing, made of hammered red metal and adorned with more dings and scrapes than anyone cared to count. It had served them well, all these years in the bunker. And it would serve them well for more years to come.

Though Gabe didn't like to dwell on that last part. He preferred to cling to the fiction that they would be able to leave. Soon. At some point. Any day now.

He plucked the wrench from the toolbox's top shelf and handed it to his father.

"Here, Dad."

The elder Correa reached for the wrench without taking his eyes off the circuit breaker in front of him. His hand flailed a bit before Gabe placed the wrench in his palm.

"Thanks, kid."

Gabe pushed his glasses up his nose and went back to reading his comic book. (His glasses slid down roughly every twenty-seven seconds and would keep sliding right off his face if he didn't keep pushing them up.) (Also, he had read this comic book no fewer than 436 times. He knew every twist, every turn, every misaligned color no matter how slight.)

"You paying attention?"

"Nope," Gabe said, flipping the page. The paper was soft now, almost as soft as cotton. "Don't need to."

His dad snorted as he finally turned away from the circuit

breaker. "All right, kid. If you're so smart, you fix this thing."

Gabe peered at his father over the top of the comic book. "Seriously?"

His dad wiped his hands on his faded jeans. "You should know how to do these things on your own."

Because I won't be around forever, was the unspoken second half of that sentence. Life was ephemeral. They knew that better than anyone.

"Okay," Gabe said, because it was better than dwelling on the melancholy subject of mortality. He took the wrench from his father and slid into the space he'd vacated. So much of the bunker ran on mechanical power, but every now and then, the electric side of things reminded Gabe that it was likely designed by a half-mad lunatic who fancied himself the Nikola Tesla of the 1980s but was absolutely nothing of the sort.

"I'm going to go check on the water tank," said his father. "You good here?"

Gabe hummed an affirmative sound under his breath without looking up. He was already absorbed in the task at hand.

"Don't blow anything up." A large hand settled on Gabe's head, and before he could protest, said hand ruffled his hair.

"Ugh, Dad."

Laughing, his father departed, whistling a jaunty tune that echoed against the metal walls.

Eventually, the laughter and the whistling faded, leaving Gabe alone in the corridor with nothing but his father's tools to keep him company. The silence was pure and complete. But it was oddly constructed. The twists and turns and bends in corridors that led to nowhere had a way of absorbing sound that made it seem like one was entirely alone in the world.

That suited Gabe just fine.

Usually.

He set down the wrench and dove back into the toolbox when the ground beneath his feet vibrated. A loud whir reverberated through the walls. And then, the lights went out.

Gabe dropped the pliers he'd just picked up. The sound of them clattering into the toolbox was impossibly loud in the silence.

The corridor—and the rest of the bunker beyond—was dark.

Completely, thoroughly dark. The void-of-space-level dark.

This is normal, Gabe reminded himself. *This happens all the time.*

He was, perhaps, not half as brave as he fancied he was.

But after a moment, red lights flooded from the recessed alcoves set into the corners of the walls.

Red light, Gabe remembered. The words played through his mind during each and every one of these drills. They repeated like a mantra. Or a prayer. Or the periodic table, which was really just his version of a comforting litany. *Red light inhabits the safe zone of the spectrum. They can't see red. They aren't attracted to red. Red will keep us safe.*

He didn't know what *they* were. No one did. Not really. But it didn't matter in that moment. This was just a drill. And *they* couldn't get into the bunker. Nothing could. It was hermetically sealed from the surface. Airtight. There was only one way in or out, and that was through the hatch, and the hatch was locked. His own father saw to it.

His own father who was somewhere close but not close enough to come back.

"Not even a tank could roll through this thing," the elder

23

Correa liked to say, patting the hatch's wheel-shaped locking mechanism like a proud papa. "It's built to stand up to a hydrogen bomb. Ten hydrogen bombs. Safe as houses down here."

That was a phrase Gabe never quite got. *Safe as houses.* If a regular old house couldn't stand up to a hydrogen bomb or a tank or whatever *they* were, how could a house be their model for safety? A thought best not dwelled on, but Gabe always loved a good dwell.

It was easier and far more preferable to think of these things during the drill than to consider what it would be like if this wasn't actually a drill. If this was *actually* happening.

But it wasn't.

Was it?

Gabe kicked the toolbox closed, swearing when his toe stubbed against the hard metal. He bent down to pick it up, groaning at the weight.

Leave it, whispered a voice at the back of his head.

His father would kill him if something happened to those tools. They were all they had. There was no popping into the hardware shop to pick up replacements. There was no hardware shop.

Grunting, Gabe pulled the toolbox into the nearest room, the sound of it scraping against the metal floor loud enough to make his bones shake. Even louder was the sound of it hitting the floor when Gabe dropped it and scrambled for the door. His own hands in front of his face were just dark silhouettes against the red light.

Every room in the bunker came equipped with a set of locks. Dead bolts that could stand up to a bomb.

Safe as houses.

He threw his weight against the door as the sound of a blaring alarm finally cut through the silence like a blade.

Late, he thought. Timing's off. *Someone should fix that.*

He would fix that. Later though.

Now, he had to hide. Everyone would be hiding. Even his father, wherever he was.

Don't think about that. Close the door. Throw the lock. Wait.

The door groaned on its rusted hinges. Someone should fix that too. It started to swing shut, slowly, as if operating at its own leisure.

Before the door closed, a voice called out, echoing through the corridor.

"Wait!"

Yuna?

The rule was not to wait. You never waited. If someone didn't make it to safety in time, that was their problem.

Maximize rates of survival. Minimize potential for risk.

But Gabe waited.

The door was still swinging shut, too heavy to be stopped entirely, but Gabe pressed his shoulder against it and held it long enough for a small person to dart in through the opening.

Yuna was taller than Gabe, but she was almost frighteningly narrow. Which, he supposed, was a benefit when you had to fit in small spaces.

Once she was inside, Gabe let go of the door. It slammed closed, making them both jump.

Yuna doubled over, hands on her knees. "Thanks."

Her breath came in harsh pants, as if she'd just run a marathon. She was in better shape than Gabe was (and she didn't have asthma), so he wasn't quite sure why she was breathing so heavily. Stress, probably. The drills were terrifying. That was their job. To scare them into action.

Gabe nodded, pushing his glasses up on his nose. He was sweating, though it wasn't hot and he hadn't been running. Stress, again. It did a number on the body.

"Don't mention it," he said, sounding far cooler than he ever intended. "But, like, really don't mention it. Moran would never let me hear the end of it if you did."

Yuna crossed her heart. "Your secret is safe with me. No one will ever know you were too compassionate to let me die alone in the hallway."

"Where were you anyway?"

Yuna gulped in another breath. "Garden. Visiting the plants. Wanted to make sure they weren't hungry."

It was such a Yuna way to phrase it. Checking the nutrient levels of the hydroponic systems. He loved her a little bit for that.

Now that they were safe (as houses), the adrenaline began to fade, leaving Gabe's limbs feeling oddly tired. His lungs—never his strongest asset—labored a little harder than they usually did. His breath came in wheezes that sounded as painful as they felt. He hadn't even been running. It simply wasn't fair.

He slumped against the wall. There was no guessing how long the drill would last. It could be minutes. It could be hours. He was pretty sure they did one a few years ago that lasted an entire day. Like, a full rotation of Earth. A whole twenty-four hours. Insanity.

With much more grace than Gabe possessed in his whole body, Yuna joined him, crossing her legs daintily and sitting with her back to the wall. Their knees touched. Normally, Gabe didn't like to be touched, but now, he didn't quite mind. It was a nice reminder that he wasn't alone. It was comforting in a way touch normally wasn't. And it was rare. Touching people in the bunker was frowned upon. It was perhaps their oldest rule. It was so deeply ingrained in their collective psyche that avoiding contact was practically second nature at this point. Most of the time, the rule didn't bug him. But now, he was glad to break it, even if just a little.

The silence wasn't as complete as it had been. Yuna hummed a little ditty under her breath. Even measures. Three-quarter time. A waltz.

Tchaikovsky, Gabe thought. It was one of the records Mrs. Eremenko liked to play the most.

"Do you ever think about it?" Yuna asked. Her voice seemed softened by the scarlet glow, as if the half-light swallowed up sound.

"About what?"

"Before."

The word landed between them with a dull thud.

Gabe breathed, in and out, through the nostrils and out of the mouth. Four seconds each way. His chest expanded on the inhale and collapsed on the exhale.

They didn't speak of *Before*.

Not because it was one of Moran's rules (it wasn't, which Gabe had always found a little surprising) but because it was an *unspoken* rule. A silent guideline no one had ever officially established but everyone knew to exist all the same.

It was simply too painful. It was the one wound time couldn't heal. It remained open, oozing pus across every facet of their existence. Talking about Before was like poking the edge of that wound, tugging it open to bleed again. Pouring ethyl alcohol directly on it. It stung.

"Sometimes," Gabe said. It felt wrong, even admitting it. But wrong in a good way.

"Me too," Yuna whispered. "What do you think about?"

Gabe shrugged. "Lots of things. Libraries. My bike. I could only sort of ride it, but I almost had it. Rice and beans. Tostones. Maduros. My grandma's cooking."

Yuna made a sound Gabe couldn't quite decipher deep in her throat.

He was normally not one to seek to fill a silence, but talking felt better than waiting. "What was your favorite food?"

A ghost of a smile flirted with Yuna's mouth. "Sundubu jjigae."

Gabe repeated the phrase after her. The syllables felt strange as he rolled them around on his tongue. *Soon. Doo. Boo. Jee. Gay.* Nothing was ever new in the bunker. But those five syllables? They were new. And he loved them for it. Even if he had no idea what they meant.

"What's that?"

"A stew. A spicy one. With tofu and . . . honestly, I don't even remember. A bunch of stuff. It's good though. My mom used to make it for me every Sunday."

"That must have been nice."

Yuna hummed in agreement.

They fell silent again. Yuna's fingers drummed out the counts of the waltz against her knee.

"I try not to though," Gabe said softly. "Think about it, I mean."

Her fingers went still, lying flat against the curve of her knee. Her face was lit in profile, a shadow against the crimson light.

"Probably for the best," Yuna said.

"Yeah." He didn't quite mean it. "Probably."

They waited in silence for the red light to fade, for the illusion of safety to return once more. For the chance to pretend they were anything more than rats huddled in a cave, hiding from the Big Bad Thing(s) up above.

CHAPTER 4

SASH

The drill passed with little fanfare.

Sash was in the kitchen, elbows deep in sudsy water, when the lights came on. Calling it a kitchen was generous. It was the corner of the central room that happened to have a sink and enough counter space to sort of cook. The alarms followed, not too long after. She and Misha huddled down until it passed, not a single word exchanged between them.

Questions she did not ask:

> Where were you when it happened?

> How come Dad came to get me?

> What happened to him after he handed
> me to you?

> Do you ever think about him?

She knew the answers to some of these questions. Misha had been at basketball practice. He'd always been tall for his age, and at twelve, he was the star of the local middle school's basketball team, for whatever that was worth. Sash knew for a fact that there was a basketball—orange faded brown with age—floating somewhere around the basement, but she had never seen him lay so much as a finger on it. It was as if that part of him—the part that liked to play, not just basketball but anything—had been killed off the same day everything else was. Like he'd just left it by the side of the road as he ran off, away from the stream, with Sash in his arms and their father somewhere behind them, never to return.

The one question she didn't ask, the one she could never seem to shake, bounced around inside her skull most persistently of them all:

What is it like up there now?

Seconds ticked by. Then minutes. Then the red light faded. The alarms fell silent. Back to normal, as if nothing had happened. And nothing had. Just a drill. That's all it ever was.

A tiny, rebellious part of Sash wished for the day it wasn't. She wanted to know what they were hiding from. She wanted to see it with her own two eyes. It might be ugly. It might be dangerous. But it would be something new. Something different. Something besides fake sunlight and tasteless gruel and a never-ending parade of tasks designed to keep them alive. But alive wasn't really living. That much she knew.

After the dishes were cleaned, she set about moving the tables into their "school" arrangement. All aligned toward the chalkboard before which Moran would stand and proselytize. (How did they have a decade's worth of chalk down here? Who planned for that?) Moran called it teaching, but Sash was never one for labeling things as anything but what they were. And this was most assuredly proselytizing.

Misha left with a jovial grunt in Sash's direction before the others filed in. And then the lesson began.

"Can anyone tell me why the world ended as it did?" Dr. Moran's inquisitive gaze swept over her assembled students.

Nastia raised her hand, nearly coming off her chair in her enthusiasm.

Sash rolled her eyes. Honestly.

She had little patience for teacher's pets. Especially when that teacher was Dr. Imogen Moran. And that pet was her younger sister.

The doctor tipped her head in Nastia's direction, signaling for the girl to go on.

A satisfied smile spread across Nastia's face. "They did it to themselves."

Moran nodded sagely. "They did. Let us never forget what their greed, corruption, and selfish pride cost. Like the snake that eats its own tail, society destroyed itself."

She reached to roll down a map of the earth. It was outdated, like everything in the bunker. There was a tiny copyright mark—whatever that meant—in the corner that said © 1987. A year so far away, it might as well be fictional.

And yet, they were surrounded by all manner of accoutrements from that mythical year and the handful of years before then. The rivets on the bunker's metal plates had been produced sometime in the seventies. Sash had found a spare box of them in the storage closet once. They'd gone old and rusty, like so much else down here. The map divided Germany into two segments—East and West—and from what little geopolitical knowledge Sash possessed of Before, she knew that hadn't been the case for a while. For a really, intensely long time.

Moran jabbed her long wooden pointer at the map as if it offended her.

"The nations of the world created the circumstances that led to their demise. Their failure to take care of the earth"—she paused, perhaps for dramatic effect, as if they all hadn't heard this bit a thousand times over—"and their neglect for one another are what led to their downfall."

Her gaze raked over each and every one of them, as if the collapse of civilization and the melting of the polar ice caps and the disappearance of the bees had been their fault entirely.

"The planet still bears the scars of their many conflicts." Moran's shrewd eyes slid over to Sash. "Some of us bear scars of our own."

Tugging her sleeve over her hand, Sash shifted in her seat. Even through the material of her sweater, she could feel the ridges of raised skin on her forearm. The scars weren't a secret. There were no secrets in the bunker. Everyone knew they were there. She just hated when anyone talked about it.

She couldn't think about the scars without thinking of how they got there. And she really, really didn't want to think about how they got there.

"Climate change. Poverty. War. Disease. Deforestation. Acid rain. Poisoned air. An ozone layer filled with holes. Ice caps melting, sea levels rising. A planet fighting a human infection. All of this came to pass." Moran bowed her head, as if taking a private moment of silence. When she looked up, her eyes were alight with the fervor of a true believer. "Just as the earth must heal itself, so we must heal ourselves. Only when we've achieved purity of both mind and body will we be strong enough to survive on the outside."

She glanced toward the rules pinned to the corkboard on the wall. As if any of them needed a reminder. They lived with those rules every day. They ate them. They breathed them. They slept them. They governed every aspect of their miserable, subterranean lives.

You must always tell the truth.

You must avoid the light of the sun.

You must never touch skin to skin.

But the most important rule, the one that was drilled into their heads from the moment the hatch had slammed shut all those years ago, was at the very end of the list. It fell from their lips in moments of uncertainty. It was repeated to wayward children, like a mantra, lest they forget. It rattled around in their skulls when all was silent, echoing in the quiet, lonely dark.

You must never go outside.

"The ones who did this to our home, who scarred our planet so," Moran intoned. The height of solemnity. "They paid for their sins. But we must always remember them. We must do better. We must *be* better."

She sighed heavily, as if weighted down by the great and terrible burden only a prophet could possibly know.

"They were wicked." Her lips curled into a beatific smile. "But *we* are blessed."

CHAPTER 5

YUNA

At the front of the class, Moran blurred, her body morphing into a vaguely human-shaped crimson smudge in Yuna's vision. Yuna blinked, rubbing at her eyes. A yawn tried to claw its way up her throat, but she clamped her teeth down, forcing it to retreat.

Yawning was a hard no in Moran's class. So was sleeping, talking, or doing anything other than listening with rapt attention.

Yuna nibbled at the inside of her cheek. That helped her stay awake sometimes. If that failed, she'd change tactics—snapping her hair tie against her wrist or digging her nails into the palms of her hand so hard she left little crescent-moon indents in her skin. Neither strategy was pleasant, but they were vastly preferable to the alternative.

Gaining Moran's complete and undivided attention.

That was a hard pass for Yuna.

Their desk tables were now arranged in a semicircle around Moran. A chalkboard stood behind the desk, onto which she'd written her three points of discussion. (Though it was less of a discussion and more of a lecture, but Dr. Moran hadn't asked for Yuna's opinion on her choice of terminology, and so Yuna would simply keep that to herself.)

The points were as followed:

1. The body as microcosm of the planet.

2. The planet as microcosm of the universe.

3. The universe as microcosm of the divine.

Yuna had no idea what any of that meant. And to be honest, she didn't quite care. All she cared about was staying awake.

Sleep had always been hard for her to come by. It was like her body (microcosm of the planet) had never quite adjusted to existing underground, deprived of natural light and fresh air. The bunker had light, of course, carefully regulated by timers to dim and brighten in an effort to simulate the rising and setting of the actual sun, but it wasn't the same. It never had been. Everyone else seemed to grow accustomed to it, but Yuna's brain had never come to accept the farce of their false sun.

Something dug into her thigh—not painfully, but not gently either—and her eyes flew open. Had they closed? All on their own? She couldn't remember.

Beside her, Sash shifted in her seat, knocking her knee

against Yuna's. Moran was still facing the blackboard, writing something in chalk the color of a dusty rose. Yuna glanced at Sash. The other girl was staring straight ahead, a shallow, inoffensive smile on her lips. But her hand moved, dropping something onto Yuna's lap.

A small piece of paper, folded into halves. It had been folded so many times, the creases had gone so soft it felt like it might disintegrate in Yuna's hands. Paper. Another hot commodity down in the bunker. There was only so much of it to go around. They'd taken to recycling their own, but the homemade stuff was never as good. Yuna's was especially bumpy.

With her eyes locked on Moran, she carefully (and quietly) unfolded the note. When Moran turned back toward the board to write something, Yuna glanced down at the paper.

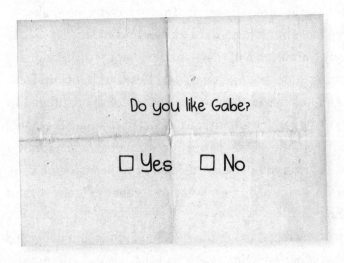

Two checkboxes. One labeled yes, the other no.

It took everything Yuna had not to audibly snort.

With one eye on Moran, she scribbled her own reply.

A third checkbox, this one labeled, "Yes, not like that."

Quickly, she folded the paper along the same well-worn creases and slid it in Sash's direction.

Except it didn't make it to Sash. The note continued its smooth slide over the metal surface of the table, coming to a halt right in front of Gabe himself.

Moran began to turn around. Without missing a beat, Gabe snatched the note off the table. It was gone before anyone but the three of them could see it.

With an owlish—and entirely too perceptive—blink, Moran asked, "Something wrong?"

Sash leaned her cheek on her fist and cracked a truly obnoxious yawn. "Nope."

Quirking her eyebrows up, Moran's gaze slid from Sash to Gabe (who blinked a bit too fast but otherwise gave nothing away) and to Yuna. Yuna met that gaze with her own, unflinching. Serene.

After a few beats, Moran sighed and turned back to the board. "Very well, then."

As soon as she started writing addendums to her list, Gabe, very slowly and very silently, retrieved the note. Keeping it on his lap, he unfolded it, quiet as a mouse. His eyes moved from side to side as he scanned its contents. Then, his lips pursed. He flattened the note against the table and scribbled something of his own underneath Yuna's contribution. Before Moran had reached the end of her sentence—"The divine is human and human is divine" (whatever that meant)—Gabe had slid the note over to Sash.

She cracked it open just enough to glimpse whatever Gabe had written and then had to bite her knuckle to keep a laugh in.

What is it? Yuna mouthed at Sash.

Sash shook her head, folding the note closed and shoving it toward Yuna.

Moran glanced at them over her shoulder for a brief moment.

"Something you'd like to share with the rest of the class, Alexandra?"

"It's Sash, and no."

Moran's brief glance turned into a cold, if somewhat bemused, glare. "Have I done something to earn your disre-spect, Alex—Sash?"

Yuna pressed her thigh into Sash's, hoping the other girl got the message.

Moran put down the chalk and turned around fully.

Oh. This was the opposite of what any of them had wanted. Yuna had desired only to make it through this lesson, as she'd made it through every other lesson, every single day since they'd settled into this bunker all those years ago.

Even Sash, with her flagrant disregard for authority, seemed to realize she'd gone a step too far. One never knew where that line was drawn with Moran. Sometimes, you could get away with bloody murder. Some days, you could barely get away with anything at all. It was a fine tightrope they all walked.

Clearing her throat, Sash sat upright in her chair. "No, ma'am."

Yuna hoped she was the only one who heard the faint thread of disdain woven through Sash's voice.

From the look on Moran's face, Yuna, in fact, was not.

Moran loosely clasped her hands together in front of her stomach. "Then, tell me, Sash, why do I deserve it?"

She spread her hands wide, gesturing toward the walls. But

also, Yuna knew, toward everything beyond their specific limits. To the hydroponic systems in the garden and the generators pulling electricity from . . . wherever it was they pulled electricity. To the powdered gruel that filled their bellies and the darkness that kept them safe.

"Have I not done enough to earn at least the smallest shred of respect?" She rounded the desk, approaching them. Yuna went still. There was something about Moran's gait that reminded her vaguely of a snake slithering through tall grass. "Have I not provided you—provided your families, all of them—with a safe haven when there was no other?"

Yuna watched as Sash swallowed thickly. The corner of Sash's mouth twitched, as if she were considering saying something wildly ill-advised. (Honestly, it wouldn't surprise Yuna, not now, not after years of minor rebellions.) But when Sash spoke, all she said was, "Of course, Dr. Moran."

Moran paused in front of Sash, forcing the girl to crane her neck to look up at her if she wanted to meet that gaze. And Yuna knew she did. Sash may have been verbally quelled for the moment, but not for one second did Yuna believe that went any deeper than the most surface of levels.

They both went still, gazes locked. Gabe caught Yuna's eye, his brows quirking upward. Yuna offered him the tiniest, most inconspicuous shrug she possibly could. This seemed like a battle of wills, but for what, Yuna was unsure. There were no victory conditions here. Win or lose, they were all locked in this bunker together with no escape in sight. It didn't make much sense to rock the boat the way Sash did, but neither did it make much sense to lord one's position over the rest the way Moran sometimes did. A very large part of Yuna wished that everyone would just take a step back, breathe a little, and calm down.

"And you?"

Yuna didn't realize Moran was talking to her until the woman's crimson gown floated into her direct line of sight. Yuna looked up. And up. And up. Dr. Moran appeared very tall when one was sitting down. Which Yuna was. What a fun dynamic this was.

"Me?" Yuna asked.

"You."

"What about me?"

Moran pursed her lips. "Have I done anything to show myself as unworthy of respect?"

"Of course not." Yuna wasn't sure if she meant it. She didn't have doubts, not the way Sash did. But Yuna always suspected that Sash *wanted* to have doubts. She wanted to be contrary. Yuna just wanted to make it through the day. Usually, that was good enough.

Moran hummed softly under her breath. Then, she nodded. "Then let's move on, shall we?"

She made her way back to the blackboard, her skirt swishing against her legs as she walked.

Yuna peered down at the note Sash had thrust into her hands. Unfolding it carefully, she read what Gabe had written.

Ouch.

And then:

I like you both too. But not like that.

CHAPTER 6

SASH

A life without music is not a life worth living.

The words had been inscribed on a wooden sign that had hung above the tall mirrors in her mother's dance studio. Sash had always felt they were a bit dark for children, but now, in the complete encompassing silence of the bunker, she realized how true they were.

"Is it working now?" Sash extended her leg to poke Gabe's thigh with her toe.

"No." The syllable was as terse as they come. "It wasn't working ninety seconds ago when you asked me, and it won't be working ninety seconds from now when you inevitably ask me again."

Yuna smirked, nibbling at the chewed end of an old ballpoint pen. The ink in the pen had long since dried up, but fiddling with writing implements was apparently such an ingrained part of human nature that the implement's ability to write was secondary to its intended purpose. "Okay, but is it working *now*?"

Gabe threw a small wrench at her like it was a dart. Laughing, she ducked her face into Sash's shoulder.

Sash's heart leaned toward the other girl like a flower craning for the sun.

Frustrated, Gabe sat back on his heels, running a hand through his hair. "I don't think I can get this thing to work."

This thing was an ancient record player they'd unearthed in one of the bunker's derelict storage boxes. The boxes were full of frivolous stuff, inessential to survival. Old comic books. Mass market paperbacks about gumshoe detectives and alien invasions and Harlequin romances. Records. Dr. Moran had sequestered those items in a corner of the bunker, locked away for when they might need to cannibalize them for spare parts: paper, stray bits of desperately outdated electronics, that sort of thing. Over the years, Sash, Yuna, and Gabe had pilfered items, one by one, and moved them to their secret place. Their hideout. Their tiny corner of their tiny world, where no one else was welcome.

It was their bunker within the bunker. A place to hide away from the rest of the world, as small as theirs was.

Drawings covered the walls in paint, layers and layers of it. For some reason, the bunker had been well stocked by its mysterious benefactor with a bevy of art supplies. Enough to last a decade. Or nearly. They'd run out of the fun colors about two years ago.

Two years, seven months, and thirteen days to be exact. Not that anyone was counting. Certainly not Sash, who felt every single one of those days like a puncture wound to the heart.

"Giving up already?" It was a mean thing to say, and she knew it. But sometimes you just had to poke the bear. For fun, naturally.

Gabe's brows inched well above the upper rim of his glasses. "Already? I've been working on this for two years. Two whole years!"

"Has it been that long?" Yuna twirled a lock of Sash's hair around her finger, seemingly oblivious to how it made Sash's heart stutter and sing. "Time flies when you're buried underground waiting out an apocalypse."

Sash snorted, settling deeper into the pillows—also pilfered from other areas of the bunker. Moran didn't seem to mind their disappearance. Things like throw pillows were luxuries, as far as the doctor was concerned. Creature comforts meant to lull you into a false sense of security, of opulence.

She glanced back down at the mending in her hands. Old socks. The toes had holes worn clean through.

There were no new clothes in the bunker. What they had now was all they were ever going to have. This one pair of socks had been repaired so many times over, it probably wasn't even the same set of socks anymore.

Working with her hands gave her something to focus on. That's probably why Gabe liked tinkering with things so much. It kept one's mind off the thoughts best left untouched. The length of time they'd been in the bunker. The length of time they had left. The tons and tons of soil and gravel and rock pressing down on them. The absent sky and the metal walls.

"Who are the Russkies?" Yuna asked, idly flipping through the pages of a new comic book to their collection. It had been wedged into the back of a box deep in the storage room. How they'd missed it all this time, Sash hadn't the foggiest.

She squinted one eye as she threaded the string through her needle. "I think they mean Russians. Babulya said the US and Russia sort of used to be at war but the Russians called themselves Soviets. Don't really know what that means though. Americans used to call them all sorts of things. Russkies was probably one of the nicer names. Babulya still seems kind of bitter about the whole thing." She bit back a curse as the thread jabbed impotently at the curve of the needle's eye. "To be honest, I don't know much about it. Mom hates when Babulya talks about it."

Gabe scoffed, looking up from his tangle of wires. "So does Dr. Moran."

"All I know is that there was a war and it was cold for some reason, and that's why Babulya came here."

Yuna flipped to the second page of her comic book. They'd all read it more times than they could count. The pages had gone as soft as silk. It had to be handled delicately or you'd run the risk of it falling apart. "Maybe it was warmer here than in Russia."

"Yeah," Sash said. "Probably."

Gabe shouted in triumph, rising to stand so quickly he nearly knocked the entire contraption to the ground. Sash and Yuna both raced to grab it before it could topple off the small worktable. "I got it!"

"You said that before," Sash mumbled, dubious.

Gabe shot her a withering look. But it was true. He had. And he'd been wrong.

"Do you think it'll play this?" Yuna held up a record. Tiffany. *I Think We're Alone Now.* On the front, a girl with feathered red hair and a light blue denim jacket—Tiffany, one could safely assume—held her hands crossed primly in front of her. Her lips were forever positioned in the most perfect of coy smirks. Like she was privy to a secret no one else knew.

"Might as well give it a whirl." Gabe took the record from Yuna and removed it from its protective sleeve. With tremendous care, he placed the vinyl record on the machine. It began to spin.

"That's new," Sash remarked.

Gabe shushed her. "Don't jinx it."

They held their collective breath as he lowered the needle.

And then nothing happened.

No sound emanated from the device. No speakers vibrated with Tiffany's voice.

Gabe made a frustrated, wordless noise as he tugged at his hair again.

"Keep doing that, and it's gonna fall out," Yuna said.

"Don't jinx *me*," Gabe said plaintively. With a sigh, he stood, his knees cracking from having been stuck in one position for so long, fighting a losing battle with a piece of technology magnitudes older than he was. "I'm going to go see if I can scrounge up some spare parts anywhere. I'm this close to fixing it." He held up two fingers, barely an inch apart. "*This close.*"

Without waiting for them to say much of anything, he made his way to the hatch for their little hideout. Once Gabe got an idea into his head, that was it. Nothing else seemed to exist.

"Good luck," Sash called over her shoulder.

"And Godspeed," Yuna added.

Silence settled between them in Gabe's wake.

After a while, Yuna broke it with a simple, succinct "Bummer."

"That about covers it," Sash agreed, falling back to rest her head against the pillow.

Overhead, strings of crisscrossed lights twinkled dimly and irregularly.

Sort of like real stars, Sash thought. Not that she really remembered what real stars looked like. She had a vague idea. A dark blanket, strewn with pinpricks of white. But the further away the source of the memory became, the fuzzier the details grew. She remembered sensations more than anything. The crick in her neck when she looked up at the sky. The way the vast, incomprehensible span of the universe made her head hurt when she tried to think about it.

Sash leaned back, settling against the mound of blankets, Yuna a warm presence to her right.

"What do you think it's like?" Sash asked, gazing up at their false sky. "Outside, I mean."

Yuna fidgeted, like she couldn't quite find a comfortable place to rest. "Like, now?"

"Yeah."

"Moran said it was a barren wasteland," Yuna intoned, voice flat. It was the voice she used when she was reciting something from memory. Something she didn't quite believe but had been drilled into her anyway.

Sash rolled her eyes. "I know that's what she said."

"You don't think she's telling the truth?" Yuna asked.

"Do you?"

Yuna hesitated. Chewed on the pen. "Part of me wants to say she's lying but . . ."

"But it's kind of hard to picture anything else," Sash supplied.

A nod from Yuna. "Do you think we'll ever go back up there?"

"I hope so," Sash said. "I think about it sometimes."

What she didn't say: *The alternative is dying down here, in a coffin of metal and wires and fear.*

More silence. More twinkling lights. One day, these bulbs would burn out and that would be it. There would be no more. No more fairy lights. No one left to make them. Just a sad green string with dead bulbs dangling off it.

"Do you remember Christmas?" Sash asked.

"We're not supposed to talk about stuff like that." The words were rote. Parroted. Yuna's voice was devoid of even the slightest trace of conviction.

Sash propped herself up on one elbow to face Yuna. The other girl rolled over on her side, her head resting on her bent arm. "I don't care what we're not supposed to talk about."

"What happens in the hideout stays in the hideout?" A tiny smile tugged at the corner of Yuna's lips.

"Exactly."

Memories were an illicit thing. Trading them was like dealing in illegal contraband. If caught, there would be consequences. So the trick was to never get caught.

With a small hum of consideration, Yuna rolled onto her back and stared up at the lights. "I remember the food."

Sash's stomach rumbled at the mere mention of something that didn't begin its life in powdered form. She settled back against the nest of pillows, an inch or two closer to Yuna than she had been before. Yuna, for her part, didn't seem to mind the proximity. "Tell me about it."

"My mom used to make this amazing mung bean jelly. Cheongpomuk-muchim."

Sash crinkled her nose. "What's a mung bean?"

"A bean . . . thing. I don't know. What I do know is that it was delicious. It came out before the rest of the meal, and one year I ate so much of it, I made myself sick and there was nothing left for our cousins when they got to the house. My mother was *livid*. But . . . Junsu told her he was the one who ate it all."

Yuna almost never spoke her brother's name aloud. It was on the long list of things they weren't allowed to discuss. Memories they weren't allowed to hold close so they didn't lose them.

But losing a memory of a person was like living through their death all over again.

"What about you?" Yuna asked. "What do you remember about Christmas?"

Sash laced her fingers over her stomach, staring up at the lights instead of at Yuna. It was easier that way, to gaze up at their twinkling and pretend that she was somewhere else.

"I remember my dad putting up the tree. He used to do it earlier than Babulya wanted him to. She celebrated Christmas in January, I think. Something about the Russian Orthodox Church. I honestly don't remember why. But one year, he caught me crying because all the other kids had trees and lights and tinsel everywhere and we didn't. So he started doing it earlier. And we left the tree up late. By the time he dragged it out of the house, it was so dry, all the needles would fall off and it was like having a second carpet."

The memory didn't sting as much as Sash thought it would. It was a dull ache, but not an entirely unpleasant one.

"I liked the way Christmas trees smelled," Yuna said. "I think I liked that almost as much as the food."

Sash hummed deep in her throat. "Me too."

After a minute passed in companionable silence, Yuna turned her head so she was facing Sash. Doing the same would have put Sash's nose mere inches from hers.

Too dangerous. Don't do it.

So she didn't.

"Why do you think Dr. Moran has such a problem with us talking about Before?" Yuna asked. "Is it because it makes people sad?"

Sash shook her head, tugging at a sore spot on her chapped lips. Pulling at it always made it feel worse, but it was a compulsion she was powerless to stop. Like wondering what it was like outside. Like remembering things others wanted her to forget.

"I don't think it's that. I think . . ." She drew in a breath. Organized her thoughts. They had been formless things once, but now they were solidifying. Taking shape. "I think it's because memories make us who we are. They define us. And Moran wants to be the one to be able to do that."

"She means well," Yuna said. "She's just trying to keep us safe."

"Do you really believe that?"

The silence that met Sash's question was answer enough.

In a soft voice, Yuna said, "I'd like to."

"We've already lost so much," Sash said. What she didn't say: *My dad. Your brother. Every Christmas for the past ten years and every Christmas left to come.* "I won't let her take those too."

CHAPTER 7

GABE

Dr. Moran smiled at Gabe from across her cluttered desk. It wasn't messy. Just cluttered. It was organized clutter but clutter nonetheless. Gabe's hands twitched with the repressed urge to reach out and tidy it up. He didn't hate much—hate was such a strong word—but he did hate clutter.

Usually, he also mildly loathed these meetings. One-on-ones, Moran called them. She did them with every denizen of the bunker on a rotating schedule. To check in, she claimed. To make sure their minds were kept as healthy as their bodies.

Humans were never meant to live like moles, Gabe thought. *So fat chance of that.*

These one-on-ones were more often than not an exercise in killing time for Gabe, but this time he had a plan. He had things to accomplish. Hearts and minds (well, one heart and one mind) to win.

The doctor laced her fingers together. She rested her elbows against the ink blotter that showed no sign of ever having blotted ink. "Have you had any revelations this week, Mr. Correa?"

It was always weird when she called him Mr. Correa. Mr. Correa was his dad. Gabe was just Gabe. But he preferred Mr. Correa to Gabriel at least.

Her use of the word *revelation* had stopped being weird a few years ago. It was a big word for the trite nonsense they covered during their talks, but it seemed to please her on some weird cosmic level, so Gabe never wasted much mental energy on it.

"As a matter of fact" was how Gabe began many of his one-on-ones, and this one was no different. "I have had a revelation."

Moran's eyebrows lifted. That was beyond the scope of their standard script.

"Well then, Mr. Correa. I'm all ears."

All ears. A weird saying. Much weirder than *revelations*. Imagine it. An entity made entirely of ears.

Gabe shook the thought loose as he pulled a rolled-up, mildly squished stack of papers from his back pocket. Blueprints, covering (almost) every usable space in the bunker. It wasn't a basement so much as an underground complex developed by a mind even more frantic about details than Gabe's. He could spot the compulsion in every meticulously diagrammed line.

"What's this?" Moran asked as Gabe flattened the papers

atop her desk, anchoring one corner with a heavy crystal paper-weight, another with a stapler (absent staples), a third with a chipped mug that read "Give Peace a Chance," and the last with a compact but heavy tome that looked vaguely like a Bible.

"This is the bunker."

That should have been obvious.

Moran's eyebrows inched upward. "I can see that."

Okay, so it was obvious.

Gabe placed his finger against one of the long vertical lines on the blueprint. "This is ventilation shaft eighty-six-C."

"And . . . ?"

"And I think I can make our air-recycling system seven percent more efficient if I reroute the flow of air from eighty-six-C to thirty-seven-F here"—he traced the line to another, wider one two inches to the left (on paper; it was a lot more than two inches in real life)—"to here."

Moran held up a hand to still his train of thought.

Rude.

"You realize this isn't why I asked you here, don't you, Mr. Correa?"

Gabe pushed his glasses up his nose. (They'd slid down. Again.)

Of course he did. This wasn't what she meant by revelations. She wanted spiritual tomfoolery. The kind for which Gabe had absolutely no time.

"Yes," he said, "but I am very passionate about not suffocat-ing, so I thought it was worth mentioning."

Moran frowned at the blueprint, then at Gabe. "How did we get from a seven percent improvement in efficiency to suffocation?"

And like well-herded prey, she had fallen into his trap. Holding back a satisfied grin, Gabe said, "Well, now that you asked . . ."

He hardly noticed when Moran tuned him out. And he only really noticed because about ten minutes into his explanation, she let her head fall forward and bonk very gently against her desk. Her voice was muffled by both the ink blotter and the nimbus of curly hair spilled around her skull. "Please. Stop. Do what you have to. Make us seven percent more efficient. Please just get out of my office."

Gabe rolled up his papers and thoroughly failed to suppress the smile on his face.

"Thanks, Dr. Moran. I promise you won't regret it."

Her only response was another dismissive wave. But right before he could close the door behind him, she lifted her head, just an inch. Her dark curls fell across her face in a way that was more than a little ominous.

"See that I don't, Mr. Correa." She held his gaze, her expression unreadable. "The bunker is a delicate ecosystem. We wouldn't want to disturb it." A shadow passed across her face. "If any one system falls, the rest will follow. We must have harmony in all things. Always, Gabriel. Do you understand me?"

He nodded, even though he was pretty sure half of what she was saying wasn't about systems or ventilation or efficiency at all. The words sounded weightier. Like there was a secondary set of sounds underneath them, outside the range of his hearing. He'd been told—mainly by his parents and sometimes by Sash—that he often missed those subtle cues. But everyone in the bunker knew about that tendency of his. If they spoke in riddles and he didn't get it, he figured that was more a them-problem than a Gabe-problem.

"Of course, Dr. Moran. Understood." Well enough.

He scuttled out of the room before she could say anything else. He had work to do.

CHAPTER 8

SASH

Moran's office was warm. Unpleasantly so. Always.

The cloying heat made Sash sticky and uncomfortable but also strangely languid, as though her muscles were glad to have a chance to relax.

Perhaps that was why Moran kept it so hot. To loosen people up. To make them both physically relaxed and physically uncomfortable, so they'd say whatever they had to say to get out of there, but without the filter that inhibitions granted.

Sash drummed her nails against the plush armrests of the chair she sat in. It wasn't across from the desk, which Sash had never seen Moran use. It was set into a corner opposite an identical plush chair, the two separated by a wicker end table draped in some kind of brightly colored tapestry. The smell of incense burned in the air. Where Moran acquired this endless supply of sage and patchouli, Sash hadn't the foggiest.

"Is there something you want to tell me?" Moran's tone implied that she knew there was something—perhaps several somethings—Sash was keeping to herself.

But Sash was happy doing just that.

She shook her head cheerfully. "No revelations today. Same as last week."

The doctor tilted her head to the side, the way Sash's ancient Pomeranian had when she was a child and the little dog knew Sash was hiding a treat in her closed fist. "Now, why don't I believe that?"

A shrug Sash hoped was nonchalant. "No idea. Projecting, maybe?"

In her head, a voice that sounded an awful lot like Yuna audibly gasped.

The inner Yuna. Far more judgmental than the actual Yuna.

But thinking about Yuna made Sash's cheeks redden. Not much but enough.

Rookie mistake.

A flicker of keen understanding slithered through the doctor's eyes.

"You understand why the rules are what they are, don't you?" Moran's voice oozed with sympathy. It slid over Sash's skin, leaving a trail of insincerity in its wake.

"You mean the rules you made up that everyone follows because they're too afraid to do anything else?"

The words were out of Sash's mouth before she could really think about them. Before she could measure their weight, test them out in the safe confines of her own skull. But now that they were out, an unusual lightness filled her chest. She'd thought it for years. Now, she'd finally said it. And it felt good.

Moran drew in a long, steady breath as she spread her fingers wide atop her desk.

"And now here we are, at the crux of the issue."

"What issue? There's no issue."

Again, the too keen look, this time paired with a condescending smile to match. Moran folded her hands together and leaned in toward Sash, as if the two of them were grand ol' pals.

"I have a proposal for you."

Sash quirked a single eyebrow. A pointed query.

"You don't insult my intelligence," Moran continued. "And I won't insult yours."

Sash's shoulders tightened, as if a cord had been drawn between them. She spared a thought for lying. For deflecting. But such a thing would be pointless when faced with the look on that woman's face. So instead, she gritted her teeth and bit out a single, terse, "Fine."

"You've been having thoughts, haven't you?" Moran asked, as if it wasn't a completely ridiculous question.

"Doesn't everyone?"

The doctor tipped her head to the side. "Thoughts of a certain nature."

Sash didn't like the way that sounded. *A certain nature.* No. She didn't like that at all. Not one bit.

"I assure you," Moran continued, "such thoughts are completely normal, especially for a girl your age."

"Oh, Jesus."

"A false prophet, but I digress."

"Please. Digress."

Moran's hand snaked out across the desk and latched on to Sash's wrist.

The touch was so startling, the physical contact so rare, that it froze Sash to her very core. Moran wasn't touching her skin—only the fabric of Sash's sleeve. But still. Weird. Weird and bad. Sash tugged on her wrist, trying to wrest it free from Moran's surprisingly strong grip, but to no avail.

"It's perfectly fine to want to be touched."

"Not by you." Sash yanked with all her might. Moran dropped her hand at the same moment, sending Sash crashing into the stiff back of the armchair.

"No," Moran said, voice low and measured. "Not by me." The doctor shook her head, sighing. "I wish it didn't have to be this way. Believe me when I say this isn't the life I wanted for any of you."

There was something about the phrasing that seemed off.

"Don't you mean us?" Sash asked. "You're locked in here with us."

Except, of course, when Moran wasn't. She got to leave at night. She got to put on that ridiculous suit and go outside. It might have been oxygen out of a tank filling her lungs, but it was closer to fresh air than any of the rest of them had gotten in years.

"Yes," Moran said. "Us." With another weary sigh, she added, "It isn't safe. Not even in here. Not entirely anyway. We were all exposed. The contaminant . . . it lives on inside our bodies. We carry it with us always."

Sash rubbed her wrist, wiping at the spot Moran had touched. She was hot all over, as if the contaminant—whatever it was—was heating her up from within.

"You don't want to get your friends sick, do you?" Moran asked.

Sash's jaw clenched so tightly, she thought something in it might crack if she exerted only a little more pressure.

"Keep your hands to yourself," Moran said, a kindly smile gracing her thin lips. "That's all I ask. The others look up to you. You should set a good example."

No, Sash thought. *That's not all. That's not even the half of it. You ask for that and so much more. You ask for everything we are, everything we could be.*

But this, she wisely did not say.

With a nod she didn't mean, Sash stood up.

"That'll be all for today." Moran was already turning away, shuffling a stack of papers on her desk.

Sash retreated, turned the doorknob in a trembling hand, and left.

CHAPTER 9

YUNA

"And you, Yuna," Moran said, a fine thread of exhaustion woven through her voice. "Any revelations this week?"

Yuna stilled her feet. Even though she was sitting, she was still running through the petite allegro steps Mrs. Eremenko had taught them during the morning ballet class. Not really running through them, of course, but marking them. That way, they stayed fresh in her mind for the next class.

"Nope."

Her gaze drifted down back to her feet. *Was it four changements? Or three?* Her timing was off, but she wasn't sure where she'd lost it. *Maybe during the echappés?*

A pointed—and not at all quiet—throat clearing tore her attention away from her fidgeting feet.

"Oh." Yuna sat upright, hands laced delicately in her lap. "Sorry. I was just thinking about ballet."

"Did you have a good class this morning?"

Yuna nodded. "Yup."

Moran's lips stretched into a shallow, secretive smile. "You know, you're an awful tough nut to crack."

"Oh, I don't really like nuts." Yuna blinked. "I'm allergic."

A tittered laugh tumbled from Moran's lips. "Of course, dear. It was just a turn of phrase."

"Oh. Okay, then."

Maybe it was the counts that were off? It's possible she misremembered them. Usually, counting off the music was such an innate thing for her, but everyone was wrong every now and then.

"Anything you'd like to share about your friends?"

Yuna cocked her head to the side. "Like what?"

Was it the glissades?

Moran shrugged. Spread her hands in a questioning gesture. "Anything at all. Any concerns you might have."

Yuna paused to give the question thought. After a long, silent moment, she said, "I think Gabe needs new glasses. He was squinting at the chore board the other day." But then she frowned. Remembered their current circumstances. "But where would he get them?" A shrug. "Oh, well. What can you do?"

No, not the glissades. The assemblé?

"You're a vault," Moran intoned, more to herself than Yuna, "aren't you?"

Yuna blinked again. "I don't know what that means."

Moran sighed. "Of course not." She waved Yuna off. "I

think that's enough for the day. You can go."

Yuna didn't wait for the doctor to change her mind. So, she left.

It was definitely the jetés. That had to be it.

She'd track down Mrs. Eremenko and ask, just to be sure.

CHAPTER 10

SASH

Sash was passing the bowl of canned peas to her mother—always canned peas, those seemed to exist in the bunker in an inexhaustible supply—when the lights went out.

Darkness fell over the room, so complete it was as though everything ceased to exist outside of each person's isolated bubble of fear.

The darkness is good, Sash told herself. *The darkness is safe. The things in the light can't get us in here.*

She wished she still believed that.

Moran's voice pierced through the black shroud enveloping the room. "No need to panic. I'm sure it's just a hiccup in the generators."

Sometimes it was a hiccup in the generators. Sometimes it wasn't. Sometimes the lights just went off without warning for no discernible reason. It wasn't ideal but it was still better than hearing the faint whir of the air filtration system die down. That happened rarely, but lately, these hiccups seemed to occur with greater and greater frequency. Already, in the past month, the lights had gone out three times. That wasn't normal.

"The bunker is falling apart," Gabe whispered. Someone shushed him. In the darkness, Sash couldn't tell who, but she was willing to bet it was Mrs. Correa. The woman didn't like that kind of talk. She was easily upset by the thought that their lives were anything less than ideal. How she could have convinced herself of that when they were all buried under-ground, essentially as living corpses, Sash hadn't the faintest clue. Self-delusion was a powerful thing, she supposed.

A hand found its way into Sash's lap, seeking her own out.

Her head instinctively swiveled in the direction of where it originated.

Yuna.

Sash opened her closed fist, fingers bumping into Yuna's where they groped uselessly at her thigh. The moment their hands touched, Yuna's latched on to Sash's with a strength belied by how small and delicate Sash knew her to be.

"Everyone, keep calm."

It was what Dr. Moran always said when this sort of thing happened. *Stay calm. Everything will be fine. Nothing to see here.* (In this case literally, because they couldn't see a single thing even if they wanted to.)

"Why?"

The question was out of Sash's mouth before she had even really formulated the thought.

A profound silence greeted her query. So rich and deep was

that silence that Sash felt as though it might smother her to death, like a nice, soft pillow to the face.

"What in God's name do you mean?"

The doctor's voice cut through that inky black darkness with the precision of a well-fired arrow.

But now that Sash had started this, she had to finish it. There was no other option. No other avenue to explore. No other recourse. They were going to have this conversation. Now. Here. With nothing but the darkness holding them back.

"I mean," she started, unsure exactly what she meant, but trusting that by the end of her sentence she would somehow find her way there, "why should we stay calm?"

The veil of shadows did nothing to mitigate the acerbic force of Dr. Moran's chuckle. "What else would you suggest, Alexandra? Panic? What, pray tell, would that accomplish?"

Under the table, a solid boot lashed out and kicked Sash square in the shin. It hurt. A lot. She knew those boots well enough to know that they had metal bits at the front to fortify the toe. And she didn't need to see Misha to know that he was shooting her a glare hot enough to melt steel.

Thankfully, her inability to actually see said glare rendered it powerless.

Take that, Misha.

"I'm not saying we should panic," Sash countered.

"Then what are you saying? Mind your words, dear. They have more power than you know."

"I'm saying we need to talk about what this means."

"Sasha, sit down." Her mother's voice was as brittle and clipped as it ever was. But more, it sounded tired. More tired

67

than it usually did. The woman seemed to mostly run on will-power and spite, both sprinkled with a heady amount of fear. But fatigue laced its way through her words.

"Mom."

"Sasha—"

"This keeps happening!" Sash didn't mean to shout. It sort of just happened. But she felt not a single ounce of regret for allowing it to. "The lights keep going off."

"A simple anomaly with the power," Moran said, as if a single simple anomaly didn't have the potential to stand between the lot of them and at least half a dozen ways to die. "It'll be back on shortly."

"That's not the point. This used to happen once a year. Maybe twice. Then it was once every couple of months. Now it's happening every few weeks."

"Sasha," Misha hissed. He tried to kick her again, but she was too quick. His boot connected only with the empty air where her legs used to be. She'd moved them to the side, knowing his anger wouldn't be so easily dissipated.

"And that doesn't even get into the problems we've been having with the air," Sash said. That was the trickiest point. The one they were universally all more afraid of. They could live in the dark. It had protected them this long. But they couldn't live without air.

"There are no problems with the air." Moran's tone invited no argument.

But she was going to get one anyway.

"Well," Gabe started, "actually—"

"Actually *nothing*," Moran barked, cutting him off. "We have nothing to worry about."

Baba Olya let loose a jagged little laugh. "At least until we all suffocate down here like rats."

"There is nothing wrong with the air," Moran reiterated. Her tone dared Gabe to contradict her.

He was far smarter than Sash. He even didn't try. Instead, Gabe said absolutely nothing at all, slamming his mouth shut with such force that Sash actually heard his teeth slam together.

But Sash wasn't Gabe. There was nothing she loved more than powering through an obstacle with sheer brute force.

"We've been in this bunker for ten years. We have to talk about the fact that we can't stay down here forever." Even though no one could see it, Sash shook her head. "We never talk about it. That's nuts. Don't you see that? It's insane. What's the plan? Do we just wait until we run out of food? Drinkable water? Air? Then what?"

"Sasha," her mother begged. It wasn't something she did often. "Please."

"Mom, we have to—" Sash stood. She realized her mistake the second the emergency lights flickered on.

Yuna's hand was still in hers.

Dinner was the one time everyone took off the gloves. They were allowed to at least eat without them. It was the one time of day Sash felt the most human.

Now, gloveless, she and Yuna were still holding hands. Touching. Unequivocal physical contact. Illicit, delicious, verboten skin-to-skin fraternization.

The doctor's gaze dropped from Sash's face, trailed down her arm, and landed squarely on their joined hands.

Yuna let go as if she were holding something hot. As if Sash's very touch burned.

The sky turned white.

Her eyes felt like they were bleeding. Something scalded her arm.

She buried her face in her father's shoulder and screamed.

Moran's eyes roamed upward, locking on Sash's. "Alexandra. It would seem you've forgotten one of our most important rules."

A heavy silence descended upon the room.

"I—" Sash's eyes darted to Yuna, who worried her lip between her teeth.

Yuna's mother whispered something in rapid, angry Korean at her daughter. Sash didn't understand it, but she didn't need a Korean-English dictionary to know it was an admonishment. The color faded from Yuna's face.

"It wasn't Yuna's fault." The words left Sash in a rush. "I grabbed her hand. I wasn't thinking. I—"

Moran held up a hand to silence her. "That is no excuse, Alexandra."

Sash's usual retort about her preferred mode of address died on her tongue.

With slow, deliberate steps, Moran approached. When she was close enough for Sash to make out the fine lines crowding the corner of her eyes, she spoke. "Perhaps you need a reminder of the dangers of skin-to-skin contact."

"I—what?"

Before Sash could say much more, Moran gestured for Misha. His strong hands—gloved now—closed around Sash's arm. He yanked her forward, ignoring her yelp of surprise.

But their forward progress was stalled by another hand on her other arm. Sash looked down to find Baba Olya's knobby knuckles whiten with the force of her grip. The old woman fixed Moran with a stare that would melt steel.

"If you lay a finger on my granddaughter, I'll make sure to cut it off."

Moran's lips twitched into what could almost be called a smile. "I have no intention of harming Alexandra. I merely wish to educate her."

Olga spat on the floor, her grip tightening even further.

The act sent a ripple of shock through the room. Even Sash's feet felt rooted to the ground.

She had never seen anyone treat Moran with such blatant disrespect.

Moran simply arched a single eyebrow. "Misha. Take Alexandra to the dark room. Perhaps she needs some time to reflect on her actions."

Misha pulled on Sash's arm, ripping her away from Olga's grip. Sash bent her knees, putting all her weight into resisting.

"No, please." Her voice inched higher and higher with every word. "Not the dark room. Please. I'm sorry."

The rambled pleas tumbled from her lips one right after the other. Fear sang through her body, heady and sharp.

The dark room was the worst part of the bunker. Nothing penetrated it. Not light. Not sound. Nothing. There was only a blackness so overpowering it felt like it would crush you. It felt like it would pour in through your nose and your mouth and your eyes and drown you.

Sash had been locked in there once. She'd been caught playing hide-and-seek with Gabe and Yuna without her gloves on, and Moran had sent her for a time-out in the dark room. For two days, she'd been left there, without food, without water. Without sound. Without light. She'd been eleven years old.

She never wanted to go back there again.

Her legs failed her. She sagged to the floor, her knees slamming into the hard metal. She'd have bruises later. But now, she barely felt the pain.

"I'm sorry," Sash said. "I made a mistake." Her words were thin and reedy. Her chest rose and fell in short sharp breaths.

Panic, her mind distantly supplied. *This is what panic feels like.*

Moran tilted her head as she stared down at Sash.

Get up, whispered a voice at the back of her head.

But she couldn't. The thought of being left in the dark room was too much to bear. It was the one thing Moran could lord over her, and they both knew it.

The doctor's expression softened as she approached Sash. The sound of her long skirt whispering against the textured metal of the floor grated Sash's ears.

"If we aren't punished for our sins," Moran said, "how will we ever learn?"

Sash shook her head, closing her eyes. For a brief moment, it felt like she was already there, drowning in darkness. "It was a mistake. I won't—It was a mistake."

Moran hummed thoughtfully. After an achingly long moment, she said, "Very well. See that you do not make it again."

And then she swept away, her long skirt slapping at Sash's face.

The doctor settled into her seat, a beatific smile on her face. "Now, shall we get back to our dinner?"

CHAPTER 11

YUNA

Hours later, Yuna still felt sick.

She'd said nothing as Sash had pleaded on her knees not to be sent to the dark room. She hadn't followed Sash after she'd fled the room, her hand clasped to her mouth. She'd stood back and let her friend be punished for something they had both done.

Moran was like that. Singling people out. Sash always seemed to be a particularly enticing target for the doctor's ire.

And Yuna had said nothing in her defense.

Shame sat heavy in her chest. She should have done something. Anything.

But she hadn't. She'd been a coward, as quiet and compliant as her mother and father were whenever Moran decided to pursue one of her punishing whims. Now, she stood between them as she watched Moran prepare to do what only she could.

Leave the bunker.

Go to the surface.

See what was left after . . . whatever it was that drove them down here like moles.

A deep and implacable yearning filled Yuna, coursing through every vein and artery in her body, as she watched Moran prepare. It was strong enough to chase out all other feelings, including her shame. The sense memory of sun warming her skin had long since faded into something abstract, distant from the realm of physical possibility. It was like the taste of her grandmother's kimchi bokkeumbap. A flimsy recollection, divorced from its finer details. A thought that existed only in theory. A memory without flavor.

Misha stepped up to help Moran put on her suit. It was a cumbersome thing, like a costume out of one of their comic books. Like an astronaut, Yuna mused, from those dog-eared issues of *Popular Science* that Gabe loved so dearly.

The suit was an industrial shade of light green, topped with a helmet that looked like a soft-sided tank. Moran held out her arms as Misha slipped a pair of heavy straps over them, settling them on her shoulders.

A hazmat suit, Yuna thought. *Hazardous materials. That's what's out there. That's all that's out there.*

Even so . . . Yuna's jealousy was so profound, she could taste it. She could roll it around on her tongue. She could bite into it. She could chew on it.

Moran turned to them, her face obscured by the clear front of the helmet. Her voice carried through the layers of respirator equipment rigged into the suit. Mr. Correa's ad hoc solution, Yuna was fairly certain. He was good with that sort of thing. And he was teaching Gabe to be as well. One day, Gabe would take over.

Which would mean that at some far-flung point in the future, they would still be down here, living off powdered gruel and the withered fruits of a sun-starved garden.

No, whispered a voice at the back of Yuna's head. *Don't.*

Yuna shook herself to dislodge the thought. Her mother's gaze cut to her, sharp enough to draw blood.

Moran's breath left her besuited body in a tinny rush of air. Her words reverberated against the inside of the hazmat gear, echoing against her frail bones.

"Though the surface is cruel, the shadows of night will keep me safe." Moran's gaze drifted to each person in the turn, not the least bit diminished by the filter of see-through plastic that separated them. "For this, I thank the blessed dark."

A chorus of mumbled, "We thank the blessed dark" rose up from those gathered around Moran.

It was never formalized, this call and response. Dr. Moran had never asked them to do it. They had just started doing it. Yuna couldn't remember who the first was. Probably Misha or Sash's mom. They seemed like the types. Maybe Gabe's mom, Mrs. Correa, on one of her bad days. She had them sometimes, when the cloud slid over her eyes and she wore calluses onto her fingers tracing her rosary beads over and over and over again.

Misha wrapped his large hands around the hatch and turned the wheel. It squeaked loudly in the deafening roar of silence that enveloped them. It swung open under his palms, its thick metal body taunting them—or maybe just Yuna—with the possibility of a world beyond it.

What's out there? Yuna wanted to know. She wanted to know it more than anything. Sometimes, she was better at silencing that question than she was right now. But every time she saw that hatch swing open, she couldn't help but think it. *Of all the things we left behind, what's left?*

Yuna's feet shuffled. Her mother rested a hand on her shoulder. In comfort or in warning. It was hard to tell. So often, those two were indistinguishable down here, hidden away from all the things that might hurt them.

Yuna sighed without even realizing she was doing it. Her chest hurt. It was best not to think about why.

Moran's heavy boots clomped up the stairs, one by one, with painstaking slowness. When she reached the hatch, she turned to look at them.

"And into the blessed dark, we go."

Always *we*. Never *I*. As if all of them went out there with her. As if she carried each of their hopes and fears and prayers with her as she went.

One boot lifted, arced. Crossed the threshold. Then, the other. Yuna's heart clamored inside her rib cage; the muscles in her calves twitched with the urge to go, to run, to leap and lurch and fling her body through that open door. If she perished, so be it, so long as she did it with sky above her head and fresh air in her lungs.

But she didn't do any of those things.

She stood in one spot, rooted to the artificial metal ground beneath her feet, watching as Misha swung the hatch closed behind Moran and her hazmat suit.

When the doctor returned the next morning, she'd have the same look on her face that she had worn every morning for the past 3,627 days.

She shed the protective layers one by one, bequeathing

each into the waiting hands of Misha and Mrs. Correa.

When her face was bare, she turned to the crowd that had assembled once more. Her lips pressed into a hard line. Dark circles smudged the skin beneath her tired eyes. She sighed. Everything they needed to know was contained in that single, sad exhalation. The truth hardly needed to be verbalized, but she gave it to them anyway.

"I'm sorry," she said. She was always sorry. Every time this happened.

"It still isn't safe." It never was. It was a fact that never changed. It was as constant as the metal walls that cradled them underground. As constant as the darkness pressing in around them on all sides. As constant as the dozens of feet of soil crushing them slowly, slowly, slowly.

"We'll have to stay down here just a little bit longer."

Just a little bit. As a lie, it was the most constant of them all.

CHAPTER 12

GABE

Dr. Moran had given him permission to go spelunking in the air vents, so as far as Gabe was concerned he was doing absolutely nothing wrong.

He kept repeating this thought to himself over and over as he crawled through the ducts, bony elbows banging against ancient metal plating. (Well, more like several decades old.) The ventilation system smelled like something from a movie he'd seen as a kid, way back when in the Before times, about the least stodgy archaeologist Gabe could possibly envision having adventures in far-flung lands. *Indiana Jones*, that's what it was. The smell wasn't bad per se. Not like something had crawled in here and died. It was just old. Old and undiscovered. Someone had built it, many moons ago, but it had been forgotten, this passage. Left waiting for someone else to find it, to unearth its secret. Waiting for someone like Gabe.

Gabe, who was doing absolutely nothing wrong.

(Okay, so the doctor hadn't exactly agreed to a spelunking expedition, but he hadn't seen fit to bog her down with details. And she'd said, "Do what you have to," which was as much permission as Gabe needed quite frankly.)

He was doing this for all of them. Not for himself. Not for his own curiosity. The bunker was old. Falling apart at the seams. If there was a way to improve the airflow, to keep them alive (buried) down here longer, he had to figure it out. He had to twist and turn the problem over in his hands until he could take it apart and put it back together again.

So, really, he was doing nothing wrong.

Why, then, had he felt the need to wait until nightfall to go about his task? Not that there was ever truly a "night" down in the bunker anyway, just a time they all agreed to go to bed in complete darkness. Why had he not told anyone save Moran that he'd discovered something on the blueprints? (Not that he'd told her specifically what he'd discovered, but he'd put them on her desk. So really, she could have seen it plain as day if only she had been inclined to look.)

And an even bigger question: Why had he not told Sash and Yuna? Why hadn't he brought them along? Why was he not clambering through these ventilation shafts with Sash on one side of him and Yuna on the other? Why were their voices not filling out this accursed darkness as he labored forward, into the unknown?

Okay, so that was more than one question, but all of them still stood.

And Gabe didn't really have any answers. He just had a feeling. Something deep in his gut that told him to march forth, into the shadows, to see what there was to see with his own eyes and no others.

Maybe there was nothing to see. Maybe he was just a little fool overwhelmed by wishful thinking, driven batty by the monotony of their lives, day in and day out, spent in the same place with the same people doing the same things, following the same rules, eating the same food until one day there would be nothing left.

That's it, isn't it? a voice at the back of his mind queried. It's fear that drove him into this duct alone. Fear that made him search it out in the first place. Fear that kept his mouth shut.

Sash was so brave. Yuna was too, in a completely different way. Gabe didn't want to be the only one who wasn't. He didn't want to be the only one who was afraid.

And he was. Constantly. Every morning he woke up, fear was the first thing to greet him at the door. Its insistent fist pounded at his rib cage, demanding to be let in.

It was still there now, humming at the back of his skull. But it wasn't the only thing insistent in there. There was a louder thrum, a deeper urge driving him forward.

Curiosity.

His knees ached with every inch gained. But that thrum got louder and louder as he followed the lines of the blueprint he'd committed to memory, deeper and deeper into the bunker until he felt that seismic shift inside him, that crossing of a dotted line that signified he was officially off the map.

There was something illicit in what he was doing.

You must always tell the truth.

That was one of Dr. Moran's irrevocable, unbreakable rules.

And he hadn't broken it. Not really.

He just hadn't told the *whole* truth. And that wasn't a lie, was it?

(Yes, it was.)

Because it wasn't just efficiency in air filtration Gabe was chasing. It was something else. Something bigger.

Something unknown.

The details in the blueprints didn't add up. He'd done the math, the geometry, the scaling more times than he could count, and it never added up. There was something there that wasn't covered by one set of blueprints. It wouldn't be the first time.

When Gabe was twelve, he'd stumbled on his father's stash of papers, the ones Moran had given to him when he took on the lion's share of work to keep the bunker running.

To keep them all alive—

There had been two documents that looked very similar. Similar, but not identical. They'd reminded him of the picture books he'd loved as a very small child, the kind where you had to compare two nearly identical wild hodgepodges of imagery and find the tiny differences between them.

"Dad, why are they like this?"

A shrug before the papers were removed from his hands. "Cornelius Percival Moran was a nutjob."

A light smack on his father's arm from his mother. "Cornelius Percival Moran is the reason we're alive. Show some respect."

Gabe continued his forward trek (crawl) through the darkness. The flashlight hanging around his neck—powered by a small hand crank on the side—flickered in and out, casting broken shadows against the metallic walls of the air vent. It was shoddy lighting, but it was bright enough for Gabe to just make out the three-letter symbol stamped near the seam of every panel.

CPM.

Cornelius Percival Moran.

The man who had ordered the construction of this bunker decades prior to anyone ever needing it. The man who had died long before he'd ever get the satisfaction of knowing his endeavor would eventually save lives.

The light flickered out once more, plunging Gabe into total darkness. But this time, it didn't flicker back on. He reached for the flashlight, fumbling against the cord around his neck.

It's okay. Darkness is good. Darkness is safe.

("And for this, we thank the blessed dark.")

Gabe adjusted his weight, moving his center of balance from one hand to the other, trying to grab the handle of the flashlight.

And that proved to be a mistake.

The change was too much for the rickety air vent paneling. One minute, his knees and palms were resting on cold, hard metal. The next, they were resting on nothing but air.

Falling, Gabe knew, was a thing that happened fast. The laws of physics demanded it thus. And yet, it felt as though he were collapsing in slow motion, suspended in a merciless, unmitigated field of blackness.

Then he landed. Hard.

Everything hurt. His shoulder hurt and his knee hurt and his face hurt and, most of all, his hip hurt. It had borne the brunt of the fall. Better than trying to catch himself with a hand and breaking his wrist but . . .

"Ow."

He groped at his neck for the flashlight, but it was gone. Slipped off in the fall. With the arm that stung less, Gabe felt around for something solid. He inched forward, fear so high and thick in his throat he thought he might choke on it. Maybe this was it, this was where he died. Maybe this was why they said curiosity killed the—

His fingers brushed something. Cold, hard metal. Right under his palm.

Hastening forward, Gabe's foot caught on something, nearly taking him out (again). The flashlight. He dropped to his knees—"Ow"—and with shaking hands, he cranked the power on.

The beam of light sliced through the darkness, searing Gabe's eyes. He squinted against the brightness, tears blurring his eyes (from the glare and not from the pain, he lied to himself) as they alighted on the thing in front of him.

A hatch.

A door.

Smaller than the one out front but nearly identical in every other way.

Same wheel handle.

Same locking mechanism.

Same rounded rectangular shape.

Gabe settled his hands on the handle, curled his fingers around the peeling paint. And turned.

CHAPTER 13

SASH

One minute she was asleep. The next, she was not.

Sash lay in bed, staring at the bunk above her. Nastia's soft snoring was the only sound she could hear. Normally, the audible, rhythmic rise and fall of her sister's chest lulled Sash gently to slumber, like an organic metronome.

But not tonight.

I heard something.

She squinted into the semidarkness. It wasn't completely dark. Soft red lights set into the wall granted her enough light to just about see her surroundings. Red light was safe. Red light was the *only* light that was safe. And normally, it was enough to chase away the nightmares of the dark room. She hadn't had one for years, but Moran's threat at dinner had brought them roaring back. But usually, opening her eyes to see the red light was enough to pull her from their grasp. Tonight, it wasn't a nightmare that woke her.

It was a sound.

The door was closed, as it always was. In the other bunk bed against the opposite wall, Baba Olya slept, a scrap of unfinished knitting clutched in her hand. Her arthritis was getting worse, but she kept on knitting through the stiffness and pain. It calmed her nerves, she claimed. It was the only way she could sleep at night, buried under however many layers of sand and soil and sediment. Whenever she ran out of yarn—which was often, considering that their supplies were limited—she would unwind the last thing she made and start over. Usually it was a sweater, or a scarf. (Though it wasn't like they ever experienced anything one could rightfully call weather down here). It was the action that mattered, not the end product.

In the bunk above Olga, Sash's mother lay curled on her side, facing the wall with her back to Sash. She always slept like that, her body tight and small like an armadillo. She was quiet now, so quiet Sash couldn't hear her breathe. It was too dark to see really, despite the dim red track light that was always on. It glowed faintly from the recessed area where the floor met the walls, hooked directly into the bunker's generator.

Sometimes her mother had nightmares that left her whimpering. Other nights she woke half the bunker with her screaming. But tonight, she was as silent as death.

Then what did I hear?

As quietly as she could, Sash pushed her blankets down to her waist and sat up. They were the same blankets she'd been sleeping under for almost ten years. White, with dinosaurs cavorting across the length of them in various primary colors. A yellow triceratops. A blue T. rex. A red stegosaurus. Green ferns separating them at regular intervals. The cotton fiber had gone soft with repeated washings and some of the colors had begun to fade. The stegosauruses were more pink than red at this point.

Sash strained her ears to listen, to check if whatever noise had awoken her came again.

It didn't.

Go back to sleep, she told herself.

But something else whispered at the back of her skull, some voice that was hers and not.

Get up.

She did.

The metal floor was cold even through her socks (knitted lovingly by her grandmother). She inched forward, hyperaware of the bunk bed's propensity to creak whenever any significant amount of weight shifted on it. But it was quiet as a tomb as she slid out from under the covers and tiptoed across the room to the door.

Her fingertips grazed the cold metal of the doorknob when it happened.

Boom.

Boom.

Boom.

Sash froze, her hand just barely touching the door.

That was it. That was the sound. That was what had woken her up.

A tendril of fear unfurled languidly in her stomach as she

waited, holding her breath to see if that rhythmic pounding came again.

It didn't.

Probably just the generator.

There were all manner of strange sounds in the bunker. How the lights stayed on was something of a mystery to Sash. She knew there were generators *somewhere*, hooked up to *something*, but the details had never really troubled her before. The Correas handled all that.

She could go back to bed. She could crawl under the covers and pretend she hadn't heard a thing.

It was nothing. Probably nothing.

But . . .

Her hand closed around the doorknob and turned it, pulling the door open by painfully slow inches. Behind her, someone shifted, their sheets whispering together in a soft susurration that seemed impossibly loud in the silent, dark night.

She went still, waiting.

A snore.

A huff.

Someone rolling over, burrowing deeper into their mound of blankets.

Then nothing. All the Eremenkos were snug in their beds, oblivious to . . . whatever was happening.

Now or never.

Sash opened the door just enough to slip through.

The same dim red track lights ran the length of the hallway . . . or at least they should have. But they were off.

Sash swallowed a thick, curdled lump of dread in her throat. She began to walk down the hallway, her right hand on the wall, her left extended before her and groping blindly in the darkness.

It's nothing, she thought. *Something's up with the generator. I should just go wake Gabe or his dad and—*

Boom.

She jumped, her socked feet slipping on the cold hard floor.

Her heartbeat thudded so loudly it reverberated through her skull, drowning out all other noise.

Something's outside.

The thought came unbidden. Unwanted. Unthinkable. Except, she thought it. And now, she could not unthink it.

There was nothing outside. All that existed, all that survived, was right here. In this manmade burrow beneath the ground, hidden far from the penetrating rays of the sun.

Maybe it's someone pulling a prank.

The thought felt flimsy in comparison to the first. Like a scrap of tracing paper placed over a neon sign in a futile attempt to shield it.

But even so, she had to check.

Sash tiptoed to the other bedrooms. A peek through the small round windows set in each hatch showed rows of bunks identical to the one she shared with her brother.

The Correas were right next door to theirs. Two bunk beds, sleeping four. Mr. and Mrs. Correa against the right-hand wall with Gabe and Lucas against the left. Mrs. Correa's hand hung down over the side of her thin mattress, her wedding ring gleaming amber in the faint red glow from the track lights. Mr. Correa's hand lay, palm up, by the side of his head, directly below her dangling fingers, as if at some point those two hands had been touching.

We aren't supposed to touch.

The thought came unbidden. Uninvited. Unwelcome. But there all the same.

All four Correas were fast asleep. A soft snore rumbled from Gabe's bunk as he mumbled something in his sleep.

"Divide by two . . . carry the four . . ."

Sash left him to his mathematics.

Her socked feet carried her farther down the corridor. Yuna and her family were all accounted for, all asleep. She may have lingered for just a moment in the doorway, admiring the fall of Yuna's hair over the side of the bunk. It was long enough to brush the ground at this point. It was due for a cut, but Sash hoped she'd keep it just a little bit longer.

She forced herself to leave. It was creepy watching people sleep, even if they were all sleeping on top of one another like puppies in a pile.

Moran's office door was at the end of the hall, right before the bend that led to the common area.

Anyone leaving the bedrooms would have to walk past her door to get anywhere else in the bunker.

Sash's fingers hovered over the handle, remembering the feeling of the lash across her knuckles when she had tried to pick the lock six years ago. It had taken weeks for the welts to heal. Her mother may have looked like a fragile music-box ballerina, but she had a surprising amount of upper-body strength.

But the memory wasn't strong enough to keep Sash from closing her hand around the knob and trying to turn.

The door was, as always, locked.

Boom.

Her head jerked in the direction of the hatch.

Maybe it was Moran. Maybe she'd gone back out again and was trapped and needed to be let back in.

Surely, the sound was something as quotidian as that. The nightly ritual, gone somewhat awry.

But uncertainty drummed out a beat in Sash's chest.

Her breath rasped out harshly as she felt her way through the darkened hallways to the supply closet. There was a flashlight in there. The kind with the hand crank that didn't need batteries, which was good because they'd run out of batteries about three years ago.

The sound of the crank was impossibly loud in the silence. Every grind of its motor made Sash's stomach turn as if it was rotating along with it. Once it had enough juice to light her way, she continued to the hatch, her pulse thrumming in her ears loudly enough to drown out the frantic sound of her own breathing.

Boom.

Sash jumped. Her socks skidded against the metal floor. The flashlight tumbled from her hands, clattering loudly enough to wake the dead as it fell.

The hatch was just up ahead.

And there was no mistaking where that sound was coming from.

The hatch. The sound was coming from the hatch. There was no question.

It's just Moran, she told herself. *It's just Moran doing some stupid experiment. She locked herself out and now she needs to be rescued. The savior becomes the saved. Blessed dark, my ass.*

How Sash wished she could believe that.

The bulk of the hatch came into view like a shadowy threat at the end of the corridor.

The flashlight came to life in Sash's hand, the beam so blindingly white it stung her eyes.

Sash's feet slid against the metal floor, snagging here and there on an uneven rivet holding the floor plates together.

Every fiber of her being screamed at her to run in the other direction, to hide deep within the belly of the bunker, somewhere far in the twisting nonsensical hallways. So deep no one could find her.

Certainly not whatever was making that noise. A noise that sounded too much like knocking for Sash's comfort if it were actually anyone but Moran making it.

But of course it wasn't anyone but Moran.

Sash took one step forward. Then another. And another. Her feet had gone unbearably cold through the worn cotton of her socks. It was just the cold metal. Not the fear, crawling up her throat like bile.

The hatch loomed ahead, the chipped red paint of the heavy metal handle lurid against the drab green of the door.

"It's just Moran," Sash whispered to no one but herself.

Her limbs trembled only a little as she climbed the stairs leading up to the hatch.

Just Moran.

Swallowing thickly, she rose up on her toes and looked through the hatch.

Her breath fogged up the glass for a moment. All she could see was her own reflection. Hair a mess. Eyes a touch too wide.

Nothing. There was nothing out there.

Not Moran. Not some nameless monster. Just the inverse of a scared, silly girl, jumping at things that go bump in the night.

"Stupid," Sash told herself. "Just stupid."

She was ready to go. The flashlight clicked off in her hand. Not enough cranking. Only the bare minimum. But it was fine. Because there was nothing out there. *Nothing to see here, folks. Move along. Be on your way.*

A fine idea, Sash thought, to do just that. But she glanced back through the glass window of the hatch once more, just for good measure.

This time, something looked back.

CHAPTER 14

YUNA

Not every aspect of living in the bunker was entirely terrible.

Yuna would never admit so aloud within earshot of Sash, but there were moments she liked. Maybe even truly enjoyed.

Like ballet.

Staying in shape was one of Moran's rules. It wasn't a bad one. (Another thought never to be spoken in Sash's presence: Not all of Moran's guidelines for life were devoid of merit.) It went hand in hand with her ideas about purity of mind and body. The body was a temple. The owner of said body was its caretaker. If they were ever going to survive on the surface, they had to be in peak physical form.

To outrun the monsters. Yuna pressed her lips tightly together to hold back the giggle threatening to spill out. She didn't think monsters were funny, but she did think the thought of outrunning them via a series of gracefully performed glissades was.

Mrs. Eremenko clapped her hands in time with the scratchy recording of piano music emanating from the record player in the corner.

"Tombé, pas de bourrée, glissade, assemblé! I said assemblé, Nastia, not . . . whatever that was."

There wasn't a mirror in the drained swimming pool, but Yuna had a vivid imagination. She pictured the line of them— her, Nastia, and even little Lucas, struggling to keep up—bobbing up and down in her imagined mirror's reflective surface, toes pointed, knees extended, arms cutting through the air as they moved through their prescribed port de bras.

Gabe had been granted special permission to skip these classes. Asthma, Dr. Moran had said. It wouldn't do to have him collapse on the pool's hard, tiled flooring. He did have to go to yoga and Pilates, also taught by Mrs. Eremenko, but the ballet he avoided. It was just as well. Yuna would never say it to his face, but he was terrible at it. No ear for music, that one. Only the tiniest sliver of dexterity.

Normally, Sash would be lurking toward the back of the room, but today, she was nowhere to be found.

We can't stay down here forever.

Sash's words had been rattling around in Yuna's brain ever since that disastrous dinner.

So far, Sash hadn't been made to pay for them. That was rare. Usually, that sort of back talk wasn't tolerated, but Moran had shown herself to be *un*usually magnanimous about the whole thing.

Perhaps because she knew—they all knew—that Sash was right.

They couldn't stay down here forever.

There wasn't an infinite amount of food.

There wasn't an infinite amount of air, especially if the circulation system went out.

And despite Moran's assurances, there might not be an infinite amount of water. The doctor said there was an underground stream that fed their system—groundwater that remained safe for human consumption after the Cataclysm— but all they had to go on was her word. Yuna had never seen it with her own eyes. The stream might have been less than a stream and more of a generous lake, feeding them for the better part of a decade, but eventually, it could run dry. And if it did . . .

Well, the thought hardly merited further explication. It was dark enough as it was, and frankly, Yuna had precious little patience for dark thoughts. They were pointless. They accomplished nothing. They were a plague upon the mind, distracting oneself from vastly more important things like—

"Your arms, Yuna." Mrs. Eremenko's voice reverberated against the walls of the swimming pool. "They're flapping about like dead chicken wings."

To drive her point home, she flailed her arms up and down in a wild gesticulation only vaguely reminiscent of dying poultry. "Support from the below. Not from the shoulder."

"Yes, right. Sorry." Yuna made the appropriate adjustment and continued with the exercise.

Tombé, pas de bourrée, glissade, assemblé. Jeté, jeté, jeté, jeté. Waltz step and waltz step and waltz step and waltz step. Piqué arabesque. Tombé and sous-sus.

"Not beautiful but serviceable."

High praise coming from Mrs. Eremenko. She was nearly

impossible to please. This was the closest Yuna could hope to come.

The physicality of it took Yuna out of herself. When the sweat was beading against her brow and sticking the Transformers T-shirt to her back, she could forget where she was. For the most ephemeral of moments, she could pretend she was anywhere else other than where she was, buried far underground, deep enough for no sunlight to penetrate. She had, in this moment, a tiny suspension of disbelief, one in which she could pretend that daytime was more than just a half-remembered fantasy.

Mrs. Eremenko clapped out the beats, shouting at them to keep on time. "The music is not a suggestion, Nastia. The music is master."

"There is no music," the younger girl grumbled, so only Yuna could hear.

She snickered, not enough for Mrs. Eremenko to notice, but enough for Nastia to feel at least a little bit validated.

But to Yuna, there was always music. Inside, where no one else could hear.

The class wound down, ending as it always did, with a reverence in the direction of the nonexistent pianist. Mrs. Eremenko was nothing if not a creature of habit. That was how ballet class traditionally ended everywhere in the world, back when there was a world in which to have ballet class. And so that was how they ended every class here. With a reverence. But without a pianist.

Afterward, Yuna wiped at her brow with a rag that had once been white before it had been through the wash a few thousand times. Mrs. Eremenko came over, her brow pinched, her lips flattened into a hard, displeased line.

"Where is my daughter?" The consonants were clipped and harsh. The question was proposed with the air of not truly expecting an answer but mildly—and Yuna couldn't stress *mildly* enough—hoping to find one anyway.

"I don't know," Yuna said.

And truly, she didn't. Normally, they were joined at the hip, but for the past few days, Sash had been oddly cagey. Jumping at little noises. Fading away halfway through conversations she was clearly less than invested in. Yuna had tried to ask what was wrong, but Sash only shrugged and said everything was fine. A lie. Yuna wasn't always the greatest judge of that sort of thing, but it was so obvious this time around that it was almost offensive.

"Hm" was all Mrs. Eremenko said.

"I saw her by the hydroponics," Nastia offered from where she sat on the floor, stretching her hamstrings. "Mumbling something to herself like a crazy person."

Mrs. Eremenko frowned. It made her look a solid ten years older. "Your sister is not crazy."

Nastia shrugged. "Sure was acting like it."

Further conversation was precluded by Nastia bowing her torso over her quadricep and touching her forehead to her knee. Conversation over.

"I can go look for her," Yuna offered.

But Mrs. Eremenko was already shaking her head. "Don't. You're a good girl. Stay that way."

With that, she pivoted her heel with all the grace of a true ballerina of the Bolshoi and left, sweeping out of the room with her caftan billowing in her own self-made breeze.

Hm.

Well.

Yuna was going to look for Sash anyway.

She started in the usual places. Sash's bunk. Too obvious. The bed was made but only just barely. The disdain with which the quilt had been tossed over the mattress was abundantly evident. The kitchen. Empty save for Mrs. Correa, meticulously measuring out dried beans. They were nearly out. A pleasant thought for another day. The library, if one could call it that. (One honestly couldn't.) Nothing.

Frustrated, Yuna turned around and made her way down the corridor to the generator room. When she turned the corner, she nearly collided into Sash herself.

"Dude," Yuna said, catching her hands on Sash's elbow. The other girl seized up, as if even that minor act of physical contact was too much.

A flash of memory burned through Yuna with the intensity of lightning. The night of the blackout. Her hand in Sash's. The warmth of another person's skin against her own. (How long had it been since she'd felt something like that? Too long.) The glare of the emergency lights as everyone saw. The viscous shame that settled low in her gut when Moran caught her eye.

Stop it.

"Where have you been?" Yuna asked. "Your mom was looking for you."

Sash furrowed her brow. In that moment, she looked astonishingly like her mother. A thought Yuna knew was best left unshared.

"I've been . . ." Sash glanced over her shoulder. Then the other. Her gaze wandered the room, not quite locking on any one thing in particular but with an intensity that made Yuna think she was maybe seeing *through* things instead of just seeing them. "Around."

"Around?" Yuna repeated. "What do you mean 'around'?"

They lived in a bunker, for God's sake. There were only so many places one could go.

Unless . . .

No.

Not an option.

But before Sash could answer, a heavy tread signaled that they weren't alone. Yuna recognized those footsteps before their owner rounded the corner.

"Hi, Misha." Yuna liked the face people made when she threw out their name before their faces had a chance to catch up. They'd all been living in the bunker so long that Yuna couldn't possibly fathom not being able to recognize people by their distinctive treads alone, but apparently, it wasn't a skill universally acquired.

"Yuna," Misha said by way of acknowledgment. And then, there it was. The face. Puckered lips. Consternation in the set of the eyes. Nice. When he turned to his sister, his expression soured even further. "Mom was looking for you."

"Cool," Sash said. "I don't care."

Misha's face contorted into that trademark Eremenko brow furrow. They all did it. Except for Olga. She didn't frown. She only ever scowled. "What is wrong with you? First, that display during dinner—"

"You mean during the third blackout we've had this month?"

Yuna wished she could fade away into the ether, but alas, she could not. She was trapped, here, in the middle of an Eremenko sibling tug-of-war.

"Don't be a brat," Misha said.

"I don't have any other hobbies," Sash countered.

"Can the two of you just not?" Yuna cut in.

She just really hated confrontation. There was no point. They were trapped in here with one another whether they liked it or not. The only thing sniping at one another would accomplish was making everyone miserable.

Misha shot Yuna a glare, but it was softer than the one his sister earned.

"You're on scrubbing duty," he said.

Ah, yes. Scrubbing duty. The act of painstakingly cleaning every surface of the bunker on hands and knees. For safety, Moran insisted. Contaminants could be anywhere.

"I was on scrubbing duty last week," Sash said, affronted. It was the most direct emotion Yuna had seen the other girl display in days. In a way, it was its own comfort.

"That's why you shouldn't be a brat." Misha didn't wait for his sister to counter with an argument. He was a wise man. He dropped that nugget and turned and left.

What was it with the Eremenkos and dramatic exits? Yuna might never know.

"Ugh." Sash shook herself. "I'm so sick of scrubbing this place down. Especially when . . ."

But the thought never manifested into words. Sash dug her teeth into her lower lip and made to leave.

Yuna grabbed Sash's forearm before she could escape deeper into the bunker—or "around"—and evade further questioning.

"What's happening, Sash? Tell me."

Sash studied Yuna for a good long moment. A moment so long it sort of stopped being good, actually. Sash opened her mouth.

Closed it. Opened it again. Did another one of those around-the-room glances that made Yuna think she was either being extremely paranoid or, depending on the circumstances, precisely the amount of paranoid she needed to be.

When Sash finally spoke, her words failed to bring even the tiniest amount of peace to Yuna's frazzled heart.

"Things aren't what they appear to be."

"What?" Yuna asked.

But Sash only shook her head, that haunted look creeping back into her eyes. She pulled her arm free of Yuna's grasp. Without another word, she turned back in the direction she had come.

She didn't need to tell Yuna not to follow her to make it clear she didn't want to be followed. And so, Yuna didn't. But the words stuck to the insides of her skull like honey. She hadn't tasted honey in years, but she remembered what it felt like. Thick and sticky. Once it got on her tongue, it was there to stay.

Things aren't what they appear to be.

It meant everything. It meant nothing. Yuna hated that sort of ambiguity. And so, with as much metaphorical muscularity as she could muster, she set it down and walked away.

CHAPTER 15

GABE

The door had been stuck shut.

(Or locked in a way he couldn't see.)

(Or it wasn't connected to anything and trying to open it was a fruitless endeavor. A fool's errand.)

He'd tugged and pulled and grunted for an hour. At least, he thought it was an hour. Time was odd and elastic in the bunker. The human body relied on sunlight to maintain its circadian rhythms, and Gabe knew that all of theirs had been out of whack for the better part of a decade. It made judging even small units of time difficult. Five minutes could feel like five hours. Five hours like five seconds.

But no matter how much time had passed, the door had refused to budge. The only thing he'd managed to knock loose was a small panel nearly hidden behind the wheel.

A closer look revealed it was electric in nature but untethered to anything. A very old, very primitive digital lock. Maybe from the 1980s. Maybe even earlier than that. It looked like it had never been properly configured, never attached to a power source. Just another dead end in the series of dead ends that comprised the bunker.

Gabe couldn't remove it from the wall, but what he could do was commit it to memory. Every detail. Every shape. Every input and output. He rolled those details over in his mind. All through the morning ritual and the thin gruel breakfast and the physical education class he skipped. He was rolling them over in his head right now, only half hearing whatever story his father was telling him about an office softball team he'd been on Before. (Also illicit. Also forbidden. The rules were as elastic as time when no one was looking.)

The team had been called the Absolute Zeros. A clever name for a bunch of science nerds working at a biochemical plant. Fitting, too, since according to his father's tales, they never won a single game.

His dad was relaying the gripping tale of the time he stole second base, only to fracture his ankle at the end of his slide. Gabe pored over the electrical panel before him, only half listening to the tale. It was seated on a plastic storage box that doubled as a table. Nothing in the bunker was single use. Everything that could serve multiple purposes did.

Waste not, want not.

The panel was designed to be multipurpose. It could be used for the lighting system, the water filtration tanks, or the power generator. It would go where it was needed, a stalwart soldier made of circuits and copper.

Touching one end of the panel caused a minor spark to flare up at the other end.

Interesting.

Gabe liked working with gadgets. There was usually a right way to make them work amid a thousand wrong ones. Finding the right way was often through process of elimination. Failure could sting, but only if you let it. The sweet thrill of victory when you discovered the solution . . . that was a glory all its own.

"And then Barry said—Gabe, are you listening to me?"

The tool in Gabe's hand slid as he jerked his head up. A mild shock zapped through his arm as one metal bit touched another metal bit it really shouldn't touch. "Ow—what? Yeah."

A quirked eyebrow was his dad's response. Then a sigh, as he set aside his own task—breakfast. There had been a brownout of the red lights that flooded the bunker during the morning ritual, and fixing it had taken the better part of the morning meal. The schedule Moran set for the bunker was usually airtight, but on this occasion, the elder Correa had been allowed to prepare his own runny serving of gruel to eat at his leisure.

("For services rendered," Moran had said.)

"What's on your mind, kid?"

Gabe tugged his lip between his teeth, mostly to keep his thoughts inside his head until he knew which ones to let out.

Don't mention the blueprints.

Don't mention the door.

Don't mention—

"Why did you call Cornelius Moran a nutjob?"

His father blinked, brow furrowed. "When did I do that?"

"Ages ago," Gabe said. "When I was twelve."

"Ages." His father huffed out a small laugh. "A whole five years. A lifetime."

Half of one, if you squinted. Fifty percent of the time they'd spent in the bunker, a life all its own, so divorced from the world beyond that it counted as its own epoch entirely.

"I found some blueprints for the bunker, and they weren't the same. There were differences here and there. Odd ones. I asked you about it, and you just shrugged it off and said he was a nutjob."

"He was eccentric, I guess you could say."

When it looked as though his father was going to leave it at that, Gabe prodded. "Eccentric how?"

His dad scratched at the stubble on his chin. Gabe was well into his late teens and had yet to grow even the slightest bit of facial hair. He wasn't jealous. Truly. It looked like a tremendous hassle to have another involuntary bodily function to maintain.

"Have you ever heard of the Winchester Mystery House?"

Gabe shook his head. "Nope. Was it some kind of amusement park ride? Like a haunted house or something?"

He remembered amusement parks but in bits and pieces. The smell of kettle corn popping. The roar of a roller coaster he would never be brave enough to ride. The sticky sweet taste of cotton candy on his tongue. The unbroken heat of the sun bearing down on his skin.

"Or something." His dad ran a hand through his hair, tussling the too-long strands. It was grayer now than it had been when they'd first entered the bunker. Significantly so. "It was built by Sarah Winchester, widow to a guy who manufactured one of the most popular firearms in the world, the Winchester rifle."

"Where was it?" Gabe asked. "The house, I mean."

"Somewhere in California." His dad scratched his chin, his face screwing up in thought. "Can't remember where though."

California. What a place. It sounded imaginary. Fictional. As fake and as far away as Narnia or Atlantis or Midgard. Cal-i-for-nia. Gabe rolled the syllables around in his mind, vowing to try them out later when he was alone. It was so odd to talk about places that used to mean something.

"Anyway, she was as crazy as the day is long, so people said. She ordered construction on a house that got bigger and bigger as time went on. Some people said that construction continued nonstop for almost forty years."

"So it was just a big house," Gabe said. "What was so special about that?"

"It wasn't the size that made it unusual. It was how the widow Winchester demanded it be built. Doors that led to nowhere. Hallways that bent in on themselves. It was like a fun house but without the fun."

Gabe didn't remember what a fun house was. But he nodded along, all the same.

"Some people thought the house was haunted by every soul killed with a Winchester gun, and that the constant, nonsensical construction was her way of avoiding them."

Something cold tap-danced on Gabe's spine. A labyrinth populated by lost spirits. A broken mind building a palatial fortress out of sheer will and too much money.

Sort of like the bunker.

"What do you think?" Gabe asked.

His father shrugged. "I think it's a clever story that got people to pay the price of admission to see a weird old house."

Gabe nodded again, mulling the thought over in his head. His father wasn't a dreamer. He was not prone to flights of fancy. He was usually right about these things. "So you think Cornelius Percival Moran was just nuts? Is that why he built this bunker the way it is?"

"Could be. Personally, I think he was just a run-of-the-mill paranoid rich guy with an expensive hobby. But I'm glad he had one, otherwise we wouldn't be here today."

Here. In the subterranean version of a haunted fun house. (Without the fun.)

"I'm going to go take a look at the power lines." His father brushed some dust that probably wasn't there off his jeans. The air-filtration system was cracking at keeping that type of particulate at bay. "Once I finish this delicious, delectable breakfast."

The question spilled out of Gabe before he could stop it. "Is there really only one way out of the bunker?"

His father paused, spoon frozen halfway to his mouth.

"Why would you ask that?"

That chill returned, shimmying along Gabe's spinal column. He shrugged, hoping it was nonchalant. "Just curious."

With a sigh, his father set aside his bowl, unfinished. When he turned to Gabe, there was concern in his eyes, but something else too. Something worse.

Pity.

"I know you're scared. I am too. All the time. And I know it isn't easy watching Dr. Moran walk through that door every night, but she's doing it for us. As far as I know, she isn't sitting on any secret, unknown exits. We've got to trust her. She knows what's best. She's kept us alive this long."

Gabe bit his lip, trying to keep the rest of his words in, but he couldn't. His father's admission of fear loosened something critical inside of him. "We can't stay here forever."

A lone, sad nod. "No. But we can for a little longer. Until it's safe." The elder Correa stood, picking up his bowl as he went. With a ruffle of Gabe's hair (a holdover gesture from Gabe's childhood that he was far too old for now, *thankyouverymuch*), he turned to go.

"Do me a favor, kid."

"Yeah, Dad?"

"Don't go around asking anyone else stuff like that. About doors. It'll just get everyone worked up. We're all stuck in here together. Might as well not rock the boat."

Gabe dug his teeth into the tender flesh of his cheek, holding back all the things he could have said.

You raised me to be curious.

You raised me to ask questions.

You raised me to think for myself, to figure things out, to look for ways in which they're broken and try to fix them.

But all that came out of his mouth was: "Okay."

With a half-hearted smile, his father rested a large hand on Gabe's shoulders. "We'll get out of here one day, kid. I promise."

He left, with Gabe watching him go. The door clicked shut behind him.

One day, Gabe thought. The words left a bitter taste in his mouth. One day.

The taste lingered at the back of his throat as he turned to the mess of wires and circuits and sensors in front of him.

Another tiny project to keep their lives going one more day.

A fruitless endeavor.

A fool's errand.

He picked up his tools and began to work. It was a simple panel. Easy enough to alter to suit one's needs. Easy enough to adapt it for another purpose. Easy enough to turn it into something it wasn't.

Anything that was locked could be unlocked. All you needed was a key.

CHAPTER 16

SASH

The comfort of their little hideout made it easier to push away the thoughts that had been plaguing her since the other night. Since the banging sound and the hatch and the thing she thought she saw moving about in the darkness.

It was a dream. It had to be.

There was nothing outside.

No people.

No animals.

No monsters.

It was just a dream.

But no matter how many times Sash told herself that, no matter how many times she repeated those words like a mantra, they refused to feel true. They felt—like so many things in the bunker—like a lie.

Stop thinking about it, she told herself. Futilely, but it had to be said all the same.

It was a dream. Just a dream.

It wouldn't be the first time she'd had a dream that felt too real.

(Waking up, throat hoarse, teeth aching from the screams—)

The others would find her in strange places. Tucked away in a tiny cupboard in the kitchen. Curled up in a ball under Baba Olya's bunk.

(The skin on her arm blistering so surely, so vividly—)

Once, standing in front of that hatch, small hands clasping the wheel, knuckles white, eyes wide but unseeing.

(*Take your sister and run—*)

Sleepwalking, Baba Olya had called it.

Night terrors, Mrs. Correa proclaimed.

Memories, Dr. Moran said. Of a time best left forgotten.

Sash hadn't forgotten it. Not one painful second. She held the memories close, turning them over in her hands, making sure they were still sharp enough to cut her palms.

It was just a dream, she told herself. *Nothing more.*

"What do I have to roll to convince the king to abdicate his throne and hand me his crown?" Yuna asked.

Gabe blinked at her over the game master's screen. It was really just three pieces of scrap they'd hammered together with a bunch of rusty nails they'd found in a long-forgotten storage space deep within the bowels of the bunker, but it did its job and it did it well. "Diplomacy, I guess. But also like . . . don't?"

"Why not?" Yuna asked.

"Because."

"Because is not a reason."

Gabe huffed out a frustrated sigh. It was not his first of the night. It would not be his last. "It is when the dungeon master says it is."

"I'm a bard." Yuna shrugged. "I do what I want."

The chalk snapped in Gabe's closed fist. "That's not what a bard does!"

Yuna chewed the wooden, eraserless end of her pencil. "That's what a chaotic bard does."

"Rules exist for a reason, Yuna."

"Oh, forget the rules." Sash fought the urge to dramatically flip the table as she said it. It would have made for excellent theater but poor sportsmanship. Though it would have been extremely in character. Her paladin was a bit hotheaded too. Life imitates art, or in this case, tabletop gaming imitates life. "We've been playing by the same stupid rules for ages. It's the same game, over and over. Don't you ever get tired of it?"

This was easier, so much easier, than rubbing the pads of her fingers on the sharp edges of a memory—or a dream.

Roll the dice. Play the part.

"Are we playing this game or what?" Gabe asked.

"Or what," Yuna said.

"Yeah, or what," Sash agreed.

With an incoherent sound of frustration, Gabe slammed the *Advanced Dungeons & Dragons Player's Handbook* shut. Like everything else in the bunker, it was a relic of another time, though this one to a world that never actually existed. Its dark cover was cracked and faded. The toothy, jewel-eyed demon that grinned out was barely visible anymore. "Why is it that we never do what I want to do?"

"We're a democracy," Yuna quipped. "And our votes just happen to align with alarming frequency."

"You're insufferable, you know that," said Gabe, piling his papers and character sheets together and tucking them into the *Player's Handbook*. The hardcover copy was ideal for protecting their treasures, fictional though they might be. "I have to pee."

"Aw, come on, Gabe," Sash said. She didn't even bother trying to sound anything other than cajoling. Gabe *hated* cajoling. "Don't storm off in a huff."

Gabe stormed off in a huff, the *Player's Handbook* tucked under his arm.

Sash and Yuna watched him go. They waited in silence for him to realize his error.

Twenty-five seconds later—Sash counted—Gabe stormed back in, his scowl even darker than before. With nary another word, he stuck the book back on the shelf, sliding it between a battered copy of Darwin's *On the Origin of Species* and a July 1984 edition of *Reader's Digest*. With another glare tossed their way, Gabe turned on his heel and stormed out. Again.

"Bye, Gabe," Sash called to his retreating back.

He replied with a rude gesture, entirely unfit for polite society.

Moments passed in silence between them. Warm, comfortable moments.

Yuna canted her head to the side. Her hair slipped over her shoulder. Sash balled her hands into fists so she didn't reach out and push that disobedient lock of hair back.

"You weren't really talking about the game, were you?"

"I . . ." Sash paused. "No. Not really." She sighed. "Aren't you sick of this place?"

Yuna laughed. When she smiled, the crooked tooth on her bottom row of teeth—the one she was achingly self-conscious about—showed. Sash had only the warmest of feelings for that crooked little tooth. It was perfect somehow in all its imperfection.

"Of course I'm sick of this place," Yuna said. "Any sane person would be."

A rueful grin tugged at Sash's lips. "You realize that discounts like . . . half of our combined families, right?"

Yuna snorted a tiny, soft laugh. The sound made something deep in Sash's chest flutter. But in an instant it was squashed by the memory of the other night.

"I saw something weird the other night."

"Did you walk in on Gabe acting out scenes from the old G.I. Joe comic again? You know he hates it when we acknowledge he does that."

"No. Not that." Sash sat upright, plucking at the loose threads in the rug. "I heard a sound. Like a banging noise. I got up and went to go investigate. It sounded like it was coming from the hatch, so I—"

Yuna bolted upright. "Please tell me you didn't open it."

"I didn't!"

Maybe you should have.

Breathing a sigh of relief, Yuna sagged. "Good."

"I just . . . peeked out the window."

"What did you see?"

Sash tried to remember. She did. But it had been so dark and her heart had been pounding so hard she hadn't been able to see anything else. She could practically taste her pulse. "I don't know."

Yuna made an inquisitive noise at the back of her throat.

Silence fell between them as Sash tried to give what she had seen, what she'd felt, shape. But she came up short.

Then the door banging open made them both jump.

Gabe froze in the doorway, eyebrows raised. "What's the matter with you two?"

Thrusting a finger at Sash, Yuna said, "Sash heard noises the other night."

Gabe paused, blinking. "What kind of noises? And when?"

There was no shock in Gabe's tone. No surprise. Odd, Sash thought.

She squirmed, settling herself a fraction of an inch farther away from Yuna. Not out of shame—Gabe never cared if they touched—but from habit mainly.

"I don't know. I didn't check a clock or anything. It was late."

"How late?"

"I don't know! Just . . . late."

Gabe's lips thinned when he was thinking a little too hard about something. "It might have been me. I was in the air vents a few nights ago."

"What?" Yuna blurted.

Sash shook her head. "Couldn't have been you, Gabe. I saw you sleeping."

Then, she added: "But why were you in the air vents?"

"I thought . . ." His words trailed off as he swept past them—insofar as anyone could sweep in a tiny space like that—and plunged into the trunk of old books and outdated atlases they used as a table, upsetting their tabletop game in the process.

For Gabe to sacrifice an expertly laid out game of Dungeons & Dragons, it must have been serious business indeed.

He emerged with a flattened roll of blueprints in his hands. Knocking a battalion of handpainted miniatures aside, Gabe laid them on the top of the trunk. "Look."

Sash stared down at the blueprints, but they were just monochromatic lines and numbers to her. "What am I supposed to be looking at?"

Gabe sighed, rolling his eyes. "They're the bunker."

"Okay and . . . ?"

"And they're not the same. They're different here"—Gabe pointed to one of the diagrams, and then another—"and here. Leaving a gap"—another finger thrust at a bit of negative space on both—"here. I thought it was odd because the air ducts follow through both in a way that doesn't make sense. At first I thought that maybe there was an unnecessary redundancy in the system, that air was being wasted on a space that wasn't used, but . . ."

He shook his head, eyes alight.

"But what?" Sash prodded.

"But it wasn't an unused space. Not really. I mean, *we* don't use it but—"

"Gabe. The point. Get to it."

"There's a hatch."

A resounding silence met his words.

"A hatch," Sash said.

"A hatch," Gabe repeated.

Yuna's gaze swung between them. "A hatch as in . . ."

"A door outside," Sash said without waiting for Gabe to answer.

He nodded. "Like the one out front."

Sash wished the source of the booming sound had been Gabe. That would have been so much simpler. So much more comforting. But regardless of its source, Sash wanted—no, needed—an explanation. For the noises. The hatch. The secret door. There were too many strange things happening in too short a span of time. They had to be connected somehow. They *had* to be.

"Okay," Sash said, "this is bananas, but hear me out."

Yuna propped her head on her chin, baleful as one could be. "Don't mention bananas. I don't remember what they taste like, but I remember liking them."

"Fine. This is bonkers," Sash said. "We're sitting here playing at fake quests when we could be on a real one."

Gabe frowned, affronted. "But I like D&D. . . ."

Yuna simply canted her head to the side, waiting for Sash to formulate her thought. Waiting for her to breathe her heresy into the air.

And so, she did: "You know what I think?"

"I have a feeling I do," Gabe replied.

"And I have a feeling it's insane," Yuna added.

Sash couldn't have fought the smile that tugged at her lips if she wanted to. And she didn't. "I think we should go through that door."

CHAPTER 17

YUNA

In the greenhouse, Yuna could pretend she was somewhere else.

And she wanted to be somewhere else right now, very badly. Sash and Gabe had argued about the merits of exploring the heretofore undiscovered door until it was late enough that the dimming of the bunker lights ended their conversation. Yuna had mostly stayed out of it. Conflict had never been her thing. Their exploration had an air of the inevitable about it. They were going to do it, no matter how much caution Gabe advised or how brazen Sash's plans. One way or the other, the door was theirs.

The thought should have filled Yuna with excitement. A new thing to do. They hadn't had a new thing to do in years. But the joy of it, the unbridled pleasure in the pursuit of the unknown she'd always dreamed of experiencing, was drowned out by fear.

Fear that opening the door would kill them and the people they loved.

Fear that going through it would bring damnation upon their heads.

Fear that it would lead absolutely nowhere at all.

Yuna shook herself as she worked her way through the greenhouse, trying to dislodge those thoughts. That fear.

Calling it a greenhouse was perhaps a rather generous massaging of the definition, but it fit somehow. It felt right. It felt good. Banks of specialized UV lights shone down on the rows of plants, casting them in a soft, purple glow.

There was basil and peppermint, rosemary and thyme. Three modest fields of spinach, especially designed to survive underground, according to Dr. Moran.

Yuna walked through the room, a lightness to her step that she staunchly refused to succumb to dark thoughts. Her conversation with Sash the other night had been . . .

Well, Yuna wasn't sure what it had been, but it had been something.

The two of them, alone.

"I think we're alone now . . ."

The fairy lights fading in and out, their brightness left to the whims of the bunker's unreliable electricity.

"There doesn't seem to be anyone around . . ."

Sash, opening her mouth and spilling out secrets and fears and fragile precious things she trusted Yuna not to break.

"I think we're alone now . . ."

The broken record player emitting the ghost of music, if not the music itself.

"The beating of our hearts is the only sound."

Yuna had read the liner notes of that Tiffany record so often, she could project them onto the insides of her eyelids. She didn't know what the title track sounded like, but she was positive it was a good song. A great one. A phenomenal one.

The soundtrack of her own design accompanied her through her chore list. She hummed under her breath, mentally checking boxes as she went about her business caring for the denizens of the greenhouse.

Yuna *liked* the greenhouse. Well, she liked it as much as she could like anything in the bunker. The air smelled different in here. It was still pumped through the same vents, still filtered through the same ventilation system, but it was different somehow. Cleaner. Fresher.

It was the plants. It had to be.

They took in carbon dioxide. They breathed fresh, unfiltered oxygen back out.

Oxygen was their most precious currency. Water was a close second. Food, a very tight third.

The greenhouse was largely responsible for keeping them all fed. Without the fruits (both literal and metaphorical) it bore, they'd have all developed scurvy and died ages ago.

She hummed what she thought Tiffany's song might sound like under her breath as Misha rotated out bulbs in the overhead UV lights.

"Must you?" His voice was gruff, but without any real fire behind it. They'd shared greenhouse duties for the past eighteen months. He was accustomed to her ways by now.

She nodded sagely as she leaned in to check the nearest plants. "I must."

Misha said something pithy and probably unkind in

return—that seemed to be his default—but the words didn't reach Yuna. All she could hear was a sort of low, keening alarm at the back of her head as her eyes raked over a clump of spinach.

"Misha."

He grunted in response, not really listening to her.

"Misha!"

"What?"

"Come here."

Frowning, he hefted a bucket and came over, a wrinkle of annoyance forming between his brows. But when she pointed at the spinach, the wrinkle smoothed. Disappeared. Returned even stronger.

Patchwork spots of white covered the leaves. The worst of them had worn clean through the green flesh, leaving jagged holes in the middle of each leaf.

Misha set down the bucket. "What happened here?"

Yuna hung back. "Misha, don't touch it."

He shot her a withering glare over his shoulder. "I wasn't going to."

She shrugged, covering her mouth with the excess fabric of her sleeve. There was a reason she liked baggy sweatshirts. The reason was honestly that she felt like she was being hugged all the time when she wore them, but they had their uses.

Through a pair of thick work gloves, Misha handled one of the stalks with a milder case of the white rot. "What is it?"

"Blight."

He cursed. Long and vicious and in at least two languages. Some of the Russian she recognized from Baba Olya's occasional expletive-laced utterances when Dr. Moran did something to annoy her (which was often).

"We're going to have to burn it all." Misha cursed again.

Yuna's mind felt slow. Sluggish. "But that means . . ."

The reality of the situation hit her, not with any amount of subtlety, but with all the force of thousands of pounds of dirt bearing down on them.

They were running out of supplies.

It wasn't exactly a startling revelation. The juice. Pear. The worst flavor. The porridge, thinner and thinner each month, as the water-to-grain ratio changed to favor the former.

And now, the spinach. The greens. Their food. Their oxygen.

Misha shoved Yuna back toward the door. "Get out of here. I'll talk to the doctor."

Yuna let herself be manhandled through the door. In the long, dark corridor, her breath ricocheted off the metal walls. Too fast. Too loud.

I can't stay here.

Her feet carried her forward while her mind lagged a half step behind.

I can't stay here.

We can't stay here.

She found Sash in the kitchen, her blond hair tied back in a messy bun (messy but cute), her gloved arms elbow deep in the large metal vat they used to mix that watered-down porridge.

"Hey," said Sash, blowing out a puff of air to get the errant strands of hair out of her face. They fluttered upward only to succumb to gravity once more.

Before she could stop herself, Yuna reached out and tucked the too-long bangs behind Sash's ear. The other girl's cheeks pinkened just slightly at the contact, brief and blunted by gloves as it was.

"No touching," Nastia said from the other side of the sink. She waved a soapy rag in Yuna's direction, splattering her with renegade bubbles. "Them's the rules."

Sash's cheeks reddened further. "Shut up, Nastia."

In a higher, much more annoying voice, Nastia said, "Shut up, Nastia." But with a roll of her eyes, she went back to scrubbing the tin plates. She wasn't gentle with them. Yuna hoped she didn't scrub the blue pattern off her plate.

Turning back to Yuna, Sash asked, "What's up?"

Yuna glanced at Nastia, who was very studiously not paying attention to the conversation happening two feet to her left. So much so that it was abundantly clear she was hanging on every word. "Can I talk to you for a second?"

"Sure, give me five minutes."

"We're running out of food."

Sash blinked at Yuna, her hair sliding out from behind her ear and over her forehead once more. This time, she didn't bother blowing it out of the way. After a long, awful moment, she glanced behind her at Nastia, who was still by the sink but had inched closer to where they stood. Brow furrowed, Sash jerked her head in the direction of the hallway.

Yuna followed her out into the corridor. There were so few places to find privacy in the bunker. It was best snatched in stolen fragments, which they both knew was all they had in that moment.

Safely out of Nastia's earshot—for now—Sash said, "But we have the greenhouse . . ."

Yuna shook her head. "We don't."

"What do you mean 'We don't'? How do we not?"

"There was a blight or something." Yuna glanced down at her hands. She'd switched out the gloves for a new pair, leaving the ones she'd been wearing in the greenhouse to soak in a vat of something caustic. But she still felt like the blight had somehow transferred to her. "I don't know how we didn't catch it before. I should have seen it coming. I should have—"

"Hey." Sash reached out and placed a gentle hand on Yuna's elbow. Against the rules. No touching. "It's gonna be okay."

"No." Yuna shook her head, more vehemently this time. "It's not." She drew in a fortifying breath, readying herself for the next words to come out of her mouth. "You were right."

Sash's eyebrows inched skyward.

"We have to go to the surface." The words tumbled out of Yuna, fast and ferocious, set free before she could lose her nerve. "And we have to go soon."

CHAPTER 18
GABE

This was a terrible idea.

Gabe *knew* this with a certainty he felt about little else. Oh, he thought he'd experienced certainty before. The absolute conviction that you are completely correct in a particular scenario. But this? This was a whole new level of assuredness.

Rigging the lock had been easier than he'd thought. The electric panel had required replacing, but luckily he'd happened to have a spare one on hand. (Not really spare, but the water-filtration analyzer would live another day without it.) And once the lock had been rigged, well . . . things happened extremely fast.

"Guys," Gabe whispered as he followed Yuna's bobbing ponytail and Sash's messy bun through the ventilation shaft. He wheezed, but only a little bit. His asthmatic lungs were working in tandem with his anxiety-addled brain and it was a Very Bad Combination. "Have I mentioned that this is a bad idea?"

Yuna shot him a grin over her shoulder. It was too dark to properly see it, but her teeth flashed in the reflected light of Gabe's small hand-cranked flashlight. It hung from a lanyard around his neck, thumping against his breastbone with every jerky forward motion as they crawled. He'd brought it to read the map stuffed in the back pocket of Sash's jeans. Every now and then, it started to slip out, but Yuna tucked it back in every time.

Gabe wondered if they were actually cognizant of their ongoing mating dance or if their subconscious minds were driving that particular bus.

Yuna came to an abrupt stop, causing Gabe to collide directly with her derriere.

He tried to backpedal and mostly failed, his scuffed sneakers banging inelegantly against the duct's paneling. "Oh my stars, I'm so sorry."

"Don't sweat it—"

"Gabe," Sash cut in, imperious as ever. Her hand appeared in the darkness by Yuna's shoulder, palm up, fingers splayed. "Flashlight."

"Didn't you bring your own?" It was a futile mumble. He was already slipping the lanyard over his head and handing it over.

"I did but I didn't crank it enough."

"You never crank it enough."

"Ugh," Yuna sighed. "Cranking."

With that, Yuna slid the uncranked flashlight out of Sash's pocket and began to turn it. The sound ticked through the darkened silence, oddly comforting in its familiarity.

Sash peered at the map, smoothing its many creases. They had pored over it for hours. Days. Gabe could probably navigate these air tunnels in his sleep. Sash could too, most likely. Yuna . . . probably not. She had seemed less concerned with the logistics of the operation than the wild and unpredictable possibilities it represented.

But that niggling doubt remained in Gabe's mind. It made him question what he thought he knew. Made him doubt things he would otherwise never. But one thing remained certain.

This was a bad idea.

Satisfied with her map perusal, Sash handed Gabe his flashlight as Yuna offered her back her own, now freshly cranked.

With a crooked smile, Sash said, "Thanks."

Light activated—dimly, of course—they proceeded. Even that amount of brightness made Gabe uneasy. Years of training was hard to overcome.

The dark is safe.

The dark will protect us.

Truths, universally acknowledged, at least down here, meters and meters and meters away from the sun.

Fear the light.

Fear what it hides.

Fear what it reveals.

What would it reveal though? They were about to find out.

Sash's startled cry alerted Gabe to the end of the duct. One minute she was there, two body lengths ahead of him. The next, she was gone. The grate fell out from beneath her, collapsing under her weight.

"Sash!" It was more of a whisper than a shout, but Yuna's fear was loud enough to sear through Gabe's eardrums.

Yuna tumbled out after her with far more physical grace than Gabe could hope to achieve.

"I'm okay." Sash's mumble made the horrid knot in Gabe's chest release. She was alive. For now, at least. And that was something.

With an awkwardness roughly equivalent to Yuna's grace, Gabe maneuvered himself so that his feet were the first thing through the now-open grate. He peered past his worn-out Nikes to gauge the distance, but it was too dark to see much of anything.

"How far down is it?" Gabe asked. Sweaty skin made for the perfect conditions for glasses to slide down one's face. His insisted on doing so, despite the aggravation it caused him.

"Not that far," Sash replied absently, as if her thoughts had already moved on, past this one small hurdle.

Gabe pushed his glasses back into place. "Not that far is *not* a numerical value."

"Oh, just come on."

Sash's hand—at least Gabe assumed it was Sash's hand because Yuna would *never*, Yuna was a good person, she was nice—wrapped around his ankle and tugged. Hard.

Gravity. What a fiend.

Gabe fell. Zero points for grace. Fifty points for not shattering every bone in his body. There was always a silver lining to be found, if only one had the temerity to look.

Sash peered down at where he lay on the floor, the wind temporarily knocked out of him.

"See?" The tone of hers was infuriatingly chipper. "That wasn't so far, was it?"

"I hate you," Gabe said, wholly without heat.

"I know." Sash extended a hand, which—despite his hatred—Gabe gratefully took. She hauled him to his feet with a surprising amount of strength considering her stature.

Yuna's flashlight carved a path through the darkness to point at something on the side of the very cramped room. A ladder. At the top of that ladder loomed a hatch, smaller than the one through which Moran walked every night. Blue instead of red. Covered in a fine layer of dust. Untouched for years. Until now.

"This is it." Sash's voice was lit with a fervor Gabe had never quite heard before. She'd gotten close before, when their D&D games hit a particularly good patch, or when the wistful nostalgia of their reminisces grew too bitter. But now, it was fully realized. The thing she craved most was there. Just one climb of a ladder away. They all yearned for the surface, but Sash felt things more powerfully than most people Gabe knew. Admittedly, it was a woefully tiny sample size, but it was all he had.

"Are you sure this is a good idea?" Gabe pitched his voice low, but it still seemed to carry, louder than was comfortable, in the small, quiet space.

Sash shrugged. "Nope."

With that, she stepped onto the bottom rung of the ladder. And then, the next step. And the next.

Yuna followed her and Gabe followed Yuna. Together, they advanced into the unknown.

CHAPTER 19

SASH

The first thing Sash noticed was the air. For the past ten years, the only air her lungs had known was the recycled oxygenated atmosphere of the bunker. That air was clean, but it was stale. It went around and around the filtration systems, scrubbed and cleaned and sent out again.

But the air outside, on the surface . . . it was new. It was wild. It was dusty.

Part of the roof of this new space had caved in, allowing a shaft of silvery moonlight to penetrate.

Motes of dust flitted through the air, tickling at Sash's nostrils.

She breathed in deep, and that was a mistake.

A vicious sneeze—the kind that makes it feel like your brain is trying to escape via your nasal cavity—tore its way through her. The sound of it echoed in the open space, as loud as cannon fire.

Yuna and Gabe froze, heads swiveling toward her with identical looks of stunned fear on their faces.

After a brief moment, in which all six of their ears strained to hear if the noise had summoned anything from the shadowy depths of the room, Gabe bit back a foul swear. Extremely uncharacteristic of him. He wasn't the sort of person who even knew bad words, much less deployed them.

"Sash," Yuna whispered. It was all she needed to say really. It was amazing, Sash thought, how much recrimination could fit inside that single syllable.

"What?" she rasped back. "I didn't do it on purpose."

Yuna bit her lip. Sash wished she didn't notice that sort of thing quite so much. *But alas. Here we are.*

Sash pulled her shirt over her nose and breathed in the scent of cotton. It was better than the taste of decades-old dust settling on her tongue.

Maybe Moran was telling the truth. Maybe the air was contaminated with a poison they couldn't see.

She didn't feel any different. When she looked down at her hands, there were no blisters forming, no boils taking shape. She looked—and felt—fine.

Gabe put a finger to his lips, as if they hadn't already made a tremendous amount of noise. They listened, but no sound came.

Thank God. Sash wasn't sure she believed in God. She wasn't sure what she believed, if she believed in anything at all. But in that moment, she was grateful to any divine being that had their backs, out here in the open.

The hatch had opened into a large space, almost like a

ballroom. The floor was tiled, black and white, so the square neatly lifted by the hatch would blend as soon as it was closed.

As if he could read her mind, Gabe said, "We shouldn't close that."

He tipped his chin in the direction of the still-open hatch.

"We won't," Yuna said. "That'd be dumb, wouldn't it?"

It was a rhetorical question and therefore merited no answer. But Sash gave one anyway, in the form of a loose bit of wooden planking she plucked from a pile near the wall. It was just long enough to lay over the hole in the floor, so even if the hatch swung shut behind them, it wouldn't close fully. They'd be safe.

Well.

Safe-ish.

"What should we do now?" Yuna whispered, too afraid to speak in her normal voice.

Sash shrugged. "I don't know."

But she did. It was there, fizzing through her veins like her blood itself was carbonated. Anticipation. Excitement. A tiny bit of trepidation, but not too much. Just enough to punch up the flavor.

"We should stick together," Gabe said.

Yuna nodded.

Sash gazed out over the indecently large room. "I didn't know people actually had ballrooms. Like, real ones."

"Wild, isn't it?" Gabe sidled alongside her, his bespectacled gaze following hers. Yuna joined them, huddling close.

Sash's hand sought out Yuna's without her brain directly instructing it to do so. Reaching for Yuna was instinctual. Like breathing.

"Yeah," Sash breathed the word more than she spoke it. It

smelled awful. Stale and slightly rotten. But good too. "Wild."

She nudged Gabe's shoulder with her own and gave Yuna's hand a playful tug. With a smile on her face she hoped came across as confident—more so than she felt—she said, "Let's explore."

◎ ◎ ◎

The bunker was big, but the manor was bigger.

The layout made about as much sense as the subterranean world beneath it. There were hallways that went nowhere. Doors that opened into solid brick walls. A room that was entirely made of mirrors so that a person standing in the middle of it would see themselves repeated an infinite number of times from all directions.

The oddest so far was a room completely bare except for what looked like a hyperbaric chamber. Sash had read about those in one of the books in the bunker's modest library, one that included treatment for a variety of ailments one might experience in severe weather conditions or when doing incredibly stupid, incredibly human things like trying to scale the highest peak in the world.

Mount Everest. Called Chomolungma by the Tibetan locals. 8,848 meters high.

This fact she cradled to her chest, like all the facts she could recall. They were precious, these fragments of knowledge. They made her strong. They fortified the cracks in her being, caulking the bits that leaked.

Knowledge is power.

It was something her father said. He had it written on a mug, the one he drank coffee out of every morning. He would sit at the kitchen table—a rickety wooden thing on whose underside

Sash had sloppily drawn a map to an imaginary world. Her Terabithia, she called it. Her Narnia. Her land behind the wardrobe, where magic was real and anything was possible.

In the bunker, there was so little to learn. Much to memorize, but memorization wasn't learning. It was rote. It was for automatons.

That was another thing her father used to say a lot. Anyone can memorize a fact. But it takes real imagination to conceive of something knew, something no one had ever thought of before, something—

"Sash?"

She jumped at the sound of Yuna's voice. Blinking, she came back to herself, inch by inch.

Yuna peered at her quizzically, eyebrows pinched. "Where'd you go?"

Sash breathed in deep, letting the dust tickle her nose but fighting the sneeze this time.

Where indeed? To Terabithia. To Narnia. To the land beyond a door no one was supposed to know existed.

"I'm here," Sash said.

Slipping her flashlight into her pocket, she freed her hands. One reached for Yuna, the other for Gabe. Yuna took it without hesitation. Gabe quirked an eyebrow, first at Sash's hand, then at Sash herself.

Human contact. Illicit. Forbidden. Against the rules that kept them safe. The rules they were *told* kept them safe. An important distinction.

Slowly, Gabe twined his fingers with Sash's. She squeezed their hands.

"*We're* here." A smile spread along her lips, slowly at first and then with more alacrity. Yuna's mouth followed suit. Then Gabe's. They were wobbly smiles, unsure of their welcome, unsure of their place in the world, but they were real. That much Sash knew.

"Now," she began, her heart doubling its pace, hammering out a war drum against the steel bars of her rib cage, "let's see what else is out here."

◎ ◎ ◎

They ventured up to the second floor, driven by the same need that led humans up and up and up until they touched the sky.

Apollo 11. The first manned mission to the moon. Neil Armstrong. The first person to set foot on its surface. July 20, 1969.

"One small step for man," Sash muttered under her breath as she stepped onto the second-floor landing.

"One giant leap for mankind," Gabe finished.

"Doesn't that just mean the same thing?" Yuna asked.

Gabe pushed his glasses up his nose. "Yes, but—"

"It's poetic," Sash said. "Sometimes, things don't have to be right to make sense."

"Now, *that* doesn't make any sense," Yuna said airily. She tugged Sash in a seemingly random direction off the grand staircase. "I wonder what's over here."

Heavy wooden doors lined the hallway, closed. Under their feet lay a threadbare runner that looked like it may have been red once, or maybe purple. It was hard to tell in the dark. Only one of their flashlights was on. Sash's. It was low, just enough to light their way without being bright enough for the light to spread in anything wider than a humble three-foot perimeter of illumination.

Between the doors hung ornate gilded frames. Shreds of canvas drooped from their edges, as if the paintings they'd once held had been ripped from their moors.

"Wow," Yuna whispered. "That's not creepy at all."

"Nope," Sash said. "Not at all."

"Should we go back?" Gabe asked, steps slowing.

"I didn't come this far to run at the first sign of creepy," Sash replied.

Emboldened—or at least doing a good job of pretending she was—Sash tried the first door. It was locked. So was the next. And the next. And the next.

"What are they trying to keep out?" Gabe asked. There was only the slightest tremor in his voice. If you didn't know him well enough, you wouldn't have heard it. But Sash did.

"Intrepid explorers like us," she offered, trying the last door on the left.

This one swung open under her hand. She paused, hand frozen as she shared a look with Gabe and Yuna.

"Bingo," she said.

Bingo. A normal pastime in the bunker until they ran out of bingo cards. It was the only time Sash had ever been glad to experience a shortage. She hated bingo. Well and truly hated it. It was a rotten game for rotten people. Mostly, she lost a lot.

When nothing leaped out of the shadows to devour her whole, Sash stepped over the threshold of the bedroom.

The room seemed to be preserved with museum-quality precision. The bed was neatly made. The items on the vanity were arranged by size—and probably several years expired. The clothing in the wardrobe Yuna had opened was hung up according to color. What wasn't draped from cushioned ivory hangers sat folded in neat piles on the wardrobe's shelves.

"Dresses! Pretty ones!" Yuna twirled out of the wardrobe with one of the them clutched to her chest, its chiffon skirt billowing around her ankles. Her feet moved over the matted carpet with a ballerina's grace, her toes the only parts of her body that seemed to just graze the floor. It was like she was made of fibers too cosmic, too ethereal to be anchored to something as dully tangible as solid ground.

"Ugh. I'm gonna go see if I can find something less"—Gabe waved his hand dismissively at the dresses in Yuna's arms—"this."

"What? You don't want to try on a dress?" Yuna asked. She held out a spectacularly tacky number, encrusted in orange sequins fading to yellow, as if the dress were on fire. Set on fire was probably the best use for it. "I think it would bring out the color in your eyes really nicely."

Gabe rolled those very same eyes as he turned to leave, flashlight—off for the time being—clutched tightly in his hand.

"Stay safe," Sash called out.

But time on the surface had made Gabe brave. He merely grunted a noncommittal sound in their general direction before he disappeared around a bend in the corridor.

It must be the fresh air.

Well, fresh-ish.

They were all a little drunk on it.

"Do you think he'll be okay?" Yuna asked.

No, Sash thought.

"Yes," she said. "He'll be fine. There's nothing out there. It's just us."

Yuna nodded, though she didn't look convinced. But the lure of things new and shiny and exciting was too much for her to resist.

She pivoted back toward the wardrobe and pulled out a frock that was less wildly sequined than the last. It was white, mostly plain. Vaguely Grecian. Or Roman. Sash wasn't sure. It looked like something someone would wear in a mythological story.

"I think you'd look nice in this," Yuna said, holding it up under Sash's chin.

It was pretty, sure. But it wasn't Sash. Yuna would look great in it. Lovely. Devastating. But Sash? Sash would look like a dog trying to stand on her hind legs. Or at least that's how she'd feel.

She did her best not to squirm. She did squirm, but only a little. "I don't think dresses are my style."

Yuna hummed thoughtfully, pursing her lips. "True." She tossed the dresses onto the bed with nary a second thought. "Then forget these. We'll just have to find something that is."

She turned back to the wardrobe. Tapped her chin thoughtfully. Then she dove back in, a woman with purpose.

"Oh, how about a suit?" Yuna said, voice muffled by the heavy wood of the armoire, the question half swallowed by long-forgotten mothballed fabric. "I bet you'd look just darling in a suit."

Sash smiled, digging her teeth into her lower lip to prevent it from being as wide and goofy as it wanted to be. "I don't think I could pull off anything that could accurately be described as 'just darling.' But I admire your fighting spirit."

"Hey," Yuna called from deeper in the wardrobe. "Check it out."

What she pulled out wasn't a suit. It wasn't an article of clothing at all.

It was a book. A large one.

No, Sash realized. Not a book. A photo album.

Newfound treasure in hand, Yuna sat down on the edge of the bed. Little puffs of dust rose up as her weight dented the mattress. Sash let them disperse before she got closer.

Yuna opened the album and flipped through the pages, eyes glancing over the faces of people neither of them knew. Then, she stopped, her finger landing on one photo in particular.

"What is it?"

Sash leaned over Yuna's shoulder—more so than she probably had to, but Yuna aired no complaint—and peered at the open page of the photo album.

"Is that . . . ?"

"Dr. Moran." Yuna's voice held all the incredulity Sash felt.

It looked like a school photo, the kind where everyone in a class is arranged roughly by height and gender, and no one really wanted to be there. A dozen politely smiling faces peered back at Sash from the photo. In the back row stood a girl—her frame wire thin even then, her expression sullen. Thick black waves obscured her face, but those eyes were the same. Dark. Penetrating. Like they could see right through you. The girl's uniform tie was askew, the tie itself loose around her neck. The shirt's top button was undone, its wrinkles unironed. Like every square inch of her was rebelling at the thought of being there, having her picture taken with her peers. As if she could hardly consider these people peers at all.

Or maybe Sash was just projecting.

"'Lyceum Lumnezia,'" Yuna said, reading aloud the

engraving visible over the girl's head, carved into what looked like a stone edifice. "What do you think that is?"

"From the looks of it, probably some fancy boarding school." Sash trailed a finger over the edge of the photo to where a flag-pole was half visible in the background. Frozen midflutter was a flag she recognized from the bunker's desperately out-of-date textbooks. "In Switzerland, if I remember my flags correctly."

"I guess that's where Moran went to school," Yuna said. She looked up so quickly, she nearly butted Sash's chin with the crown of her head. "This must be her room."

The words hung between them, each granting new weight to their surroundings. The dresses. Moran wore those. The bed. Moran slept in that. Or at least a version of her did, a long, long time ago.

"It makes sense if you think about it," Yuna said, worrying her bottom lip between her teeth. "This was her family home. That's how she knew about the bunker, right? She had to have access somehow. Someone had to build it. Her grandfather did."

"I guess . . ."

It wasn't incorrect, what Yuna was saying. The stamp of the elder Moran was all over the bunker. On his blueprints. On his illegibly scrawled notes in the margins. On the water tanks that fed their hydroponics system and the state-of-the-art— patent pending, according to the labels—air-filtration system. The Moran family was wealthy. Ridiculously so, if the resources available to them to build something as self-sustaining and complex as the bunker was any indication. But it was still odd to encounter traces of their former lives here.

And they had lives. They were real people. That was probably the strangest thing of all.

Yuna flipped the page. On this one, there were no photographs but clippings from a newspaper. Some were written in what looked like French—though it could have been Italian. Sash had precious little exposure to other languages in the written form. But one was in English. It was short, barely a footnote.

She leaned over Yuna's shoulder, cranking her flashlight. Squinting to read the small, aged print, she asked, "What does it say?"

"'Mysterious illness strikes Swiss boarding school,'" Yuna read aloud. "'Board of trustees to determine closure. Lumnezia police investigating.'" She made an unhappy noise in the back of her throat. "That's it."

"Huh," said Sash. "Weird."

"Yeah," Yuna agreed. "Very weird. Guess it got Moran out of boarding school though."

Sash shrugged, relishing the way her shoulder brushed against Yuna's arm. "I don't know. Boarding school seems kind of . . ."

"Glamorous? Romantic?"

"Like an adventure."

"Far, far away from your family."

"And chores."

"And schedules."

"And bunkers."

They caught each other's gaze, and a fit of wildly inappropriate giggles seized Sash. She clapped her hand over her mouth to keep that hideous, undignified noise where it belonged. Inside her. Preferably deep, deep inside, so deep no one would ever be able to unearth it ever again.

"Did you just giggle?" Yuna asked, laughter lightening her voice. Making it too loud. "Oh my God. Alexandra Eremenko. Did you just *giggle*?"

"I did not," Sash said, lying with alacrity. Her smile faded when her eyes landed back to the photo album. The page had fallen back to the last one when Yuna shifted her weight.

That picture kept staring at Sash. Or rather, the girl in it did, with her dark, haunting eyes.

"Come on," she said, tugging on Yuna's right hand. The photo album slipped from her left, cracked open on the bed. "Let's get out of here. See what else this creepy house has to offer."

Yuna responded with a dramatic shudder. "Hope it's not ghosts."

Sash offered a perfunctory chuckle. She couldn't quite shake the feeling that the manor was haunted but the ghosts were all underground, buried beneath the land on which it sat.

They made their way out of the room. As they walked by the fireplace, Sash made sure to grab a heavy iron poker that was resting against an equally heavy iron ring welded into the wall.

Better safe than sorry, she thought.

One never knew what was hiding out there in the dark. Or worse, the light.

CHAPTER 20

YUNA

They moved on from the bedroom. A part of Yuna wished she'd taken the picture, the one of Moran and her class-mates. She looked so different somehow but still the same. The same dark eyes. The same knowing expression, like she held on to secrets you could only dream of learning. It made her seem both more and less human. More approach-able somehow, but less, because how did that girl become the doctor who risked her life for them every night? How does something like that happen? How does a person *become* something else?

Life, I suppose.

She followed Sash through the corridors of the manor—and there was no better word for it, honestly. It was a manor, plain and simple. To call it a house would be a gross oversimplification.

Bright, unadulterated moonlight pooled in through the windows, illuminating the floor in disjointed shafts. Every time Yuna's foot penetrated one, a thrill went through her. Light like this was something she hadn't seen in years. It was forbidden. It was delicious. It was a rarity the likes of which she'd lost the ability to even imagine.

So absorbed was Yuna in the way her footfalls alternated between shadow and light that she didn't notice Sash had stopped walking until she collided with the other girl's back.

"Oof—sorry."

But Sash only shook her head, waving off the apology with a dismissive gesture. She had paused before a set of double doors. Massive, ornate double doors, each carved with elaborate scenes of flying dragons and swimming mermaids.

With a trembling hand, Yuna reached for the doors. She wanted to feel the grain of the wood beneath her bare skin, wanted to trace the pads of her fingers over the uneven whorls and minuscule imperfections. Wanted to know the swoop of a mermaid's tail and the jagged edge of a dragon's tooth. But when her hand touched the door, the sensation was blunted by the material of her gloves.

"What do you think's in here?" she asked.

That same smile tugged at Sash's lips, the same one she'd worn when they'd decided to come up here. The smile that said *I have no idea what lies beyond this cliff, but I'm going to leap off the precipice anyway because I'd rather die trying to find the answer than live not knowing.*

Or maybe Yuna was just projecting.

The doors were stuck from years of neglect and an overabundance of dust. It took the both of them leaning their combined body weight to push them open just shy of a foot. It was a narrow opening but wide enough for one Yuna-size person.

Sash angled her head, trying to get a good look through the gap. "No way am I going to be able to squeeze through there."

"I might." Yuna made for the narrow opening, but a hand on her arm stopped her. She turned to Sash, who was staring, brows pinched, teeth worrying at her bottom lip.

"Be careful, okay?" Sash said. She offered Yuna the poker she'd taken from Moran's childhood bedroom. "Take this."

The cold iron was hard and heavy in her hands. The potential for grievous bodily harm seemed to radiate from it.

Don't know if I have it in me to swing this thing at someone.

She hoped she'd never have to find out.

After drawing a fortifying breath, Yuna shimmied through the narrow gap between the barely open doors.

Her shirt caught on the old wood as the edge of the door scraped against her ribs. She sucked in a breath, as if that would make her any smaller. The wooden doors scraped at her as she slid past their bulk. It wasn't a pleasant feeling, but it was overwhelmed once her eyes registered what she was seeing beyond them.

It was a library, grander than any she had ever seen. (Not that she had seen that many; she had a patchwork memory of the public library in Indigo Falls, with its interlocking foam alphabet covering the floor of the children's section and its musty stacks of reference books.) It was certainly far grander than any she could have imagined.

The room itself was cavernous. The ceiling stood at least fifty feet above her head, with a second floor wrapping around the sides of the room, accessible by a wrought-iron spiral staircase in the far corner.

Stained-glass windows overlooked it all, casting hued shadows on the floor. A segment had been blown inward, littering the floor with small, glittering chunks of multicolored glass. Very expensive-looking items decorated the room. Cracked statues. Paintings in golden frames. A suit of samurai armor that looked like it belonged in a museum and a sword displayed beside it. But what pulled most strongly at Yuna's attention were the shelves.

They towered against the walls, carved of the same dark wood as the balustrade around the second floor. A few books had fallen to the ground, probably knocked free by the same force that had destroyed the windows. They lay there like forgotten casualties, their pages torn, their spines cracked.

"Books!" Yuna whisper-shouted. "Glorious books!"

Without wasting another breath, she turned back toward the doors. There was an errant piece of fallen wood—a part of the broken balustrade surrounding the second floor of the library—and with a triumphant kick, she knocked it free. It skidded halfway across the room as the door swung open under Sash's weight.

"Books? What—?"

The query died in Sash's mouth as she experienced the same moment of shocked awe Yuna had.

Yuna twirled in the center of the vast room, her arms spread wide. When she pulled them in, she twirled faster still, half raised on the balls of her feet in something that wasn't quite a chaîné turn, but was close enough that Mrs. Eremenko would have frowned in judgment—were she here. But she wasn't. It was just Yuna and Sash (and Gabe, but he wasn't *here* here, just here.)

Sash made a beeline for the books on the nearest shelf and read the names on their spines in a hushed, reverent whisper. "Mark Twain, William Faulkner, John Steinbeck, Kurt Vonnegut, George Orwell . . ."

"Sounds like a bunch of dead white guys," Yuna said, dancing over to a table in the center of the room. Books were grand, but what was on the table proved a worthy distraction even from a universe of untold—or at least unread—stories.

On the table stood a bizarre contraption, the likes of which Yuna had never seen. A wooden pedestal of sorts supported a thin brass tube. The tube met with a connecting joint before widening to a large open horn, nearly big enough for her to stick her head in. Not that she would. Who knew what tiny monsters had taken up residence in its shadowy brass depths.

"What is it?" Yuna asked, her voice a whisper.

Sash shrugged, rapping the side of it with her knuckles. "Don't know. Looks old. I mean, older than everything else."

Yuna squinted, trying to read the engraving on the side. "Give me some light."

Sash angled the flashlight over Yuna's shoulder and clicked it on.

"Victrola," Yuna read. She turned to Sash, blinking against the light before the other girl could angle it away from her eyes. "What's a Victrola?"

"Sort of looks like Gabe's busted record player." Sash pointed the flashlight to a stack of what Yuna had assumed were folders on the floor beside the device. "Guessing it played those."

Yuna bent down to pick one up.

Tchaikovsky. A waltz.

The name was like a bolt of lightning straight to Yuna's heart. It was one of the names Mrs. Eremenko would whisper fondly to herself during ballet class, as if she were listening to music only she could hear.

"Can we?" Yuna clutched the record to her chest. It was stupid. She knew it was stupid. Anyone with a half a dozen brain cells could tell it was stupid. But the chance to listen to music— real music, new music, not the same tired melodies they listened to over and over and over in Mrs. Eremenko's class—was too good to pass up.

Sash's lips twitched into that barely there smile of hers. It was like a real smile was fighting to get out, but her reputation simply wouldn't allow it. Yuna liked that smile more than a normal, uninhibited one. It meant Sash was containing something so strong, she had to fight to hold it back. But it was winning. And since Sash was the strongest person Yuna knew, that meant it had to be even stronger.

With a nod, Sash said, "Yeah."

That was all it took. Yuna plopped the record on the Victrola— not as gently as she should have—and used the crank to wind up the machine. When it felt ready to go, she released the lever and waited.

Not a second later, sound filled the library. It was an odd, thin sound, but it was music.

Her gaze caught Sash's. They stared at each other, listening to the waltz fill the impossibly large library. Finger by finger, Yuna tugged off her gloves. With her bare skin exposed to the elements, she tossed the gloves onto the table and reached for Sash. The other girl stared at her hand as if she had never seen its ilk before.

"I don't know how to dance to this," Sash said, her eyes dropping to her feet.

"It's okay," Yuna offered. "I can lead."

With a shaky nod, Sash accepted Yuna's proffered hand. Her own—awkward and hesitant—fell to Yuna's waist, her fingers half curled into fists. Tension sang through every inch of her being with more clarity than the music warbling out of the Victrola.

"Don't overthink it," Yuna said, swaying in place along with the melody. "Just follow me. Move with the music."

"You say that like it's easy," Sash mumbled, her gaze rising just long enough to shoot Yuna a sullen glare. And long enough for her unsupervised feet to trod on Yuna's left toe.

"It is if you stop worrying about it." Yuna applied just a hair of pressure to Sash's shoulders, encouraging her to move in the right way at the right time. According to the placement of their hands, Sash should have been leading, but the poor girl was clearly in no state to take on that sort of responsibility.

"This is nice," Sash said, her voice so soft Yuna could barely hear it over the Victrola's scratchy lullaby.

Yuna nodded, dropping her own gaze. She didn't have to look at her feet. She trusted them not to embarrass her. But she didn't quite trust her expression the same way. It felt like her face was doing something she hadn't agreed to but was powerless to stop. Especially when Sash looked at her *like that*. *Like that* was dangerous. *Like that* made Yuna's face do all sorts of unpredictable things.

A strange sound—an aberration, definitely not part of Tchaikovsky's grand plan—cut through the moment with none of the grace of the man's score.

Yuna froze. "What was that?"

"It was just the record. Probably had a scratch on it."

Yuna shook her head, dropping her arms from around Sash's neck. A flicker of hurt passed over Sash's face, but it was gone as quickly as it had appeared. Regret zinged through Yuna's chest, hot and tight, but it was chased away by something greater.

Fear.

"It wasn't the record," Yuna insisted.

"Then what—?"

Skkritch.

Sash closed her mouth with such force, Yuna actually heard her teeth clack together.

The sound was most assuredly not emanating from the Victrola.

"Turn it off," Sash whispered. "Turn the music off."

"I'm trying!"

But fear—thick, cloying, suffocating—made Yuna's fingers feel too large, her hands too clumsy, the flashlight too slippery. She fumbled with the Victrola, trying to find a way to silence it, but without success. After several pounding heartbeats, she settled for yanking the record right off its rotating seat. It dropped from her grasp and landed on the hard tile with a crack as loud as lightning. No, louder.

Yuna stared at it, her breath harsh in the ensuing silence. It was split in two, neatly divided into broken halves, as if she'd meant to do just that.

She hadn't. Oh God, she hadn't.

Her lips started to form words, an apology maybe, to account for the ruination of the single most perfect moment of her life.

Then she raised her eyes and saw Sash put a single finger to her own lips.

Be quiet, that gesture said. *Make no sudden moves or sounds. Don't even think too loud lest something hear us.* The gesture brooked no argument and neither did the steely look in Sash's eyes. Yuna clapped her jaw shut so hard it hurt.

They went still in the silence and waited.

Something—or someone—was in the manor with them.

And Yuna knew, deep in her gut, that it wasn't Gabe.

"Yuna," Sash whispered. "Run."

But Yuna didn't run. She stayed, rooted to the spot, her eyes wide, her breathing choppy and fast. A fine tremble worked its way through her body.

I'm panicking, Yuna realized in a distant way, like she was an observer watching this happen to someone else.

Something clicked out in the hallway, closer this time than it was before.

They didn't have time for panic.

Sash grabbed the poker in one hand and Yuna's with the other. They ran.

Moran was right.

Probably not the most opportune time for the thought, but it couldn't be held at bay, not when some abomination was hot on their heels. *We were wrong, and Moran was right.*

Yuna tripped as Sash tugged on her arm, urging her to go faster. Thankfully, Sash was strong enough—or scared enough—to keep them both upright as they fled in the opposite direction of that awful, awful sound.

Oh my God, Moran was right.

CHAPTER 21

GABE

Splitting up was a bad idea.

The thought occurred to Gabe seconds after he left Yuna and Sash plundering sequined monstrosities from the closet of someone probably long dead. Not that he had a problem with sequined monstrosities—or dresses, really. He'd left because he wanted to give the two of them a minute alone together. They'd been dancing around each other for years, either too stupid or too scared to do anything about their painfully obvious mutual crush. He wasn't going to say anything about it either.

We shouldn't have split up.

But when were they going to have a moment like this again? Alone in the world. Free to do whatever they pleased, even if those two idiots couldn't seem to figure out what it was they pleased. He didn't blame Sash and Yuna for their lack of forward progress toward what seemed painfully obvious to him. It was hard in the bunker to have even the slightest moment of privacy. And when you did get what passed for privacy—an illusion in the bunker, always—the threat of losing it was always there. Even more prevalent was the specter of the rules by which they lived. No touching, no skin-to-skin. No direct physical contact. No hugs. No kisses. No hand-holding, even through gloves.

They were oppressive, those rules. But now, he and his friends were free of them, even if only for the most fleeting of moments.

Yuna and Sash were his friends. He wanted them to be happy, even if their happiness didn't include him. Even if it did hurt a little to be the odd man out. But Gabe could live with that.

What he couldn't live with was the thick layer of dust that coated everything in this godforsaken place.

He scrunched up his face and held in a sneeze to the best of his ability. The sound he produced was more of a half-aborted chirp than a true and proper sneeze. It wasn't satisfying, but at least it was quiet. If there was anything lurking in those shadows, he didn't want to meet it.

Gabe wasn't scared. Well, he was. A little bit. Especially right now with the old bones of the house creaking with every step he took, and the baser parts of his brain lurching at every shadow. He cranked his flashlight a few more times when the beam started to tremble and fade.

You shouldn't be doing that, whispered a voice at the back of his mind. *Light is danger. Darkness is good.*

But it was a pain in the butt to walk around a decrepit old manor in the dark, and so he cranked that light up.

There's nothing here, he whispered back at that voice. (Internally. He wasn't an idiot.) *Just me and Yuna and Sash.*

He repeated those words like a mantra as he wandered the halls. His meandering led him deeper into the belly of the house, past a massive dining room (complete with chandelier), a parlor (with cushions so plump and pristine it was clear no butts had ever indented them), and a room devoted entirely to death (with mounted animal heads on the walls and racks of what looked like very old hunting rifles alongside them).

The dining room led to a kitchen, though to call it one felt like a gross understatement of what it actually was. Gabe had never seen one so large. The cabinets were made of what looked like a lightly stained wood. The countertops were granite, cool to the touch, even through Gabe's glove. The stovetop range had more burners than Gabe would ever know what to do with.

This kitchen was *vast*.

It was the only word to describe it.

A wide space, full of industrial-size appliances. A chrome refrigerator with two massive doors. An island worthy of the name.

Tall open shelves, long since picked clean of anything useful. The shelves hung off the wall by the remaining will of a few rusty nails. Cobwebs crowded the empty spaces, blending with the thick coat of dust on the rotting wood.

Above the gargantuan island hung rows and rows of copper pots and pans, gleaming like metallic roses under the moonlight that filtered in through the broken window. Fragments of glass were still scattered beneath the empty panes.

Blown inward, Gabe thought.

A shudder ran through him, somehow both cold and hot all at the same time.

Don't think about it.

But telling yourself not to think a thing was exactly like thinking about it, a futile position to take, really.

Gabe trailed his hand along the edge of the island as he walked deeper into the kitchen. On the other side of the room a heavy wooden door stood closed. It matched the rest of the room's rustic decor, save for one salient detail.

A keypad to the left of it.

Odd.

Cranking the flashlight a few more times, Gabe approached the door. He shone his beam on the keypad and his tongue went dry in his mouth.

The numbers weren't dusty. Well, a few of them weren't.

Everything in the manor they had thus far encountered had been covered in a fine layer of dust. Every surface, every windowsill, every doorjamb. But four numbers on the keypad stood out in stark relief.

Two.

Three.

Eight.

Zero.

Gabe swallowed thickly. These buttons had been touched recently enough for the dust not to be able to collect on them.

Someone has been here.

Those words zinged around in his head, bouncing off the interior of his skull like deranged pinballs.

Someone has been here. And recently, from the look of things.

Gabe's breath rattled from his lungs. His hands twitched for an inhaler that wasn't there. Like so much else, the bunker's supply had run short. That was why he didn't have to take Mrs. Eremenko's physical education classes. Too much stress on his poor lungs. Too much—

Someone has been here.

That singular thought overrode everything else his brain could concoct.

The who and why and how hardly mattered. Well, they did, but they didn't. They couldn't. Those questions—and their answers—were far-off things. Hypotheticals. Unreal.

What was real was the door and the keypad and the curiously dust-free buttons.

Gabe's hand trembled toward those buttons entirely of its own accord. His gloved fingers traced the rectangular contours of each button, savoring even that dulled sensation.

Four numbers.

Twenty-four possible permutations of those numbers.

The chance of guessing the right order: 1 in 417.

That's assuming the lock allowed for some amount of human error—but not an infinite amount—far fewer attempts than that to get it right. Ten on the outside. Three if the lock's designer was particularly unforgiving.

Don't do it, one part of his brain cautioned.

But another, louder part, shouted, *Do it.*

And so . . . Gabe did it.

His hand shook as he punched in the numbers, first in the numerical order in which they occurred.

Zero. Two. Three. Eight.

The lock beeped once. From beneath its dusty cover, the light above the keys flashed a dull red.

No dice.

Another combination, then.

Eight. Three. Two. Zero.

Beep. Flash. Red.

Gabe drew in a tremulous breath. If he was designing a lock like this, he would show no mercy. If you couldn't get it right on the third try, you had no business opening it. You clearly didn't know what you were doing. You clearly weren't meant to be trusted with whatever secrets it sheltered.

Zero. Two. Eight. Three.

Beep.

Beep.

Flash.

Green.

The flashlight tumbled from Gabe's fingers, landing on the tiled floor with all the subtle silence of stampeding bulls.

He didn't bother scooping it up. The lock was open, which meant the door *could* be opened.

And so he opened it.

Inside was a pantry. Shelves—metal and utilitarian, so unlike the warm welcoming wood of the kitchen—lined the walls.

Something on the topmost shelf drew his eye, like it was calling out for him—specifically for Gabe and no one else. He reached up, but his hands were just short of being able to reach it. After a cursory glance informed him that there wasn't a stool or ladder or anything of the sort in the pantry—and he wasn't about to leave, not with such delicious bounty right there—he set one foot on the lowest shelf and pulled himself up. The shelf groaned, unhappy to be burdened with the weight of a seventeen-year-old boy, but it lasted long enough for Gabe's outstretched hand to reach for his prize.

A radio. Compact and coated with dust, but a radio nonetheless. One of those CB radios with the mic to speak into and everything.

Click.

Skkritch.

Sounds. Not his own. Coming from outside the pantry. Maybe even outside the kitchen. It was hard to tell. He was so used to the confined space of the bunker, the exact manner in which sounds bounced off of those tightly packed surfaces, that he was having trouble judging how sound behaved in the open. In the wild.

Click.

There it was again.

A noise, like something small and solid tapping against stone. Gabe froze, his hands an inch from the radio.

He held his breath, straining his ears to see if the noise would come again. But his heart beat so loudly in the silence he could hear nothing else.

"Hello?"

No response came. Not in the form of an answering voice or another weird clicking sound.

It took several tries for Gabe to find his voice again. It had fled to some well-hidden depth within him.

"This isn't funny, guys."

It's probably just Sash being an idiot. She and Yuna are playing some dumb prank. One day, we'll all have a good chortle about it, once I stop hating them.

Gabe brushed his hands on his jeans. That was pointless,

since his jeans were also dusty. All he managed to accomplish was to introduce one layer of dust to another layer of dust so they could make friends.

His flashlight roamed over the room as he methodically pointed it at each corner.

Nothing there.

He inched forward, closer to the door.

Swallowing the sour clump of fear lodged in his throat, he debated the merits of calling out for Yuna and Sash again.

On the one hand, if they were there and he confirmed it, he could yell at them at his leisure for being such unbelievable hell spawn.

On the other, if that wasn't them making the noise, it stood to reason it was something else—or *someone*, an even more terrifying thought. Making any more sound himself would be the equivalent of drawing a nice big target right on his face.

If there was something—or *someone*—out there, he didn't want it to eat his face. He desperately did not want that.

But no other sound came.

It was just his mind, playing tricks. Minds were good at that. Fiendishly good, some might say.

He clutched the radio to his chest, closing his eyes at the wondrous sensation of its hard plastic digging into his ribs.

A radio. One he might be able to get working. There might be no one in the universe left to talk to, but it was *new*. It was exciting. He had dismantled and reconstructed practically every gadget and device the bunker had to offer. He had grown bored of their electronic innards. He knew them too well. But this? This was unknown.

With the radio cradled in his arms, he cast another glance

around the rest of the room. His earlier fear might have blinded him to other treasures waiting to be discovered by his curious eyes.

The rest of the shelves were mostly bare save for a few sacks of what looked like rice.

Rice.

Actual, honest-to-God rice.

Like a sailor drawn irrevocably to the sound of a siren's melody, Gabe went for the bag.

Rice and beans.

Arroz con gandules.

Arroz con pollo.

The soft, comforting taste of the rice porridge—arroz con leche—his grandmother had made for him whenever he got sick. It wasn't the sweet kind you'd eat for the dessert but the gently bland kind, good for settling upset stomachs.

As soon as he neared the bag, he knew something was off. The smell. It wasn't right. Rice wasn't supposed to smell like that.

He peered closer. There was a hole in the bag, its fibers raw and uneven, as if something had chewed straight through it.

Squinting in the dark, Gabe drew closer to the bag. Maybe some of the rice was still salvageable. It was dry, after all. It should have kept? Maybe? He didn't know enough about rice to be sure but—

Something jumped out of the hole in the bag.

With a startled cry, Gabe leaped backward, knocking an empty cardboard box off a shelf.

With one hand, he grappled at the shelves for purchase, and they clanged against the walls under his weight.

He had to run. He had to, but he could hardly breathe, how was he supposed to—

The thing scrambled across the floor, tiny feet tripping over stray grains of rice.

It was a rat.

Just a rat.

Gabe sighed, leaning against the shelf. The hard dig of the wood into his back grounded him, reminding him that he was just a stupid, jumpy idiot and there was absolutely nothing to be afraid of. Nothing at all.

It's just me and Yuna and Sa—

"Who are you?"

The voice sliced through Gabe's frenzied relief, hot and sharp.

It was a new voice. Not one of the same cadre of voices he'd been listening to exclusively for nearly a decade.

A new voice.

A new sound.

A new person.

An old man stood in the open doorway, his features shrouded in shadow. What Gabe could see was this:

- A long gray beard, scraggly and unkempt.

- Oversize clothing, hanging off the man's frail form like too-large rags.

- A hatchet, clutched in one hand.

- Mottled skin, oddly shiny and hairless in some places.

What he could smell was this:

- Filth.

When Gabe failed to answer him, the man banged a fist wrapped in a soiled bandage against one of the shelves. *"Who are you?"*

But how could Gabe possibly answer him? How could he gather the letters that had fallen out of his scattered brain and slap them into something resembling words? He was being confronted with the one thing that should not have been possible.

The mere presence of this man meant only one thing. That thing spat in the face of the most fundamental truth the residents of the bunker held sacred. The one thing that went unquestioned, even by Sash at her most contrarian.

They were *not* alone.

Moran was wrong, Moran was wrong, Moran was wrong.

Each word slammed into him with the force of a brick swung around in a burlap sack.

The man stepped into the pantry. Gabe's tongue was too large for his jaw suddenly, like it was trying to suffocate him. His mouth opened and closed like a guppy choking on air.

A squeak from the corner of the pantry made them both freeze. The man went still, his head twitching in the direction of the sound.

The rat. The one from the rice.

As if summoned by Gabe's thoughts, the rat darted out from the bottom shelf, aiming for the door.

But the old man—was he that old or did he just look that way?—was more spry than he appeared. Arms outstretched, he lunged for the rat. It shrieked as his claylike hands closed around its body.

And then, the man bit it.

He bit the rat.

Blood spurted around his jaw as his eyes closed in ecstasy. Under his layers of mismatched rags, his body trembled as if in the deepest throes of pleasure.

Bile rose high in Gabe's throat at the sight.

A thousand questions ran through his head, but none he could articulate in the moment.

Why?

How?

What?

What?

What?

The rat struggled in the man's bandaged and bloodied hands, its tiny, hairless legs kicked in a futile attempt to escape, its tail twitching as those hands tightened their hold.

With the man distracted by his feast, Gabe did the only thing he could think of.

He tucked the radio under one arm and ran.

CHAPTER 22
YUNA

They could have been hiding for minutes or for hours.

Time had lost all meaning to Yuna, huddled in what felt like the belly of a tauntaun. (They had a copy in the bunker of an old Star Wars novelization. Its mass market paperback pages were yellowed and thinning, but it was still good reading.)

It wasn't actually a tauntaun (they weren't real), but a closet full of fur. Coats, to be exact, of different textures and colors. Yuna assumed the last bit. It was too dark to see anything. Sash had snatched the flashlight from Yuna's hand and switched it off as they ran through the manor's twisting corridors until they'd found this place. This dark, horrible, fur-lined place.

It was also hot and musty, especially with the two of them crammed into the small space, knees knocking together and legs all tangled up.

She wanted to whisper something to Sash. To ask if she was okay. To check if the coast was clear. But she was too afraid. Too afraid to speak. Too afraid to move. Too afraid to breathe, really. She tried to hold her breath, but as it turns out, the body overrides the brain when it's suffocating from sheer stupid terror. So she breathed, but quietly, and in no way that felt satisfying to her lungs.

Her hand—still gloveless; God, where were her gloves?—fumbled in the pitch black for something to hold on to, something that wasn't a dead animal transformed into a garment for whatever rich lady had filled this closet with wearable corpses.

Fingers collided with hers before twining around them, joining their hands. Sash, too, had apparently been seeking out human contact.

It was silent now, but Yuna imagined she could still hear it. That awful noise.

Skkkrrrritch.

Like nails on a chalkboard.

Or claws against marble.

"What was that?" Yuna dared to whisper.

Sash pressed a hand to the girl's mouth, shaking her head.

I don't know, said that shake of the head.

Don't speak, said that shake of the head.

I'm sorry, I was an idiot. I never should have suggested we come up here, and I hope we don't die, was a little too complex to be conveyed with a single shake of the head, but Yuna thought she heard it anyway.

She buried her face in her knees, focusing on the Herculean

task of taking air into her lungs via her nostrils and breathing it out slowly through her mouth.

In and out.

In and out.

In and out.

Her heart was beating so loudly in her chest, she was sure that whatever was out there could hear it. It would sound the alarm to the monsters lurking in the shadows and summon them to their location, to this closet. It would stain the mink coats red with their blood. It would—

Something yanked the door open.

Yuna let out a strangled scream before a hand—Sash's— clapped over her mouth, sealing the remainder of it behind a sweaty palm.

Blinking against the half-light of the otherwise empty hallway, Yuna choked back the rest of her scream. In the open doorway stood Gabe, his chest heaving as it rose and fell with a series of strained asthmatic breaths.

"We . . . have . . ." Each word punctuated by another labored breath. "To . . . run."

Sash moved so quickly that the unfolding of her legs made them both tumble out of the closet and onto the floor at Gabe's feet.

Gabe circled Yuna's upper arm with his free hand—the one not clutching a weird black box against his chest—and hauled her to her feet with a strength she hadn't ever realized he possessed.

Once they were all upright, they wasted no time.

They ran.

As quietly as they could, through the manor's labyrinthine

corridors. Past empty rooms and empty frames and empty chairs and tables.

Yuna was too turned around to know where she was going. Too afraid for her mind to make any sense of the manor's bizarre geography. She could only trust—and pray—that Gabe's eidetic memory would save them from . . .

From what?

Yuna hadn't seen anything. She was fairly certain Sash hadn't either.

But something had been there. Something that wasn't the three of them. Something that sounded distinctly inhuman.

Her mind was still spiraling when they trampled back into the ballroom. Their footsteps felt too loud against its black-and-white-checkered floor, but eventually they made it to the hatch. It had been cleverly disguised by the pattern in the flooring, if not for the piece of rotted wood they'd wedged inside, holding it ajar. That piece of wood was all that prevented them from being sealed outside, in this horrible place with its horrible ghosts *skkkrrrritching* at the floors.

Sash reached the hatch first. She dropped to her knees and wrenched it open, knocking their makeshift doorstop aside. Her hair—loose now somehow, how had that happened?—whipped around her face as she turned to Yuna. The girl's eyes were wide, her complexion pale with fear.

"Go!"

Yuna went.

She dropped through the hatch feetfirst, landing on the metal grating beneath with a dull thud that reverberated up her calves. The shock subsided as she scrambled out of the way. Gabe fell through after her, followed by Sash, whose swinging feet nearly decapitated him. As she fell, she pulled the hatch shut behind her.

The metal door slammed closed, knocking ten years' worth of dust from its hinges. It was the loudest sound Yuna had ever heard.

The silence that followed in its wake was somehow worse.

She panted, doubling over, hands on her knees. Her hair had fallen loose of its bun during their mad dash to the hatch. A cascade of it blocked the others from her sight. She squeezed her eyes shut, but that proved to be a mistake. All she could see then were the horrible creatures her mind concocted to go with those sounds.

After a long, terrible moment, Gabe broke the silence:

"I saw someone."

Yuna and Sash both stared at him. Except he wasn't looking at them. He was inspecting the thing he'd held so tightly in his arms the entire time they were running. It looked like some kind of old electronics, maybe even older than the Betamax (they had a bunch of those in the bunker).

"That's not possible," Sash said.

It was so unlike her, Yuna couldn't help but notice.

Sash was the sort of person who always wanted to believe in the impossible. It was her imagination, her absolute unshakable faith that the world was not what they'd been told, that had led them topside in the first place.

Maybe even Sash can have doubts.

It was an odd thought. Not one Yuna wanted to welcome into her mind. Not at all.

But Gabe was shaking his head. "I did. I saw someone. I swear."

"Like . . ." Yuna swallowed, forcing the words up her throat, phoneme by painful phoneme. "A person?"

It was probably a stupid question, except in how it wasn't.

Gabe nodded, too rapidly, like one of those bobblehead dolls her older brother had once kept on the dashboard of his new car.

Don't.

Those were thoughts she did not think.

If she thought them, she would be lost.

Lost was something she couldn't afford to be. Not now. Not when Gabe had seen someone.

"He ate a rat," Gabe whispered, staring at the device in his hands. "It was still alive." He swallowed thickly. Once. Twice. He looked up at them, his eyes curiously distant, as if he were seeing something they couldn't. "There was something wrong with his skin."

Yuna dropped Sash's hand—when had she taken it again?—and stepped away from them both.

"Yuna . . ." Sash's voice was so soft. So hurt. She thought Yuna had withdrawn from her. That Yuna believed touching Sash was a bad thing.

"No—I . . ." Yuna didn't know how to verbalize what it was she felt. "What if I . . . ?" She looked down at her hands, half expecting her unmarked flesh to erupt in boils, for pus and blood and bile to come streaming out of her pores. Tearing her eyes away from her bare—bare!—hands, Yuna said, "I don't want to hurt you."

"If you're infected, we're all infected." Gabe's voice was coming back to his body, like he was pulling himself inch by painful inch out of a memory. He looked so haunted. Maybe he would be for the rest of his life, Yuna thought. However long that was.

Oh God, what had they done?

"Go, wash your hands. Find another pair of gloves. I'll give you a pair of mine if you need them." Sash pulled hers out of her back pocket (a much more sensible place to have stored them). She held them out to Yuna, who could only stare dumbly at them. "Take these."

Yuna shook her head. "No. You need them."

"I'll be fine."

"But, Sash—"

"None of us are going to be fine," Gabe blurted. "You didn't see him! He was—"

Sash clapped her hand—her bare hand—over Gabe's mouth. He mumbled something, but it was effectively smothered by her palm.

"Keep it together," Sash said, her own voice oddly steady considering the circumstances. "And for the love of all that is holy, keep your voice down."

Gabe narrowed his eyes at her over his palm. After a long, mutinous glare, his face softened and he nodded.

Slowly, Sash lowered her hand. That she wiped it off on her jeans did not escape anyone's notice. But no one remarked on it. They were all trying their best, considering the circumstances.

"What are we going to do?" Yuna asked. She hated how her voice sounded. Young and scared and tremulous. But she was young and she was scared and she was fairly certain she was about to start shaking like a leaf and never, ever stop.

Considering the circumstances.

Sash turned so she was facing them both. "We're going to do the same exact thing we always do."

"How can you—" Gabe shook his head, cutting himself off.

"After what I saw, how can you expect us to go about our business as usual? Oh, hey, still nothing to see out there!" His voice rose in pitch with every word, amplified by his burgeoning hysteria. "There *was* something! And I did see it! And it was a person. A whole, living person! On the surface! Where there are supposed to be no people! None!"

"Gabe."

Sash grabbed his face in both hands—her gloves were back on, and Yuna hadn't even noticed her don them. How odd. She leaned in close, not close enough to touch but close enough.

She spoke in a low, soothing voice. "You cannot lose it right now. Do you understand me?"

Gabe tried to shake his head, but the movement was limited by Sash's grip. "But—"

"No buts. You absolutely cannot lose it."

Squeezing his eyes shut, Gabe drew in a long, shaky breath. After a moment, he opened his eyes and met Sash's. Then he nodded.

"Okay." Sash released him and turned to Yuna. "I don't know what was up there. I don't understand what you saw." She stepped back so she could address them both. "But what I do know is that we cannot tell *anyone*. Not yet. Not until we find out more. Not until we know the truth."

"But how?" Yuna asked. "How are we going to do that?"

Sash squared her shoulders. The look on her face was one Yuna knew well. It was determination and ferocity and an unwavering commitment to whatever absurd nonsense she was about to pull.

"I'll figure something out. I promise."

CHAPTER 23

SASH

Act normal.

Sure.

No problem.

Just act perfectly normal as if nothing life-altering had happened in the dead of the night.

As if the fabric of their shared reality hadn't been fundamentally torn wide open by the sound of claws in the shadows, or the ghost of a man haunting the hallways of a long-abandoned manor house.

It had been so easy to say that to Gabe and Yuna. *Act normal.* So easy to be the one to reassure them, to hold the pieces together in the cupped palms of her hands as if she knew what she was doing.

She didn't.

⊙ ⊙ ⊙

The day proceeded as normally as she could force it to. Breakfast was a quiet, sullen affair, but Sash being quiet and sullen in the morning was nothing new. Her rotation cleaning up after the meal was equally as mundane. She was paired with Nastia this time, who did as poor a job rinsing the dishes as she always did.

Everything was normal.

Perfectly normal.

Absolutely positively normal.

At least it was until class. Until she saw Moran's smug face, smiling at them as they filed into the room, their assorted morning chores complete. She was wearing a burgundy caftan today, its tassels swinging with every movement of her arms. The loose black dress underneath it highlighted the hollows of her cheeks, the smudges under her eyes.

The same girl in that photograph. The girl from the fancy Swiss boarding school. That's who Moran was. Not some savior. Not a saint. Not what she pretended to be at all.

"Blessed morrow, all."

Blessed morrow. God, Sash hated that. Why not just say "good morning" like a normal person? Why dress it up? Why bother, when none of their mornings were good or blessed?

"Blessed morrow, Dr. Moran," the class intoned, more or less as one. Even Sash. The habit was so firmly ingrained that she didn't notice herself speaking the words until they had already escaped, free on the air.

Nastia nudged Sash out of the way as she aimed for the best seat in the class. It was nearest the pipe that carried warm water from one end of the bunker to the other. If she put her feet on the right spot on the floor, she could feel a little bit of warmth seeping upward.

"Move," Nastia grunted unkindly. Normally, Sash would have rolled her eyes at this sort of behavior. Once she hit her tween years, Nastia had become a terror. Trying to assert herself, their mother would say. Being a brat, Sash would say. Sometimes even Misha would agree with her, and he was prone to let Nastia get away with anything short of bloody murder.

Sash had asked once what Nastia remembered about the world above. About Before. Nastia had merely shrugged and shoveled another spoonful of watery gruel into her mouth, then said, "I remember a bird pooping on me once."

Now Nastia plopped down onto the chair, heaving out a dramatic sigh. With exacting deliberateness, she toed off her shoes. Her socked feet settled on the floor as her eyelids fluttered shut.

For life in the bunker, a heated floor panel was the height of luxury. And Nastia was willing to shove her own sister aside for that sliver of comfort. That one, slender moment of bliss.

This is the only life she knows. The thought settled at the base of Sash's stomach like cold sludge. *And this life is a lie.*

That was what did it.

That was what made her fling the very sound advice she'd given Gabe and Yuna (though it was more of a demand than advice) out the window. Metaphorically.

This far underground, there were no windows.

But maybe, just maybe, they didn't need to be this far underground.

Maybe, just maybe, Nastia could have grown up with sunlight on her skin and not just the poor simulation the UV lamps could provide.

The others settled into their seats as Moran began to write out her agenda for the day's lesson on the board.

Yuna caught Sash's eyes from across the room. Something must have shown on Sash's face because the girl's eyebrows pinched in that way they did when she was worried.

She had every reason to worry.

Sash was about to do something monumentally stupid.

Once they were all seated, Sash thrust her hand up in the air. Without waiting for Moran to call on her (the woman's back was still to her students as she wrote on the board), Sash opened her mouth and made what she knew was a mistake.

"What really happened during the Cataclysm?"

The chalk scraped against the blackboard with a terrific screech that made Sash's teeth hurt. Her skin felt like it was fit to crawl right off her bones.

Moran turned slowly, her usually quiet smile now a rictus scream of *Why are you trying my patience?*

"What do you mean 'What really happened'?" Moran asked, her voice drenched in sickly sweet honey. She was giving Sash a chance to take it back, to snag the question right out of the air, to stuff that impertinence right back in her pocket.

Sash, of course, did no such thing.

She spared a thought for their little hideout. She labored under no delusion that Moran somehow didn't know of it. She had to. If they'd found the blueprints, she must have at some point as well. They'd all been trapped in here like sardines in a can for a decade. At this point, there were no secrets, just harmless omissions they wordlessly agreed to tolerate for the sake of their collective sanity.

"You know very well what happened, Alexandra."

"It's Sash."

Moran's smile tightened.

And then, because Sash was fueled by pure fearless adrenaline: "I know what you told us. But I want to know the truth."

"Sash," hissed Gabe from his seat.

But she ignored him. So did Moran.

With an amused little snort, the doctor set the piece of chalk down on the lip of the blackboard and dusted her palms together. "I had a feeling this day would come. It's only natural, you know."

That . . . was not the response Sash had been expecting.

"What is?"

Moran inhaled through her nose, as if steadying herself to have a facts-of-life conversation. "This questioning of authority. It's perfectly normal. In the old days . . ."

And now, they were all holding their breaths. So rare was it for Moran to discuss the time Before in anything other than high-minded proselytism.

"In the old days," she repeated, knowing she had their full, captive attention, "you might have snuck out of the house . . ."

Sash went still. She didn't even blink. She dared not breathe.

"Or perhaps gotten a tattoo. Or passed the time with unsuitable companions."

The snare that had begun to close around Sash's throat loosened, just a hair.

"Maybe you would have imbibed alcoholic beverages or experimented with illicit substances or dyed your hair hot pink."

Nastia snorted at that. It earned a small, tight smile from Moran.

"But none of those rebellious options are available to you now." Moran held a hand over her heart. "And I sympathize. I do. I was a teenager myself once. And I understand what it's like to buck at what you think are shackles holding you in place."

The photograph flashed through Sash's mind. That young girl with her dark hair and her darker eyes, shuttled off to some Swiss boarding school, perhaps to atone for whatever *her* rebellion had been.

"But I assure you, I have never lied to you." Her eyes were steady on Sash's. Steady and open and raw, as if to say, *Gaze into my depths. See what lies beneath.* "Not once." A sad shake of her head. "A part of me wishes I could. It would be easier, to peddle pretty lies and easily digestible half-truths." A soft, wistful sigh. "But that would do you no favors. Everything I have told you is the truth. The hubris of man. His greed. His selfishness. His hunger for more. More wealth. More power. More blood and death and toil led us here. Underground. Buried, so that someday, like seedlings, we may grow again. *That* is what happened."

A masterful performance. Beautiful words strung together, saying absolutely nothing at all.

Moran turned away, pivoting toward the blackboard. As far as she was concerned, the conversation was over.

It was not.

"How did my father die?"

Gabe's head swiveled so he could catch Sash's eyes and glare. She could actually feel her own eyes gleaming with determination. It was an odd sensation, that internal gleaming.

Like a dog with a bone, teeth baring down harder and harder. Unrelenting.

Moran turned back to face Sash, her head cocking to the side. She blinked.

"How should I know?"

Sash pressed on. "You know so much about what went on up there. You say you know what the atmosphere would do to our bodies, how the air would burn our lungs, that the rain would fall like acid, melting the skin right off our bones." She shrugged. "Thought you might have an idea."

Moran was quiet for a long moment. Then: "Trust me when I tell you, Alexandra, that you do not want to know."

Nastia shifted in her seat, her gaze locked on the burnished aluminum surface of the table.

Sash spared her sister a glance.

Of course, her father wasn't just *her* father. He was theirs. Nastia may not have remembered him, but he belonged to both of them all the same. She had lost him too.

And that was why she deserved the truth.

"I do," Sash said. "I do want to know."

"Do you?" Dr. Moran asked, her voice taking on an odd lightness in its tone. "Do you really want to know what happened to him? Do you want to hear the gory details? Do you want to know how his skin crisped on the outside while his organs liquefied? Do you want to know that it happened so quickly that he was probably conscious the entire time? Do you want to know that he felt the skin sliding off his bones?"

Nastia stood up so quickly, her chair tipped backward. It clattered to the floor with a horrible, cacophonous sound. Her eyes were rimmed with red, and pink splotched her cheeks. She retched, drooping over the table. Clamping a hand to her mouth, she ran, knocking the chair out of the way with her shin.

A prolonged minute of stunned quiet followed in her wake.

That was when Sash noticed that Nastia had left without her shoes.

They were sitting there, one on its side, small and lonely. Discarded. Forgotten.

That was cruel, whispered one half of her brain.

That was necessary, replied the other.

Sash drew in another breath and immediately wished she hadn't. A stench, wicked and bright, filled her nostrils. Rotting flesh, crisping and burning. Boiling under the light of a merciless sun. It was an illusion, that smell. But that didn't make it feel any less real.

"What if there are people still out there?" Sash asked.

From the corner of her eyes, she could see Yuna and Gabe lock eyes from across the room.

This was the opposite of laying low. This was the opposite of pretending nothing happened. This was the opposite of exactly what Sash herself had advised them to do.

The question landed like a lead balloon.

"I think that's enough for today." Moran had her eyes on the door through which Nastia had fled. "You all have chores to attend to. I suggest you do them and think about how your words, how your actions, might impact other people."

The others filed out slowly, like prey animals trying not to draw attention. Sash lingered for a moment.

"You should make sure your sister gets her shoes back," Moran said, her back to Sash. "She'll hurt herself walking around in just her socks."

And that was that.

Sash wanted to ask more. She wanted to press. But she wasn't sure she could stomach it. And Moran clearly wasn't going to give her anything.

Stupid.

Impulsive.

Rash.

All the things she'd warned Gabe and Yuna not to be.

She picked up Nastia's sneakers (ladies size 6, once-white Reeboks, popular in the mid-1980s) and left.

In the hallway stood Yuna.

Sash blinked at her stupidly, Nastia's sneakers tucked under one arm.

"Hi—"

"What was that?" Yuna blurted.

With a glance over her shoulder at the closed door separating them from Moran, Sash said, "Not here."

She walked away, Yuna following close behind. Anger radiating off the other girl in waves.

No, not anger. Fury.

When they reached a relatively quiet spot, Sash pulled Yuna into the bend of a hallway that went nowhere.

Yuna flinched at the contact.

Sash let her go. It hurt to do so, but the sight of Yuna recoiling from her touch hurt even more.

"Why are you doing this?" Yuna asked.

"What do you mean, why? You know why!" An answering hiss, just as forceful, just as quiet. "You were there, Yuna. You heard what I did. You know what Gabe saw."

"Yeah, and how is this going to accomplish anything? How is

antagonizing Moran going to help us get answers?" Yuna stepped away.

Sash wanted to follow her, but she didn't. In her heart, she knew Yuna was right.

Stupid. Stupid, stupid, stupid.

Another step from Yuna, away from this conversation, away from Sash. "You're going to get us all in trouble."

Sash blinked at her. The words coming out of the other girl's mouth made her own go dry. "There are worse things than being in trouble, Yuna."

A tiny wrinkle formed between Yuna's brows as they pinched together. It wasn't a look that sat well on Yuna's face. It was a fine face, but it didn't look like her.

"Yeah," Yuna bit out. "Like whatever happened to that guy up there. The one Gabe saw. And whatever would have happened to us if Gabe hadn't found us. If we hadn't run. Is that what you want to happen?"

And now that didn't sound like her either.

"Yuna, that's not going—"

"Stop." Yuna held up a hand, silencing Sash. "Whatever it is you're going to say, don't say it. You can't make any promises. You don't know anything. None of us do."

Sash sank her teeth into her lower lip hard enough to hurt. It wasn't wrong. She wanted to argue, but she couldn't.

"But what I do know is that there are consequences to our actions." Yuna crossed her arms, hugging them to her chest. "She could force us out."

No one needed to specify who.

Moran.

"She can't kick us out of the bunker."

"She could," Yuna said with a note of panic. "I think if she convinced the others it was the right thing to do, she could."

Sash shook her head. "No. She could try, but they wouldn't let her. Our parents wouldn't let her."

Yuna's lips pressed into a hard, sad line. "Are you sure about that?"

"Of course I'm sure." She scoffed with more confidence than she felt. "Your parents would never let Moran hurt you. Neither would Gabe's."

"And what about yours?" Yuna asked softly. Like she didn't want to. Not really. "Would your mom stop her? Would Misha?"

She didn't wait for Sash to answer.

Shaking her head, Yuna said the worst thing she could have: "Maybe Moran was right."

Backing away, she added a final twist of the knife. "This isn't about you. You're not thinking. Not about me. Not about Gabe. And not about your poor sister."

"Yuna, please—"

"No." Yuna held up a hand. "I can't talk to you right now."

With that, she turned and walked away, leaving Sash standing in a hallway to nowhere, a dirty pair of shoes clutched in her hands as if they were the only thing keeping her afloat.

CHAPTER 24

YUNA

Anger was one of Yuna's least favorite emotions.

It was hot and unwieldy, like a heavy metal tray plucked straight from the oven.

It was sour in her mouth, sort of the way her breath tasted (and probably smelled) first thing in the morning. But it didn't go away when she brushed her teeth. It lingered. It clung. It *fermented*.

It followed her, persistent and awful, all the way from the hallway in which she'd yelled (sort of) at Sash to the chicken coop.

She'd *yelled* (sort of) at Sash.

It was the kind of thing Yuna simply did not do. And yet, she had done it. It was done. It had happened.

And she hadn't regretted it one bit.

Act normal, Sash had said.

And then Sash had done *that*. And what was worse, she hadn't seemed to understand why it was so bad. It wasn't a slap on the wrist Yuna feared. It was something much worse.

Exile.

Isolation.

A punishment to fit the crime.

"So much for normal," Yuna grumbled to herself. She popped onto her toes to reach for the bucket on the top shelf outside the coop. The handle flopped as her fingers brushed against it, sending it an inch deeper into the shelf space. With a bitten-back curse (much like anger, so very unlike her), Yuna strained for the bucket. She usually left it on the lower shelf so it was easier to reach, but someone—probably Misha, he was criminally tall—kept putting it back on the highest shelf, out of reach for the arms of mere mortals. She extended her arm as far as she could, but the bucket was now too far for her to get a hold on it. Her gloves made matters worse, their surface too slick for adequate purchase.

"Oh, for crying out loud," Yuna muttered.

With a frustrated sigh, she glared up at the bucket, willing it to fall.

She waited. It didn't.

"Fine. Be that way." She glanced around for something to step on. A stool or a ladder. They had a couple of them in the bunker, but they were never where she needed them to be. Now was no different.

The only thing Yuna could use to reach the bucket was the bottom shelf. With just the toes of her left sneaker, she pressed down on it. It groaned a little unhappily but it seemed sturdy enough to hold her weight. It wasn't that much. Mrs. Eremenko always said she had the body for ballet (if there were any ballet companies left in the world, which there weren't).

She placed her foot on the shelf and hoisted herself up with one hand on the top shelf. The other reached for the bucket. Her fingers closed around the handle.

"Finally, victory is mi—"

The bottom shelf cracked under her weight.

She had the slimmest moment to think *Oh no* before the shelf collapsed, sending her sprawling to the floor in a graceless lump of flailing limbs.

The air fled her lungs with the impact. Ears ringing, she lay there, staring up at the recessed lighting—tinted the slightest bit red—and tried to blink the pain away. Astonishingly, it did not work.

She sat up, rolling her spine gently as she rose, taking stock of each vertebrae.

All intact. Well, that was solid.

Her head, however, throbbed. Her fingers probed at the back of her skull, wincing when she touched a particularly sensitive, swollen spot. A wet, sensitive, swollen spot.

That's no good.

Her fingers came away, streaked red.

Her vision swam as bile rose in her throat. She'd never been good with the sight of blood. Especially blood of the unexpected variety. Some blood was okay. It followed a pattern. But this blood was the sort of blood that should stay in the body where it belonged.

She rubbed her fingers together, smearing the blood. That was worse, somehow.

But there was something else wrong. Something that wasn't

her own blood splattered against her skin and the metal of the floor paneling. Something not quite right.

Maybe it was the head wound.

Maybe she banged her skull harder than she thought.

Maybe—

The hair on the back of Yuna's neck rose.

It was a loud noise, her fall. The chickens would have hated it. Or, they should have. But they were quiet. The only thing Yuna could hear was the shrill ringing in her own ears.

Maybe they hadn't heard.

Grasping for the bucket—it had skid several feet across the floor—she scrabbled to her feet.

It's fine. They're just sleeping. Chickens sleep. Especially Winnie. She's the laziest. The best eggs, but the laziest.

Swallowing past a curious lump in her throat, Yuna turned the combination for the lock—like the greenhouse and the water-filtration room, the chicken coop had one of those—and pushed her weight against the door.

It swung open on silent hinges. She kept them well-oiled, or as well as she could, considering how low their oil supply was. The chickens hated the screech of rusty metal. Yuna stood in the open doorway, the bucket dangling from one hand, while the other clutched at the wall for support.

She took one step into the room. Then, another.

At this point, the chickens should have been clucking happily to see her.

Their little feet should have been pattering over the soft lining of their enclosure, their feathers whispering as they fluttered them in anticipation of being fed.

But there was no clucking.

No pattering feet.

No rustling feathers.

The chickens were dead.

Not just one chicken.

All of them.

The handle of the bucket slipped from Yuna's now nerveless fingers. Little food pellets spilled to the ground at her feet as she stared at the coop. The feed crunched under her shoes as she took one step forward, then another.

Maybe they were just sleeping. Or maybe they were sick and Dr. Moran would know of some way to make them better again.

Both lies, and Yuna knew it.

Yuna dropped to her knees beside Winnie. Her favorite. Her black swan.

"Winnie . . . ?"

She reached for the bird. But when her fingers brushed her feathers, Yuna knew it was a mistake.

They were lifeless. It seemed like a stupid observation, but seeing it and feeling it were two different things.

Winnie was cold. They were all cold.

They looked so small lying there. Unmoving. Winnie's black feathers reflected the UV lights like an oil slick. Her head was resting against her hay at an odd angle. Necks weren't supposed to bend like that. But her wings were askew too. As if she'd fought something off before dying. Or as if the throes of her death were so traumatic, she'd contorted herself trying to escape them.

Bile rose thick and sour in Yuna's throat. She got up and turned, her shoes skidding against the floor's metal plates.

When she reached the corridor, she collapsed, her knees

striking the hard metal with a painful thud. Her stomach heaved. She fell forward onto her hands, squeezing her eyes shut.

But that only made it worse. All she could see against her lids was the birds—her birds, she loved those birds—littering the ground.

She drew in a deep breath, and that too was a mistake.

All she could smell was blood.

The first retch caught her by surprise. The meager breakfast she'd choked down under her mother's eye surged up. Her stomach emptied its contents on the cold metal floor. Her body kept trying to purge itself of what she'd smelled and seen and felt, even after there was nothing left to purge. Her abdominals cramped with the force of her heaving. The sweat of her palms made her slip, nearly collapsing into her own sick.

She didn't know how long she was there, her knees aching against the hard floor, the rivets holding the metal plates together digging into her tender flesh.

Her body purged and purged and purged until there was nothing left for it to expel. But even then, it tried.

The smell was noxious, but at least it wasn't blood. At least it wasn't poor Winnie with her black feathers, soft, so soft—

"Yuna?"

For a moment, the voice sounded so much like Sash that Yuna wanted to cry. She wanted to fling herself into Sash's arms and scream and sob and claw at her eyes.

But when she forced them open, it wasn't Sash she saw standing before her, heavy bucket dangling from both hands.

Nastia blinked down at Yuna for a long silent moment. Then she lowered the bucket—gingerly, so as not to spill the water—and knelt by Yuna's side.

The hand brushing Yuna's hair from her face was gloved but nice and cool.

"What happened? Are you sick?"

That gloved hand paused, as if the possibility of sickness hadn't occurred to her until that moment. But once the thought was there, it was impossible to uproot.

Nastia retracted her hand and leaned back, just enough to feel like an insult.

"I'm not sick," Yuna said.

That she knew of. She could be.

Her hands, bare in the unknown atmosphere of the manor.

Her gloves, left abandoned in a library long forgotten.

Her lungs breathing in a decade's worth of air, ignorant of what particles it contained, what dangers it held.

"The chickens—"

That was all Yuna managed to choke out before another wave of nausea assaulted her.

With a swear that would have made Baba Olya blush, Nastia sprang to her knees and went into the chicken coop.

"No." Yuna retched again. "Don't—"

But it was too late.

After a long, silent moment, Nastia emerged again, her face entirely blank. In her hands, she cradled a small, feathered body. Black feathers. Like a swan. Like the color of a midnight Yuna couldn't remember.

"Did my sister do something?"

Yuna's body seized up so swiftly her retching stopped.

She rolled her eyes up at Nastia and her stone face. "What?"

"My sister." Something in Nastia's jaw twitched. "Did she do something?"

She had.

Sash had done something.

She had opened a Pandora's box.

She had led them to the surface.

She had broken the rules.

And Yuna had followed.

"No," Yuna lied, fresh tears stinging at her eyes. She'd already been crying—vomiting did that—so it all blended together. One big lie.

Nastia studied her for a moment.

Holding that gaze was a touch too painful. But looking at the dead chicken in Nastia's arms wasn't any better. Winnie looked so small, feathers still. She would never cluck again. She wouldn't ever tilt her head at the sound of Yuna's approaching footsteps. She would never lay another egg. Her eyes would never drift shut when Yuna scratched the spot on her back that she liked so much. She would never ruffle her feathers in delight or displeasure ever again. Heat stung at Yuna's eyes, and she squeezed them shut so no moisture would escape.

After a moment Nastia said, "I don't believe you."

She turned away and stalked down the hall, Winnie's broken body in her arms, leaving Yuna crumbled on the floor, soaked through with blood and tears and things far, far worse.

CHAPTER 25

GABE

In the bunker, paper was scarce. More than scarce. It was precious. It was finite. Once they ran out of paper, that was it. There were no mills left to manufacture more. They could recycle their own—and they did. But it wasn't the same. Their bunker-made paper was thick and bumpy, clumsily pulped and pounded into submission. But fresh paper with a smooth surface? That stuff was priceless.

And the things Gabe drew couldn't be tossed into the pulp pile once he filled up the page. He didn't want others to see his drawings, much less talk about them. Explosions. Scarred flesh. A sky on fire.

The Cataclysm, as Moran liked to call it.

The day the world ended outside.

The day life began down here.

Gabe peered down at the page. It was blank. That in and of

itself was a rarity. A luxury. Every other page of his sketch-book was filled from edge to edge, corner to corner. Every valuable spot of real estate was occupied by pencil. Not one single centimeter went to waste. It gave his drawings an almost surreal quality. Like something Hieronymus Bosch could only dream of. Everything Gabe knew came from the stack of moldy old art books tucked into the bunker's library. The ones with religious art had been spared Moran's recycling purges. He wasn't sure why those were worthy of survival when Isaac Asimov's collected works hadn't been, but oh well. What could you do?

Gabe's pencil hovered over the blank page, nearly touching the paper but not quite.

This wouldn't work. Simple graphite wouldn't work.

His hand hovered over the box of pastels. They were even more precious than paper. Crayon nubs could be melted down together to create bigger, weirder crayons (the colors of those always blended together into an incoherent mishmash, but Gabe normally didn't mind). The pastels though . . . those were truly irreplaceable.

But he needed color for this. It needed to be right. It needed to be vivid.

He had to commit exactly what he saw to the page before it faded from memory, like so many things they had already lost.

Gabe swiped red against the paper in a long, dark gash. The crimson was lurid against all that white. Vulgar even.

Good. Vulgar is what it all was. Going to the surface. Breaking the seal on a hatch that had been closed for at least the past ten years. The man. The rat.

His skin, putrid and peeling. Patched with inflammation. Scarred by a life misspent on survival.

How did anyone live like that? How could anyone live like that?

He didn't have any answers. All he had was one of the last few pieces of paper in the bunker and a precious set of pastels that would be gone by week's end.

And so he drew. His hand darted across the page, frenzied, wild. For once, his fingers moved faster than his mind, guided to give form to the image in his head before he could over-analyze it out of existence.

He didn't hear the hatch to their little hideout open. Didn't hear the soft footsteps of someone approaching. Didn't notice that he was no longer alone until a figure leaned over, blocking the meager light from the bulb overhead.

"What are you doing?"

Gabe jerked his head up to find his brother blinking at him owlishly.

"I'm, um . . ." He looked down at his pastel technicolor hands, stained with the evidence that he'd wasted one of their most precious possessions.

Lucas furrowed his brow as he leaned in closer to see what was worth such a tremendous sacrifice.

Gabe didn't realize how badly cramped his hands were until Lucas reached for the drawing and slipped it from Gabe's soiled fingers. Said fingers were too slow to respond, to stop it from happening, to stop him from seeing what none of them were ever meant to see.

"What is this?" Lucas asked.

Gabe wanted to snatch the drawing out of his brother's hands, but he couldn't. The paper was too fragile. It would tear. And so he pried Lucas's fingers free, one by one, as gently as he possibly could. The boy hardly resisted at all.

"It's nothing," Gabe said.

"You wouldn't use the pastels for nothing."

Twelve-year-olds shouldn't be that astute. There were so many stupid rules in the bunker. Why couldn't that be one of them?

"It's a monster," Gabe said. And that was true. "It's just something I made up. Nothing for you to worry about it."

That was a lie.

"Looks scary," Lucas said, tilting his head at the picture, as if trying to reason his way through its jumbled parts.

It was, Gabe didn't say. *It's the scariest thing I've ever seen. And I barely even saw it.*

Him, his mind corrected. *Barely even saw* him.

Because the man was a person. A human being. Even if his humanity seemed like something left by the side of the road many moons past.

What had happened to him?

What made him like that?

How did he survive?

And the most terrifying question of all: *How many others did?*

But Lucas was unplagued by those questions. Unburdened by doubt. He merely shrugged and hopped up to sit on one of the old trunks that held a stack of board games, most of which were missing several key pieces. He reached into his pocket and pulled out a small panel full of wiring. Gabe recognized it as his father's. It was a minor thing, a tiny bulb at one end, connected to a series of wires. He'd used it to teach Gabe about electrical engineering. And now, it seemed, Gabe would use it to teach Lucas. Just like that, a trade was passed along family lines. Just in case something happened to one of them, there would always be someone who knew how to rewire the bunker's mechanisms.

We're going to be in here forever, Gabe thought. But then, the thought amended itself. *We're going to die in here. We're going to die in here or out there.*

"You were mumbling in your sleep last night." Lucas kicked his heels against the trunk, creating a weird echoing thump that bounced back at them off the walls.

Oh. Oh no. Gabe swallowed thickly before he trusted himself enough to speak without saying anything overly incriminating. "What did I say?"

Lucas merely shrugged. "Don't know. I couldn't really hear you. I hit you with my pillow and you stopped."

A sickly sort of relief swept through Gabe.

He had no recollection of this happening, but he was glad it did. Never had he been so relieved to be so deep a sleeper that he could sleep through an apocalypse, which he had.

He hadn't given anything away. Nothing but the drawing, but even that, Lucas seemed not to question. But then, the boy's entire diet of extracurricular reading had involved the same dozen issues of the Uncanny X-Men they'd all read cover to cover more times than they could count. Lucas was no stranger to two-dimensional violence.

It was all he knew.

"What do you remember," Gabe began, settling the stubby remnants of the pastels back in their tin, "about Before?"

Lucas's face screwed up in concentration as he tried to focus on the task at hand. His tongue peeked out from between his pursed lips. "Before what?"

The question slammed into Gabe's chest with the force of an expertly thrown fastball.

Before what?

Before was such a gargantuan concept to Gabe. To Yuna. To Sash. To pretty much everyone in the basement, it was safe to assume.

But not to Lucas.

He'd only been two. He'd been old enough to totter around after Gabe on chubby toddler legs, stalking him from room to room with the sort of starry-eyed adoration younger siblings typically grew out of somewhere between the ages of four and six. Gabe wiped his palms on his jeans. They had been his father's before Gabe had grown into them. Now they were his. One day, they would belong to Lucas if they were still in the bunker then.

They would still be in the bunker then.

"Before the bunker," Gabe said softly.

Lucas glanced up at him. He blinked for a moment, considering the question. Then he shrugged and turned back to the clock.

"Nothing really."

"Nothing?"

Another shrug. "What? I was almost a baby."

"Yeah." Gabe's stomach clenched. Lucas had been so small, but he'd had these pudgy little hands Gabe could wrap one of his around entirely. "Fat hands."

Lucas glanced up at Gabe. Briefly, because 90 percent of his attention was still on the wiring panel. "What?"

Gabe shook his head. "Nothing."

With a frustrated, wordless noise, Lucas flung the panel toward a pile of raggedy blankets in the corner. Gabe fumbled for it, but it landed safely on the soft mound of fabric.

"Lucas!"

With all the petulant force of someone nearing their early teens, Lucas said, "What?"

Cradling the panel, Gabe shot his brother a look. "This is the only one we have. If this breaks, that's it. There's not another one."

But there could be.

Shamefaced, Lucas looked down at his hands and nodded. "I know. I'm sorry. I just—I don't get it." Peering back up at his brother, he added, "You and Dad always make it look so easy, and I just don't get it. I must be stupid or something."

And just like that, Gabe's irritation dispersed.

"You're not stupid. Here. Look."

Bringing the panel back over to Lucas, he showed him how it was done. Which wires needed to be rerouted and where. Which small switches needed to be flipped. What elements needed grounding.

Under Lucas's hands, the bulb lit up. A tiny red glow.

Red, weeping sores.

Blood splattering against cold stone.

"Go," Gabe told Lucas, giving him a gentle shove toward the hatch. "Get out of here and show Dad what you did. He'll be proud."

Still smiling down at his little red light, Lucas grabbed Gabe into a one-armed hug, pressing the side of his face into Gabe's collarbone. "Thanks!"

Before Gabe could react, before he could hug him back the way he should have, Lucas was gone.

◎ ◎ ◎

This is nuts, whispered a traitorous little voice at the back of Gabe's head. It was his voice of reason, his voice of caution. A voice he was staunchly ignoring right now.

And he was ignoring it in the name of science. Or at least that was what he had convinced himself. Well, half convinced himself. Doing something in the name of science and doing something for the pure, unadulterated curiosity the mere thought of it inspired were close cousins, but they weren't exactly the same thing.

But how could anyone expect Gabe to have such a won-drous device in his possession and not use it? How? It was unthinkable.

He stared down at the radio, hunkered amid a fortress of old dinosaur sheets and threadbare pillows. It looked ridiculous in their little cave, surrounded by ancient comic books and plastic figurines with peeling paint. Heavy and black and square. Out of place. Old but new. And newness was a rarity—an impossibility—in a life suffocated by the familiar.

Two voices warred inside his head. The first, calm, rational, responsible: *You shouldn't be doing this.*

The second, louder, frantic, desperate: *Do it. Do it, do it, do it.*

It wasn't, of course, for science.

He couldn't not think about the look on Lucas's face when Gabe had asked him about Before.

Blank. Like there was nothing there at all. Like Before was a concept he'd read about in a book but never really experienced. Like it was an abstract notion, a thought exercise.

But it wasn't like that at all. It *was* that.

This—the bunker, the scarcity, the constant fear thrumming in the background like the generators that kept them alive—was all Lucas knew.

He could know more.

It was a thought Gabe couldn't stomach. That Lucas's world was so small. That he couldn't remember anything but these walls. Didn't recall the feel of wind on his face or what the stars looked like.

The first gift Gabe had given him the day his parents brought him home from the hospital had been stars. Fake ones, made of carefully folded paper and tied to string. A mobile to hang above the crib.

You can give him stars again.

If an incredibly disturbed rat-eating man had survived up on the surface, maybe someone else had. Someone who didn't eat rats. Or at the very least, someone who cooked them first.

And if people had survived, then maybe—

No.

It was a dangerous thought. Even more dangerous than what he was considering doing.

Hope. Now that was dangerous. The only thing that had gotten him through all these years, buried underground, was that this was the only life left to them.

This was it.

The bunker.

To dream of anything more was folly.

Real stars this time, not paper ones.

Gabe licked his lips. They were oddly dry. Drier than usual. (They were always dry; recycled air had that effect on the skin.)

His tongue flicked out to moisten them, catching on the chapped skin.

His heart hammered in his chest.

There's no one out there, whispered a vicious little voice nestled at the back of his skull, like a poisonous snake hidden in high grass. *You're all that's left. You and everyone in this bunker. Humanity's last stand. What a pathetic sight. All those people hiding underground like rats burrowing in the dirt, clinging on to the hope of a world that doesn't exist. Not anymore.*

But it didn't feel true. It didn't feel true when Moran told them as much, after the hatch closed behind them all those years ago, and it didn't feel true now.

Because it wasn't.

He knew that now. And knowing was half the battle.

Gabe reached out a trembling hand and picked up the microphone. His thumb depressed the switch on its side. A burst of static crackled faintly before fading into nearly inaudible white noise.

And then, he began to talk.

SASH

Sash felt sick.

Not as in fever, chills, and cough sick, but a worse kind. The kind you couldn't flush away with medicine (not that they had any of that left, not after all these years). Her stomach roiled about like a turbulent sea.

Don't touch me.

The way Yuna had said that.

Another roil, this one particularly enthusiastic. Like a giant wave that could knock experienced sailors clear off a boat.

Had she ever been on a boat? She couldn't remember. Her father had one sitting in the garage of their old house, but did she recall ever being on it? He'd work on it on weekends, fiddling about with rudders and paint and other things Sash had been too young to understand.

For the first time in however long she could remember, Sash

skipped her chores. She'd been meant to clean the supply closet, but that was a depressing job, and honestly, it was done every day. It could go a day without. She just couldn't look at their dwindling barrels of oats and rice. Their bare cupboards. Their empty shelves.

Instead, she had left Yuna (Yuna had left her) and found a quiet spot to read. Not the hideout, though that would have been the obvious choice. But she hadn't wanted to be found. She'd wanted to be alone. She wanted no distractions. No more shouting. No arguments. No more idiotic gestures, like confronting Moran in front of half the bunker's residents.

All she wanted to do was read.

There was a disused electrical supply room in the far-west corner. Whatever mechanisms it had been connected to were either broken or severed or never finished in the first place. As far as anyone could tell, it was utterly useless. For a few years, it had served as a closet for old clothes, but as those piles were worn down under the demand of growing children and thread-bare fabric, the closet had ceased to have much of a purpose. Now, it housed a few old sweaters and one jersey of some kind, blue and orange, for a team called the Knicks.

A basketball team, Misha had told her once, a long, long time ago. On the back was written the number 33 and above that, the name Patrick Ewing. Sash had no idea who he was, but Misha had insisted on keeping the stupid jersey intact all these years.

She sat on it as she read. And read and read. Absorbed in a book in a way she hadn't been in years, even after everything they'd been through, everything they'd seen. Everything they'd done.

But solitude had worn its way through her, and eventually she was forced to set the book down. She needed someone to talk to. Someone who wasn't Gabe or Yuna. Who wouldn't glare at her with recrimination or disappointment or anything in that general family.

Sash glanced toward the tiny room where her grandmother liked to sit, rocking herself as she muttered in Russian to her knitting. Always the same length of thread she'd been working and reworking for years.

But the rocking chair was empty.

That was odd. Olga Eremenko was nothing if not a creature of habit. Every day at two o'clock on the dot, she took her tea in her room, away from the doctor's watchful gaze, her own eyes distant as she went through the ritual she'd brought with her from a far-off land. Warming the pot. Steeping the leaves. Laying out a single, crumbly, stale biscuit. Breathing in the aroma of tea as she poured it into her chipped cup, another relic of the old country that had survived countless wars, a trip across the sea, and a panicked flight underground. And when the tea had run out, she'd maintained the ritual of heating water and serving it out of her ceramic pot. She still called it "taking her tea" even when the leaves were nothing more than a memory.

"Hey, Mom?" Sash called out. She tried to squish down the sickly seed of worry blossoming in her gut. It was nothing. Maybe the elder Eremenko simply wanted a change of scenery. Maybe she was off with Misha, haranguing him about the length of his hair or the American accent he could never scrub from his Russian or some other trait she decided to fixate on that day. "Where's Babulya?"

"She's in her room," came her mother's response. Her nose was buried in a book. An autobiography of Rudolf Nureyev that

Sash knew for a fact her mother had read cover to cover approximately nine thousand times. The spine was cracked and the pages hopelessly soft from years of dog-earing.

"No, she's not."

With an exasperated sigh, her mother set the book aside—facedown, adding a fresh crack to the spine, something that would have driven Gabe up a wall. She stood. Even standing was a production for her. Her long, lithe limbs unfolded with the grace of a swan spreading its wings to take flight across the stage of the Metropolitan Opera House. Or maybe the Mariinsky Theatre, or the Palais Garnier, or any of the countless venues that were as real to Sash as Narnia and Terabithia. She had never seen them in her life. And she never would. For a brief, delirious moment, she wondered if any of those buildings were still standing. She imagined red velvet seats covered in years of dust and heavy curtains riddled with cobwebs. Gilded ceilings collapsed, allowing the wicked rays of the sun to filter in, lighting a stage that was never meant to bathe in their warmth.

Her mother waved her hand at Sash to get out of the way. Sash stepped aside so they didn't brush against each other as her mother passed. Even that bit of contact was forbidden. Too risky to accidentally touch skin to skin.

A warm hand in hers as they swayed to the music, fresh air in their lungs, and solid ground beneath their feet.

Pausing in the door, her mother frowned. "She's not here."

"That's what I just said."

"Don't get smart with me, Sasha."

"It's Sash." At her mother's glare, she added, "Sorry, reflex."

Rolling her eyes, her mother went back to her chair and picked up a new book. It was the second in a series of Regency romances, though they had no others in the series. It was one of the more popular tomes in the bunker with the adults. The children were forbidden from reading it, so naturally they'd stolen it once, in a particularly daring heist that still brought a smile to Sash's lips. Gabe had acted as a lookout as Yuna and Sash had crawled on their bellies toward the book, even though no one else had been in the room with them. It just felt more dramatic that way. They'd read it aloud in the hideout, Gabe blushing furiously every time two characters kissed.

"I don't know where your grandmother is," her mother said without looking up. "Probably in the kitchen, complaining about bare shelves in the Soviet Union again."

Baba Olya was not in the kitchen. Sash had come from there after deciding that she wasn't in the mood to clean its pantry.

Sash stood there awkwardly, the angular heft of the book tucked into her pants digging into her spine. Her sweatshirt was thick and loose enough to hide it, so long as no one touched her. And no one was going to touch her. It was forbidden.

Don't touch me.

"Hey, Mom . . ."

"What?" A turn of the page. Not a single glance upward.

Would your mother save you?

Sash swallowed thickly. Then she shook her head. "Never mind."

She turned to go without another word, following her footsteps back to the place where she'd hidden before, curled up with a book, both so like and extremely unlike her mother. Her limbs were less graceful. Her muscles less flexible. Her every moment less studied.

Her book far more illicit.

She tucked herself away in the closet, closing the door behind her. Her only illumination was one of the small hand-cranked flashlights—the same one she'd taken topside—but it was more than enough to read the words.

Her fingers brushed against the title, though they'd already memorized the feel of the raised text, the architecture of that title.

1984.

She opened the book and picked up where she left off, reading aloud to herself in that small, dark space.

"'Nothing,'" George Orwell wrote, "'was your own except the few cubic centimeters inside your skull.'"

CHAPTER 27
YUNA

Gabe was the one who found her, lying there in front of the chicken coop beside a puddle of her own sick.

He hadn't said anything. He'd checked to make sure she was still breathing and then stepped over her legs to peek inside the coop. When he came back out, his face was several shades paler. But he'd only helped her to her feet and to the bathroom, where he got her cleaned up. Then he ushered her to their hideout and put a warm cup of water between her trembling palms.

The last bag of tea had gone to Grandma Olga three years ago. All they had now was water that was just short of boiling.

"I did something."

That was how Gabe broke the silence.

Yuna peered at him over the rim of the cup.

"What?"

He told her.

And now she knew what it felt like to spill scalding hot water all over her thighs.

"You did *what*?"

Gabe shook his head, rising to pace the small area once more. He'd done that seven or eight times by this point. He was going to wear a hole in the floor paneling.

("You'll tunnel straight through to China," Mr. Correa liked to quip whenever anyone paced in the bunker.)

(Except Yuna had looked at a globe once—an out-of-date globe, but still—and directly opposite their location was the middle of nowhere in the Indian Ocean.)

"I have to tell Sash," he said, sitting down and then standing just as abruptly.

"Wait, Gabe—"

But he was already at the hatch.

And the hatch was already swinging open before he could touch it.

Sash poked her head through the door, her gaze racing from Gabe to Yuna. Then, with a pained expression, back to Gabe.

"My grandma is missing."

"I sent out a transmission on the radio I stole from the manor."

"The chickens are dead."

A heavy silence descended on them all, weighed down by the heft of their revelations.

"I have to tell Moran," Yuna said, putting the now mostly empty tin cup aside. "I mean, if Nastia hasn't already."

Sash stiffened. "My sister was there?"

"Of course she was there. We do the chicken coop together. You know that."

"You can't tell Moran," Sash said. It wasn't a request. It was an order. As if Sash was really the person to be delivering those.

Yuna frowned. "She's going to notice if all the chickens are dead, Sash. There won't be any eggs."

Sash brushed her hands against the thighs of her jeans. She did that when she was nervous. Her palms had a tendency to sweat.

"Wait, hold on," Gabe interjected, holding up a hand. "What about your grandma?"

Sash's head jerked back to him. "I can't find her."

"We're in a bunker," he said. "Where could she possibly have gone?"

"I don't know, Gabe! That's the problem. I thought she was just breaking her routine, and I left it for a while, but then I went to look for her again and she's not *anywhere*. Not in the kitchen. Not in the bedrooms. Not in the common area. Not in the supply closets."

"How would Grandma Olga fit in a supply closet?" Yuna asked.

"She can't. And she hasn't." Sash exhaled a shaky breath. "Something happened to her."

"We have to tell someone," Yuna said again.

They all knew she wasn't talking about just the chickens. Or Grandma Olga. Those things wouldn't stay secret for long, if they were at all.

Because there was a reason all these strange things were happening. There had to be. Mysteriously dead chickens. Missing grandmothers. Foolish messages to whatever ghosts haunted the toxic afterlife aboveground. For ten years, life in the bunker had proceeded without change. Every morning, the same routine. Every day, the same. Until they'd broken the pattern. Until they'd done something to smash through all that sameness.

Until they went to the surface.

Them.

They did this.

They were the anomaly. They had to be the cause of every anomaly that followed.

Sash's eyes cut sharply to Yuna. The look stung, as if her gaze was a real, palpable slap. "Are you out of your mind?"

"No," Yuna said. "I'm not out of my mind."

Gabe released his breath in a tired exhalation. "Sash . . ."

"What?"

"Maybe Yuna's right."

Now Sash looked between Gabe and Yuna as if they'd *both* lost their minds. But Yuna was feeling distinctly sane. Keeping this to themselves—that they'd gone to the surface, that they'd brought something back with them, something that was deadly, was already killing—*that* was the senseless choice.

"We have to tell someone," Yuna insisted. "We have to. We can't not."

Sash laughed. It was jagged at the edges, cutting up her throat on the way out. "Tell who? Dr. Moran? Oh, I'm sure that'll go well."

"Okay, not Moran, but somebody?"

Sash sputtered, throwing her hands wide in exasperation. "I ask you again . . . who? My mother? She'll tell Moran. Misha? He'll tell Moran. Your parents? They will *definitely* tell Moran. The Correas—?"

"Something chased us in that house, Sash!" Yuna shouted.

She clapped both her hands over her mouth. Yuna could

count on one hand how many times she'd raised her voice in anger at someone. And never with Sash. Never, not ever.

"It could have been dogs . . . ," Sash said, but her voice was soft. Tentative in a way it almost never was. "Maybe they survived, like that one guy . . ."

"If they were like that guy, then they probably weren't regular dogs anymore," Gabe said softly, pushing his glasses up his nose. He pulled his lower lip in between his teeth. "He was messed up. Like, really messed up."

Yuna thought about the chickens, killed by something that defied explanation.

About Grandma Olga, missing in this small, finite space.

About the way her skin itched and itched and itched when she got back, no matter how much she scratched.

"I'll say it again: I think Yuna's right," Gabe added.

The betrayal etched across Sash's face burned itself onto Yuna's retinas. "I can't believe this. I can't believe you two—"

"Winnie's dead!"

Yuna could feel her voice inching higher, her tone getting more and more frantic with each word. "We brought something back into the bunker, and it killed her! It killed all of them! What if it—"

A hand wrapping around Yuna's wrist stopped the rest of the words in her throat. "Don't tell her."

The look in Sash's eyes was so raw, so scared, that Yuna almost agreed on the spot.

"Sash, this is bigger than us." Yuna glanced down at Sash's fingers looped around her arm. The nails were jagged and short, chewed down to the pink parts. Not normal for Sash. None of this was normal. "People are dying."

"Not people," Sash said. "A chicken."

The hand on her arm didn't feel quite so warm anymore. It felt stiff and cold, but maybe that was just Yuna's brain projecting.

"She was special to me." She tugged on her arm, freeing her wrist from Sash's grasp none too gently. "And I don't think she's gonna be the last."

Without waiting for Sash to say anything—to beg, to plead, to apologize—Yuna pivoted on her heel and left, crawling through the hatch. She didn't look back. Not even once.

CHAPTER 28

GABE

Gabe rolled over on his pallet, clamping his thin pillow to his ears. To say sleep had been elusive in the days since their outing was an understatement of epic proportions. But how could he sleep? How could any of them?

Every time he closed his eyes, he saw the man.

Rags wrapped around the open sores on his weeping hands.

One eye nearly swollen shut from some kind of bulbous, leaking growth.

The rat, kicking its back legs frantically in a vain bid for freedom.

Blood spilling between the man's fingers.

The guttural moan that Gabe would never, ever forget.

Flopping the pillow down, he stared up at the bunk above him. Lucas had asked for the top bunk for his birthday last year.

It was such a sweet, humble request that Gabe had given in readily. A soft snore drifted down from above.

Lucas could sleep without a problem. He didn't have any guilt to lug around. Any secrets to carry. Just a small life in a small world.

Gabe sat up and looked over to where his parents slept, three feet away, in bunks of their own. His mother's hand hung down from her mattress. They weren't allowed to touch skin to skin, like anyone else.

But sometimes he caught his parents shucking off their gloves and holding hands, late at night, when they believed both their sons were asleep.

Gabe knew. Lucas knew. No one said anything. It was a minor infraction, really. And no one had died from it yet.

My grandmother is missing.

Winnie's dead.

Hauling himself out of bed, Gabe slipped his sneakers on and tiptoed out of the room. It was too early for chores, but he couldn't just lie there, listening to his brother's soft breathing.

(And wondering when and how it might stop.)

Sash and Yuna weren't talking. And honestly, he couldn't stand to look at Sash now. Yuna was always tapping her toes to Tchaikovsky in a way that seemed more anxious than absent-minded, and she'd withdrawn from them both. For the moment, he was on his own.

It was odd, feeling lonely in a place where you were never truly alone. And yet here he was, curled up with the messy wires in what they called the generator room but was actually a tiny closet overstuffed with equipment that could easily explode in the wrong hands.

The wires were getting old. It was all getting old. For the past six months, the motor had been making an odd sound it had never before produced. The complicated network of machinery that connected their generator to a power source (the underground stream Gabe had never seen but the existence of which he'd never had reason to doubt) was showing its age. Rust was held at bay through years of careful, dedicated maintenance, but there were only so many things one could do to halt the flow of time.

A loud bang on the door made him jump, nearly electrocuting himself—and, potentially, several other people in the bunker—in the process.

"What the he—?"

The door was yanked open by a figure whose bulk blocked the low lighting in the corridor outside.

Misha towered above Gabe, their positions making him look even more oppressively tall than he already was.

"Family meeting."

He grabbed Gabe's arm and yanked him to his feet, none too gently.

"Hey!" Gabe barely had time to put his tools down as Misha marched him forward. "Watch it."

Misha merely grunted and released Gabe's arm. He didn't need to look to know that a ring of finger-size welts was probably marked on his arm.

They were the last to arrive in the all-purpose dining-room-classroom-meeting-hall.

Family meetings. Laughable. A joke. That was what they called these things. Normally, they consisted of an airing of grievances, the likes of which could go on for hours. Too many people in too small a space. Reallocations of chores to keep people from getting bored enough to dash their skulls open against the wall paneling. Or impromptu sermons from Dr. Moran, whose meditative musings were delivered to them in half-baked ramblings Gabe never really listened to.

But he wasn't laughing now. No one was. He spotted Yuna and Sash sitting with their families. Sash briefly caught his gaze, but Yuna refused to look up, her own eyes locked on her twisting hands, safely encased in gloves he recognized as her mother's spare pair.

Taking a seat by his own parents—his mother's hair still had the telltale misshapen muss of sleep on it—Gabe looked toward the woman standing at the front of the room. She stared at them all, stoic. Imperious. Unflinching.

"Do you know why I've called you all here this morning?"

Silence met her query as they looked at one another, wondering who had committed the sin that had summoned them from their beds at this ungodly hour. Gabe didn't have to look very far.

"There has been a death in the family, as I am sure you all know."

Olga.

Dr. Moran bowed her head. The others followed suit. Gabe lowered his but kept his eyes raised over the frame of his glasses. Mrs. Eremenko's face was even stonier than usual.

"Olga Eremenko was our stalwart companion for years," Moran intoned. "She was a constant in our lives—"

Everything in the bunker was constant, Gabe thought.

"—and she will be missed. May she find peace in the embrace

of the blessed dark." Moran sighed softly, as if in mourning. "A moment of silence, please."

"How did she die?"

The question was so frank, so sudden.

Sash was the only one not bowing her head. Ironic, perhaps, since she had loved Olga more than anyone in that room.

"Excuse me, Alexandra?"

"You heard me," Sash said. "How did my grandmother die?"

"Sasha." Mrs. Eremenko's voice was as hard and sharp as cold steel.

"No, Mom. I want to know." Sash looked back at Moran, steady and composed. At least, if you didn't know where to look. Beneath her chair, the toe of one sneaker dug into the soft bit of flesh behind the opposite ankle. A nervous tic. "What happened to my grandmother?"

"Heart failure," Dr. Moran said without missing a beat. "She passed in her sleep."

"If it was just heart failure, why weren't we allowed to see her?"

Dr. Moran studied Sash for a moment. She took one step down from the dais at the front of the room. Then another. And another. Until she was standing before them with an intimacy she rarely exhibited.

"Because I had reason to believe her flesh was contaminated."

Gabe's pulse felt like it stuttered and stopped.

Sash stared up at Moran, for once absent a retort.

"Why?" Yuna's mother asked. "What happened? Are we safe?"

"For now," Moran said. "But I do believe someone is trying to poke holes in that safety."

She turned in place, gazing at each person in turn. "Who among us has broken our most important rule?"

The silence in the room thickened into a nearly palpable sludge. If he breathed in too deeply, Gabe was certain that it would flood his trachea and fill his lungs to the point of bursting.

Dr. Moran's sharp gaze traveled from one individual to the next, as if she could divine their secrets with a hard stare alone.

And maybe she could.

"They did." Nastia's arm thrust in Sash's direction, her finger pointed in accusation. "My sister and Yuna and Gabe."

Sash flinched in her seat as if struck. "Nastia, what the—?"

Then Moran issued her order, her tone as solid and unforgiving as steel. "Grab them."

Misha's hand landed on Gabe's shoulder with a heavy thud. Nastia had one of Sash's arms while her mother took the other. The older woman's expression was unchanged from their moment of silence. Like nothing could penetrate whatever fortress walls she's been fortifying for the last ten years. Yuna didn't try to stand. Her mother's hand wrapped around her upper arm while her father sat silent, his hand on Yuna's shoulder in an echo of Misha's on Gabe.

"Wait!" Desperation grappled its way up Gabe's throat, spilling from his lips in the form of the worst words he could have possibly chosen: "What proof do you have?"

Victory flashed through Moran's eyes.

Oh.

When it took visible effort to restrain the satisfied smile tugging at the corners of her lips, Gabe knew he'd made a terrible miscalculation.

From the folds of her dress she pulled out a tome.

A mass market paperback, the kind with the cheap paper that yellowed and started to smell musty sooner than more expensively bound books.

On the cover, Gabe just barely managed to read the title: *1984* by George Orwell.

"I'm glad you asked, Gabriel." She set the book down on the table in front of Sash. "Do you recognize this, Alexandra?"

Sash didn't look at the book, which was damning in its own right. "No."

"That's odd," Moran said, "As I found it among your belongings."

"Why were you looking in my belongings?"

Wrong question, Sash, Gabe thought but didn't say. What would have been the point? She was determined to dig her own grave, and theirs along with it.

"I had reason to believe someone close to Olga brought the contagion into this place. This safe haven that we have defended—that I have guarded with my life—for years." Anger—true and blazing hot—laced its way through each one of the doctor's words. "That someone put every soul in the bunker in danger."

She set one gloved finger on the book's well-worn cover. "I know everything that happens within these walls. I know everything they contain. Every tool, every light, every grain of rice. Every book. And this one"—she tapped the top whorl of the eight—"was never among their number."

Sash shrugged, or tried to in her mother's and sister's grasp. "I found it. You must have missed one."

Dr. Moran leaned over and whispered right in Sash's face,

closer than even her own rules allowed. "I miss *nothing*." Then she stood and projected her voice for all to hear. "You went outside. You and perhaps your friends."

Gabe's internal organs curdled.

"But I have only proof that you did, Alexandra. Not the others." Dr. Moran turned to Yuna, who trembled like a dry leaf in a winter gale. And then to Gabe, who felt about three seconds off from vomiting all over his hand-me-down shoes. "Unless they would like to speak for themselves."

"We did it," Yuna said softly. So softly that Gabe thought that maybe he'd misheard.

But from the way her mother crossed herself, mumbling in rapid-fire Korean and the disappointment shuttering her father's face, he hadn't.

If Yuna could be so brave . . .

"We all did," Gabe said, words coming fast, too fast for his fear to stop them. "We went outside."

"Gabriel!" Beside him, his mother recoiled as if struck. His father stared at him in dumbfounded shock.

"It wasn't their fault!" Sash's voice rang out over the rest, clear and resonant and strong. "I made them do it!"

Moran paused, one dark eyebrow inching upward ever so slightly.

"What did you say?"

Sash swallowed thickly.

Don't do this, Gabe thought. But he didn't say it. Because he wasn't as strong as she was. None of them were. Not him. Not Yuna. Not their parents. No one.

"I said . . ." Sash had to swallow again before she could get all the words out. Maybe she was scared. But she didn't look it. She just looked angry. Angry and righteous, like something out of the book of Greek myths Gabe had read from cover to cover so many times, he could scroll through its text on the back of his eyelids if he tried hard enough. "I made them do it. It was my fault. Blame me. Not them."

Yuna twitched, as if to move forward but Gabe's sharp gaze stopped her. "Sash—"

But Sash only shook her head. "They didn't want to go. I forced them to." When she delivered her coup de grace, she made sure she was looking Moran right in the eye.

Gabe loved her a little for that.

"It's like you said. The others look up to me. I was supposed to set a good example, and I didn't and I'm sorry."

But when she said the last few words, Sash turned her attention away from Moran. To Gabe and Yuna.

"Are you so determined to fall on your sword?" Moran asked.

Another thick swallow. And then, a nod. Singular and sure.

"I am."

No, Gabe screamed inside his head. *Don't do this! Not for us. Please!*

But he kept the words to himself. Silent. Complicit.

"You will take her away," Dr. Moran said, nodding to Misha.

Misha released Gabe's shoulder, but another weight settled on Gabe, even more burdensome than the last.

"But first, I feel a demonstration is in order."

CHAPTER 29

SASH

This isn't real, argued the insipid, optimistic part of Sash's brain.

But it was. It was very real. And it was undeniably happening.

Misha held her as her own mother and sister dragged a large metal barrel to the center of the room, in front of the dais from which Moran issued her sermons and edicts.

"Nastia, would you get the other books please? As we discussed."

With a nod, Nastia leaped to her feet (*Too enthusiastic; what was wrong with her?*) and left the room. She returned a moment later, arms laden with books, some from the bunker's communal library. But others were from the hideout. The comic books. The encyclopedia. The penny dreadfuls and the trashy sci-fi.

The doctor flipped a switch in the corner that activated the exhaust fan above. It was meant to stop them from suffocating in the event of a fire, to suck away the smoke.

Sash had never imagined it would be used like this.

"Mom, what are you doing?"

But her mother said nothing to her. It was like Sash had ceased to exist. Into the barrel, her mother threw a few used rags and then proceeded to squirt a bit of clear liquid from a squeeze bottle onto them, filling the room with the acrid smell of lighter fluid.

"No!" Sash struggled against her brother's hands on her shoulders. She managed to get free of one, but Misha wrapped his forearm around the front of her torso, trapping her against his chest. She elbowed him in the gut as hard as she could, but it earned her only a pained grunt in response. He held fast, keeping her from lunging at Moran. "Stop this! You can't do this! Mom!"

Mrs. Eremenko angled her head away from her daughter. Something in Sash's chest seized.

She hates me.

A part of her had always known. She'd seen it in the resentful glances. Heard it in the reproachful silences. Felt it in the detached, fleeting moments of contact as Sash grew up in the shadow of a dead man, whose ghost her mother saw every time she looked at her.

"I can do this," Dr. Moran said, her voice a cold, calm contrast with the crackling maw of the furnace behind her. "And I will."

She picked up the book on the top of the pile.

Audubon's *Birds of America*, with its faded stork illustration and elegant lettering on the cover.

"Please," Sash begged. "Please don't."

Something akin to pity flitted across Moran's face. "I'm doing this for you, Alexandra. For us all."

And then she tossed the book into the flames.

Sash let out a fractured scream.

They're just birds, insisted a voice at the back of Sash's mind. It was the voice that cautioned her to stay quiet, to not ask questions, to fade the way her mother had. It sounded like Moran. *Not even real birds. Fake ones! Flat ones! They're just drawings. A bound pile of drawings. Paper and ink and glue.*

But they were so much more than that.

And Moran knew it.

She met Sash's gaze and smiled. Sickly and sweet.

"Tell me," Moran said as she picked her next sacrifice off the table and flipped through its pages. When she looked up, there was something in her eyes that chilled Sash to the bone. Malice. Pure and simple. Straightforward. Cruel. "Are you proud?"

With that, she fed Louisa May Alcott and her *Little Women* into the flames.

Moran shook her head, making a tsk-tsk noise that grated on Sash's nerves like fingernails on a chalkboard. "If only you had learned to trust in the safety of the blessed dark."

She tossed books in after another.

A Prayer for Owen Meany.

Kurt Vonnegut.

Wide Sargasso Sea.

Philip K. Dick.

Great Expectations.

Dorothy Parker.

Call of the Wild.

An entire set of Jane Austen.

All of it, consigned to the flames.

Tears stung Sash's eyes, mingling with the smoke and the ash. Hate, pure and potent, bubbled up inside of her with an intensity she had never known before.

Dr. Moran saved the best for last.

She picked up the book, the one that had caused all this trouble, and held it between two gloved fingers as if it was dirty.

And it was. At least, nearly everyone in this room believed that it was. And that was good enough.

George Orwell's *1984*.

A half-remembered line from the book flitted through Sash's mind: *"The best books . . . are those that tell you what you know already."*

Dr. Moran is evil. She is a liar.

And now, she's making me—making us—pay for discovering the truth.

"You're right. I went to the surface. And I didn't die. My skin didn't melt off my bones. My blood didn't boil in my veins. My lungs didn't burst in my chest." Fresh tears welled up, clinging to her lashes. "Mom." Her mother angled her face away, avoiding Sash's gaze. "Mom, look at me. I'm here. I'm still here."

But her mother refused to look at her. So did her brother. And her sister. And everyone who wasn't Yuna. Even Gabe's eyes were riveted to the fire, enthralled in the most horrible way by the destruction of all those words. Of all that knowledge.

"Don't you see?" Sash's voice climbed several octaves as their blank faces stared back at her. Uncomprehending. Disbelieving. Some downright hostile.

Like Misha.

His blue eyes gleamed with cold fury when they finally settled on her.

With hate, she realized.

The knowledge that her brother—the one who'd tucked her into bed at night when her mother's wounds had been too raw, who'd bandaged the burns on her arms, who'd read her every children's book the bunker could boast of and then made up his own stories when he'd ran out of those—could look at her with such hate slammed into her so hard it stole her breath.

I'm dead to him, she thought. *Or as good as.*

But still . . . she had to try.

"Moran is lying to you." Her voice broke over the words as she pushed them out, each painful syllable at a time. "She's been lying to you—to us—for years."

"Shut her up, Misha." The words were almost startlingly informal coming from Moran. But he did as requested. His hand clamped over Sash's mouth with merciless force, silencing the rest of her plea, futile as it was.

Flipping open the book, the doctor glanced at the pages, shaking her head sadly. Then she tore out the first page. And then the next, and the next, feeding each one to the flames with deliberate slowness.

Moran made sure to capture Sash's gaze when she spoke, a satisfied smile tugging at the corners of her lips. She quoted from the very book that she was burning, page by terrible page:

"'It's a beautiful thing, the destruction of words.'"

Sash wanted to weep. To scream. To claw Moran's eyes out of her skull with her bare hands, to feel soft tissue raking free under her fingernails.

But Sash couldn't do any of that, even if she somehow

managed to break free from her brother's punishing grip, because at that moment, the lights went out.

Red safety lights flooded the space, bathing them all in crimson shadows.

A fragment from one of her comics floated through her mind. One about a group of people on some colony in outer space. One that was burning on a pile with all the rest.

This is not a drill.

"Danger, Will Robinson."

A loud bang sounded from the ceiling.

But there was nothing up there. Nothing but a mile of dirt.

Sash tried to yank herself away from Misha's grasp but his fist only tightened.

No one was paying attention to her. All eyes were on the woman still holding a mangled copy of *1984*.

"Doctor, is this—?"

Moran snapped the book shut and tossed its remnants into the fire. Just like that, it was gone. She held up her newly free hand, silencing Mrs. Correa's question.

"Everyone, you know what to do," she said, her voice solid with authority. "We've practiced for this."

CHAPTER 30

YUNA

They *had* practiced for this.

But in that singular moment of chaos, none of those hours spent running drills seemed to matter.

What the drills hadn't accounted for was a break in the routine. A calculated moment of cruelty. A fire, blazing bright like a signal beacon in the darkness.

They scattered away from it like cockroaches when a light's been turned on.

Light is danger.

Light is poison.

Light is death.

The words went through Yuna's brain over and over as she fumbled away from the group in the middle of the room, away from her parents who she did not recognize, away from the sick glee emanating from Moran as she destroyed the things that had kept them alive—and not just surviving—all these years.

The dark *was* a blessing. And chaos was an opportunity.

She slipped away from her mother's sharp-nailed grasp and threw herself into the shadows. They all did, seeking safety in the one thing they knew they could trust. The darkness.

The last thing she saw before the hustle of bodies blocked her view was Misha hauling Sash through the door.

That was *not* what they had practiced.

Drills were standard. They were the same, every time. Whichever room you were in is where you holed up. If you weren't in a room with a hatch, you ran to the nearest one. Yuna had peeked at the blueprints for the bunker once over Gabe's shoulder when he was fretting over ventilation shafts and power conduits, or whatever it was he liked to fret over. The bunker wasn't one structure, but a series of them, linked together with a network of interconnected corridors. Each room was its own, self-sustaining mechanism. Air could be shut off or turned on. The electric grids were conjoined but could be operated autonomously.

A series of panic rooms, Yuna remembered Gabe calling it.

It seemed a fitting term now. Each room could be sealed away through several inches of metal.

But Misha left.

The hatch was still open behind him. She sprinted for it without thinking, with only the tiniest nascent sliver of a plan forming in her mind. The hatches were designed to swing closed on their own when the alarm sounded. Not much time.

The door snagged at her sweater as she bolted through it, as quickly and silently as she could. It slammed shut behind her, leaving her in the corridor, bathed in the red glow of the safety lights. At the other end of the hall, she saw Misha round a corner, his sister in tow.

To the dark room.

It's where sinners were sent to repent for their misdeeds. Where naughty children were locked away, left in the blessed dark to think about what landed them there.

Yuna had spent a single night in it once.

She couldn't take Misha in a fight. But if she pulled off what she was hoping to, she wouldn't have to.

◎ ◎ ◎

She should have waited for Gabe.

The thought followed her all the way to the hatch—the secret one. She had nothing on her person to assist in this harebrained endeavor. Not even one of their manual flashlights. Just her wits, frazzled as they were.

The thought followed her through the shafts and resounded in her skull as she turned the hatch and climbed the ladder up and up and up. It echoed, loudly and persistently, as she opened the trapdoor in the floor of the manor's ballroom.

But there hadn't been time. With the way things had gone with Moran's inquisition, there was no telling what she would try next. (Moran had really nailed the inquisition thing down too, from the torturous interrogation to the ritualistic burning of heretical texts.)

Yuna had seen her chance and she took it, even if it meant taking it alone.

But when she emerged into the semi-fresh air of the house above, the thought recurred for one final jab.

You should have waited for Gabe.

She looked around for the loose piece of wood they'd used to prop the door open before. It was right where they'd left it (kicked, in their mad dash). Good. Perfect for an encore.

Biting her lip, she gazed around the ballroom. It had looked big before, but it seemed so much larger now with only Yuna in it. She felt utterly dwarfed by its cavernous size. No matter how quiet she tried to keep her footfalls, each step bounced off the walls to scream back at her.

(Sash throwing herself at Moran's mercy to save them, to save her.)

If there was something to be found in the manor, something to prove that Sash was right, that Moran had been lying to them all along, Yuna had to find it.

(Red lights, ringing alarms. The frightened procession of souls away from the light and into the dark.)

(The dark that was sacred. The dark that was safe.)

It didn't feel safe now, as Yuna retraced their steps from ballroom to the bedrooms on the second floor. It pressed in around her as if trying to soak into her skin, to contaminate her through her pores. It followed her up the grand staircase with its swooping wooden balustrades and its rotting carpeting. It nipped at her heels as she tiptoed through the corridors, past the empty picture frames and the fractured Grecian busts.

The moonlight was less impressive than it had been the night they'd come up here. It was barely enough to see by as it filtered in through the soaring arched windows. If Yuna looked down, she could only just barely make out the shape of her sneakers against the ground.

When she reached the door to Dr. Moran's bedroom—her childhood bedroom—she paused.

This was probably a bad idea. Another one to add to the growing list.

But she didn't know where else to look. Where to start. Especially not now that she knew she wasn't alone up here, on the surface. There were rats and men who ate them and whatever that thing was that she and Sash heard.

(It wasn't human. She knew what humans sounded like, and that had not been human.)

The door was ajar, just like they'd left it. Yuna stepped into the room. There was the massive four-poster bed with its dusty rose-colored drapes and its mahogany wood, nearly black in the gloaming. The wardrobe with its bounty of hideous dresses, most of which had gone out of style decades ago. The gilt-edged mirror in which she'd danced, the glittering frock catching the starlight as if she were a thing that had fallen from the cosmos to shine down on Earth.

Everything was, again, almost exactly as they'd left it.

Almost.

The photo album, the one with the picture of Moran looking sullen in the Swiss Alps, was *not* where they had left it.

Yuna had the distinct memory of leaving it open on the bed. She hadn't bothered putting it away, because why? When no one lived in this house. When no one was ever supposed to be in this room.

(When they were the only people left on Earth.)

The album was now sitting atop the writing desk tucked into

the corner. Closed. Its edge perfectly aligned with that desk, the album centered before the chair as if waiting for someone to find it.

Yuna's skin prickled into goose bumps.

They were not alone.

This shouldn't have felt like a revelation, but it did. It very much did.

Stop it. Focus.

She had come here with a purpose. She had to see it through, no matter how scared she was.

(And she was very scared.)

Yuna stepped farther into the room, glancing around.

If I was a dirty, dark secret, where would I hide?

She started with the desk. It seemed obvious (too obvious) but she did it anyway. After closing—and locking—the door behind her, she went to work, yanking open drawers and rummaging through their contents. Report cards and love letters from a series of heartbroken admirers and small notebooks filled with text Yuna couldn't hope to decipher.

One was wedged into the top drawer, its cover less dusty than the rest.

Jackpot.

Yuna flipped open the book and began to read.

And read.

And read.

DAY 92

The air is still too hot.

Beneath that, a series of numbers Yuna didn't understand. Temperatures, probably.

Oxygen levels are low. Supplementary O_2 necessary.

More numbers, these in a different metric. She scanned them without committing them to memory. They weren't important. It was the words that mattered. The words.

Sediment shows significant signs of contamination.
Difficult to determine when soil will be arable again.
Volume of substrate in water at toxic levels.

Even more numbers now. Strings and strings of them. They seemed bad. Yuna didn't know the first thing about chemistry but these seemed like chemistry. And they seemed *bad*.

The experiment was a rousing success.

"Experiment," Yuna whispered.
The word ricocheted inside her head, over and over and over.

EXPERIMENT, EXPERIMENT, EXPERIMENT. DAY 217

Have noticed an interesting phenomenon. The atmosphere still contains a significant amount of substrate, with traces of reagent present. Unexpected. Attribute to an uncharacteristically dry season. Minimal winds. The sunset is violently red. The color seems to keep the unfortunate creatures at bay.

"Two hundred seventeen days," Yuna muttered. Thirty days in a month, roughly. Divide two hundred seventeen by thirty and you get . . .

Her mind was blank. Math was Gabe's thing. Not hers. She

was bad at it. She couldn't think in numbers. Her brain didn't want to hold them. She needed—

A pencil.

It took more fumbling than it should have to unearth one from the messy drawer. Her hands were shaking too violently for coordination.

(Violently red.)

On the back of what looked like a Christmas card, the skinny kind that had a special flap for money, Yuna scribbled two hundred seventeen. Then thirty. Divide one by the other and you get . . .

"Seven months."

The pencil slipped from her fingers, rolling off the desk to land on the floor, its descent muffled by the plush carpeting under foot.

Seven months. They'd lived in the bunker for seven months before adding the red lights. Yuna had been too young to wonder where they'd come from. As she got older, she'd started to think they'd always been there. But they hadn't. They'd been added. Seven months after they'd fled down there, all of them, in a hasty rush, running through town with the sky on fire.

Not the sky.

The plant.

The chemical plant where nearly every person in Indigo Falls worked. The plant founded by—

"Cornelius Percival Moran."

It was the name written on the corners of the bunker blueprints. The initials, C.P.M., were stamped on every other wall plate. A signature from the man who built it.

Yuna pushed the Christmas card aside and flipped through the journal, landing on a page about halfway through.

DAY 1,096

Substrate levels in water have gone down significantly. A shame. It's almost drinkable now. Wouldn't recommend it. Would burn you inside out.

Numbers, numbers. More numbers.
Soil levels have stabilized. Still not arable. Likely will not be for at least another year.

Drinkable water. Soil arable in another year.
Boundary for the experiment seems to have stabilized at town limits, as expected. Soil beyond this point substandard but nontoxic to humans. Habitation possible.

Yuna did another calculation, the pencil (retrieved from the floor) shaking so wickedly in her hand, the numbers were hardly straight. Not neat and self-assured like the author of the journal.

Moran. It was Dr. Moran. This was her room. This is her room. She wrote in this. She wrote these things.

One thousand ninety-six days.

Three years.

Three. Years.

"Habitation possible," Yuna whispered. "Beyond this point."

Bile rose thick and cloying in her throat. She turned to the last page, her hands now trembling with such ferocity she ripped the edge of it.

DAY 3,635

Animal trials on toxin complete.

Chicken deceased within 7 minutes.

Human subject less than ideal. In remarkably good health for its age but still, age advanced.

Moment from ingestion to cessation of cardiac activity: 18 minutes.

Remains disposed of in incinerator. Will keep generators running off auxiliary power for a few more days.

Toxin likely to take longer in younger, able-bodied subject. Will record findings later in the week.

Yuna's breath clogged her own throat, it was coming too shallow, too fast.

DAY 3,636

They don't deserve me.

The experiment best scrapped.

Will try again in another town.

It's Lumnezia all over again.

And that was it. The last entry. Yuna closed the journal, sitting back in the hard wooden chair.

Three years.

The area around Indigo Falls had been habitable three years after the Cataclysm.

"Not a cataclysm," Yuna said to herself. She needed to say it out loud. Needed to hear the words.

Seven years.

Seven years.

They had stayed in the bunker seven years after that point. Seven long, hard years. Seven years of deprivation. Of food shortages. Of gloves. Of never-ending, heart-stopping fear at the brush of a bare hand against one's own.

The chair's legs scraped against the floor as Yuna stood. It clattered to the ground, but it made no sound.

No.

That wasn't right. It made a sound. It had to.

She just couldn't hear it. She couldn't hear anything over the roar in her ears.

Seven years.

Seven years.

Seven years.

Seven years.

Her lungs weren't working. They weren't pulling in air. They weren't scrubbing it of oxygen dioxide, they weren't pushing straight, uncut oxygen into her blood.

Stumbling back, she looked at the journal lying open on the desk.

Seven years.

Go.

The voice in her head sounded an awful lot like Junsu.

Go.

It was the last thing her brother had said to her.

The sky had opened up and screamed, and he had told her to go so she had. She'd gone. She'd run. She hadn't looked back. She hadn't known she'd needed to. That that moment was the last time she'd ever see him.

Skkritch.

Yuna froze.

That wasn't Junsu's voice.

Click, click.

Skkritch.

Yuna held her breath, going as still as she could. Her muscles quivered under her skin, ready to bolt. Like a rabbit hiding in tall grass, praying the scary thing passes it by.

Click.

It was closer now. Whatever it was, it was closer.

She could hide. She could fold herself into the wardrobe and go still. It had worked before. Whatever it was had passed Sash and her by, had failed to notice them, failed to find them.

Seven years.

No. She couldn't hide.

They had to know. And they had to leave.

As quietly as she could, Yuna grabbed the journal and tucked it into her jeans.

Go.

And so, she did.

CHAPTER 31

GABE

Silence was a terrible thing. A great and terrible deafening thing. It was deep enough to drown in, powerful enough to tug you under.

To call it deafening seemed odd to Gabe, but fitting too somehow. It roared in his ears for those minutes—hours?—as they waited in the cold, lonely darkness for the threat to pass them by.

And though they didn't see it or hear it or smell it or taste it, they knew, every last one of them, that it was a threat. It. Whatever had tripped the alarms, whatever had driven them underground in the first place, whatever it was keeping them here, in this industrialized coffin designed by a madman, buried like the living dead.

The silence followed Gabe throughout the lockdown as he sat huddled with his family in their bedroom, sitting on the floor cross-legged, separated from them by some vast, undefinable distance. Lucas had tried to sit next to Gabe, to rest his head on his shoulder, but their mother had tugged the boy away. The two of them sat less than a meter away from Gabe, but it might as well have been a mile. It felt like there were two realities now. The one before he'd broken the rules and the one that came after. He had crossed a line into a place where they could not— would not—follow. And on the other side of that divide, he sat alone, wishing desperately that he wasn't.

Bang.

He jumped where he sat, his arms tightening their stranglehold on his knees.

"What was that?" Lucas whispered before his mother clasped a hand around his mouth.

No one was supposed to talk during lockdown drills.

But this isn't a drill, is it?

A long moment of sharpened silence passed between them, huddled in the dark like frightened rodents.

Bang.

Another loud metallic clang sounded from overhead and below and all around them. Gabe started again, but less this time. He knew that sound.

Lucas whimpered, his voice muffled by his mother's hand.

"It's the pipes," Gabe whispered.

At this point, he had already broken so many inviolable rules. What was one more?

"Shut up," his mother hissed. Gabe reared back as if struck.

"Linda." His father's voice resonated in the silence.

That was the last sound he heard for hours, save for the harsh rasp of frightened breathing and the soft muttering of his mother's prayers to herself, her voice trapped inside her body.

They sat in the dark—that blessed thing, that sacred thing—and waited. Full dark. Red light may have been safe, but the absence of it was even safer. They had to trust in it. They had no other choice. All their choices had been stripped away. And when Gabe had snatched one for himself, this was what happened. His friend punished for being brave enough to shoulder the blame for all their sins. His family treating him like a pariah.

He wasn't sure how much time passed before the red lights came on, painting his mother and Lucas in crimson shadows, like he was looking at them through a prism of blood.

The PA system in the bunker crackled to life as Moran's voice filtered through: "All clear."

Gabe's mother stood, pulling Lucas up with her. Without a second glance back at her other son, she left, tugging Lucas out of the room by the hand. Lucas, at least, looked back.

More slowly, his father rose, bracing his hands on his thighs, the way he'd started doing in the last year or so.

"These old knees," he sometimes said.

He didn't say it now.

"I'm sorry," Gabe blurted.

He wasn't. Not really. Not for going outside. Not for questioning the truths they'd been told all these years. Not for the ache of discovery that led him to break their most sacrosanct rules. But he was sorry for the disappointment that colored his father's every movement, from the way he straightened his back slowly to get out of the kinks to the way he wiped his glasses off with the hem of his T-shirt.

"You should check on the filters," said his father, still wiping down his glasses, longer than was necessary. "That sounded like a stuck pipe." Sliding his glasses back on, he added, "I'm going to go check on your mother."

With that, he left.

Gabe waited for a moment. For what, he didn't know. But when nothing more happened—no more recriminations, no more confessions, no more accusations—he rose, brushing off his jeans.

He couldn't fix what he had broken. He couldn't save Sash from her own beautiful, foolish bravery. He couldn't undo the things he had done. *Wouldn't*, even if he had that power.

But what he could do was unstick a stupid pipe.

◎ ◎ ◎

The filtration system was located in an oversize closet, large enough for the three tanks that cleaned their water, enabling them to drink it. The spring that fed it was the same underground reservoir that powered their lights and kept their air circulating and breathable. It was their oasis in the desert. The source of all their power.

And now, it was their damnation.

The water was black.

"What the . . ."

From his vantage point atop the short step stool he'd used to lift the lid of one of the tanks, Gabe frowned down at the darker-than-it-should-be liquid.

It should have been clear. He should have been able to see straight to the bottom of the tank. It was not. He could not.

Leaning down as close as he dared, he sniffed at the surface. A not entirely unfamiliar metallic scent stung his nostrils.

What is that?

The sense memory hit him before he could properly decipher that smell into something specific.

Open sores, weeping into the crisp night air.

Bandaged hands, knobby knuckles.

Jaundiced eyes, sclera stained, gone wild with something unnamed.

Bile rose thick in his throat. He clamped his mouth shut, holding in whatever his body wanted to expel with his hand. Nothing, there was nothing in it to expel, no matter how badly it wanted to.

He breathed in, eyes closed, painting the backs of his lids with innocuous images—Flash Gordon comics, the Very Hungry Caterpillar, Harold and his purple crayon, the Bat signal blazing across the Gotham skyline—until the nausea passed.

It's fine, he thought to himself. *You're fine.*

Both lies, but necessary ones.

He couldn't afford to lose it now. Whatever *it* was. The fragile adhesive holding the rational parts of his brain together. He glanced back at the filtration system. There didn't appear to be anything wrong with it. He had just checked it the day before.

And the other tanks didn't appear to have anything wrong with *them*, either. Their water levels were low, but the water itself was clear. It was only the first tank, the one that drew directly from the spring that was—(*don't say contaminated, contaminated is bad, contaminated means there's been a breach, contaminated means we aren't safe*)—not quite right.

Descending the step stool, Gabe pulled a pair of waterproof gloves from his back pocket. He kept them tucked away there, ready for whenever he came into this room. The clarity of the water was integral to their survival. One of the first things his father had taught him was to never contaminate (*that word*) it. He pulled on the gloves, making sure they rolled all the way up to his elbow.

There was something lodged in one of the pipes. Something small and dark, seeping billowing clouds of vicious liquid into the tank. It had to be small. The pipes were relatively narrow in this part of the mechanism. Cost-effective, according to Cornelius Moran's notes. Like money had ever been an issue for the family who had built this bunker, had lived in that gilded palace above.

Gabe reached his arm into the tank. His hand disappeared from view, swallowed by the blackened water.

He groped blindly for the source of the obstruction. The water lapped at the sides of the tank, disturbed by his rummaging. His breath trickled through his nose—not his mouth, he didn't want to taste that smell—in short spurts, oddly loud in that small room.

Something brushed against his hand. He started, his sneakers sliding against the step stool, nearly upending it. His other hand clutched the side of the tank, steadying himself.

Don't touch it, his rational mind screamed. *Don't touch it, don't touch it, don't touch it.*

He put his hand back into the tank.

A groan emanated from the pipe. Bubbles formed on the surface of the dark water, further obscuring Gabe's view.

Not that he could see his hand anyway. And besides—

Something—no, several somethings—rushed past his hand. It took his mind an excruciating moment to realize what they were.

Bodies.

Tiny, bloated, furred bodies.

Rats.

They poured out of the pipe, feet scrabbling against Gabe's skin, pricking through the rubber of his glove. Some floated to the surface while others fought, clawing at each other to breach the surface.

With a choked scream, Gabe threw himself backward. The stool slipped, sending him toppling to the ground. The rats flowed over the side of the open tank, hitting the ground with meaty little thuds. A few bodies stayed where they were, but enough of them got up, cushioned by their brethren as they swarmed.

Right at Gabe. Who was still on the floor. Frozen, mouth slack-jawed and stupid with fear.

The feel of the first one climbing up his pant leg is what did it. That wretched, frozen moment shattered. Sound rushed back in around Gabe, an incoherent roar of blood in his ears.

They were on his jeans. Clinging to his sweater.

There was something wrong with them.

Something wrong, something wrong.

He batted at them as he tried to stand, but the floor was wet now, so wet. The soles of his sneakers skidded against the water on the ground. His knee slammed, not into the metal paneling of the floor but into something else, something hot and soft and wet, and he would have screamed if he wasn't so afraid to open his mouth. He could feel them, on his skin, trying to find something? What? Warmth? Food?

Groping at the side of the water tank, Gabe pulled himself up, spinning frantically as he swiped his gloved hands against his chest, his legs, flailed wildly at his back.

One of the rats touched his neck, its small, sharp claws scrabbling for purchase. It was in his hair, too close, too close.

He ran, his hands knocking into his own body, his head, his everything so hard he could feel the bruises wanting to form. He slipped on something else, he didn't want to know what, before he reached the door.

The hatch.

They couldn't get past the hatch.

He couldn't let them.

It swung open under his hands. He was fast, but they were faster, running, shrieking, spilling over each other like they were made of something more liquid than flesh and bone and sinew.

Gabe threw himself through the door, not looking back as he slammed it shut behind him, spinning the handwheel to lock it.

He collapsed against the far wall, eyes riveted to the closed hatch. Droplets of water and something else, something darker and thicker, peppered the bottom.

The doors were thick. At least five inches so. That was how they were designed, back in the Cold War when madmen with more money than sense were constructing bunkers for a doomsday scenario they would never live to see. But even then, even over the harsh rasp of his own breathing, Gabe could still hear them scrabbling, fighting, screaming to be set free.

◎ ◎ ◎

He scrubbed his hands until they bled.

The sight of the water in the basin turning pink made him heave into the toilet. He'd done this so many times he thought he might start losing vital organs to the process.

The cold metal panels were a balm on his hot skin. He could still feel the rats, pawing, clawing, scratching.

If he could rip his skin off his bones and flush it down the toilet he would.

But he couldn't.

What he could do was this.

◎ ◎ ◎

He had a nervous tic. Twirling pencils. Graphite was one of those precious commodities in the bunker, one of the things they were running out of and fast. Lessons never involved note-taking. Well, they had, once upon a time. A long, long time ago, when their stores had felt ample and their quarantine like it had an expiration date. He'd kept one in the hideout for precisely this purpose. Twirling. Around and around and around until the maelstrom of thoughts slowed enough for his body to turn them into action.

The radio crackled to life.

Gabe froze, his body seizing with such force that the pencil in his hand snapped.

That wasn't—

That couldn't possibly be—

He stared at the radio again, waiting for it to make another noise, like a child at the circus waiting for a trained cat to jump through a hoop.

A burst of static punched through the speaker, making him jump.

He wasn't crazy.

This wasn't a hallucination, or a dream, or wishful thinking. This was real. It was happening.

He knocked the mic off its perch in his haste to get to the radio.

Sending a quick and fervent prayer to any deities that might have been listening, Gabe adjusted the volume controls.

Please. Please, please, please.

There was a wordless crackle. And then, noise.

It was a phrase, seemingly repeated, but too broken by bursts of static to mean much of anything.

"Four—nine—sector—four—nine—exclusion—zone—"

Gabe cracked the volume up as high as he dared. He had the headset on, sure, but he wasn't positive it would cancel all noise. And he wanted to be able to hear anyone approach if they did.

He didn't want to think of what Moran would do if she found him with a radio. A radio, of all things! And he'd turned it on, broadcasting their location to who knows where.

He fumbled for the microphone, dropping it not once or twice but three times as his hands shook with the wild abandon singing through his veins.

"I don't know if anyone's out there, but if you are . . ." Gabe squeezed his eyes shut, praying for the first time in years. Not to a deity, not to the divine, but to whoever was listening. His hands steadied on the mic as he did the only thing he could think of to do, the only thing that felt right. "We need help."

CHAPTER 32

SASH

Sash didn't know how long she screamed until she simply couldn't anymore. Her voice cracked. Went hoarse. And then, agonizingly, crumbled into a broken rasp. Her forehead slumped against the metal of the door with a dull thud that reverberated all the way down to the roots of her teeth.

"Come back." Calling the words a croak would be generous. They clawed their way out of Sash with painstaking effort, each consonant scraping at her raw throat.

Her nails scrabbled against the unrelenting bulk of the door. It was an industrial hatch. Impossible to force open, especially when all you had in your arsenal was your own legs. She could try kicking the door down, but she'd sooner break a knee than the lock. But still, that knowledge didn't stop her from pounding against the solid metal frame, fists bruised and battered and swollen by the time her voice ran dry.

Fist thudding uselessly against the door, Sash sucked in a lungful of stale air. Staler even than the rest of the bunker. No one ever came into this room. Not on purpose anyway. The air didn't cycle through it the way it did in the other, more habitable rooms.

The thought was enough to make Sash's chest seize.

She shook her head, hair rucking against her sweaty skin.

It was hot in here too. Or maybe that was the fear ratcheting up her body temperature. It could do that. Sometimes it made you feel cold, but other times, it burned you right up from the inside.

Keep it together. You're fine. You will be fine.

The voice inside her head was nearly as shattered as the one that actually made sound.

They can't leave you in here forever.

Summoning that particular thought proved to be a mistake. Hot on its heels was its counterpoint. Its shadow self.

They could keep you in here forever.

Sash squeezed her eyes shut, though it made little difference.

They might just forget about you. Leave you here all alone. To starve or to suffocate.

She wasn't sure which would come first.

Gabe. Gabe would know. Gabe always knew stuff like that. Odd details. Stray scraps of trivia.

Her feet shuffled away from the door as she put out her hands to test the limits of her space.

The room was small and dark, but neither of those adjectives did it justice.

It wasn't just small. It was downright claustrophobic, even by the standards of someone who had lived most of their life in a basement. If she stood up on her toes, her hair brushed the ceiling. If she laid down, legs stretched out their full length, her toes hit the wall. If she extended her arms to either side, the tips of her fingers would brush against cold hard metal.

And it wasn't just dark.

The blackness was so opaque it made Sash dizzy. She closed her eyes, not to fight the shadows, but to allow her mind to embrace them. If she opened them, her mind tried desperately to sort out some shape or form, but there was no illumination for her brain to use to make sense of anything.

It was the sort of darkness she had never known. There was no ambient light that could penetrate the bunker, no soft morning sunshine or velvety twilight glow. But whenever someone entered a room, a light was triggered. Not a very bright one (to conserve energy, naturally) but enough to see. The light bled out of the recesses set into the ceiling and walls, cleverly hidden so as not to be obtrusive.

But light was always there when she needed it.

Now, she had nothing.

No light.

No sound but the rasp of her own breathing.

No one to come for her when she called. They were all in the room when Moran had ordered Misha (*her own brother*) to take her away. They had all watched. They had all said not one word in her defense. Not even Gabe. Not even Yuna. Not even her own mother. Her *mother*.

Heat pricked at the corners of her eyes.

You knew she never loved you.

The thought came so suddenly, the force of it had Sash swaying in place.

She had never manifested the thought so plainly. Oh, she had flirted with the notion. Danced around the idea with a quick-footed grace her mother would envy. But never had she phrased it as such, not even to herself.

Sash wrapped her arms around her stomach and sank her nails into the tender flesh of her sides.

"Stop it," she hissed to no one but herself.

How long had she been in here? It felt like minutes. It felt like hours. Either seemed as likely to Sash in that horrible, elastic moment.

She always blamed you.

Her fingers curled into fists on her lap. She dug her knuckles painfully into the meat of her thighs.

It's your fault.

The voice whispered through her head, slick and oily and viscous. Clinging to the nooks and crannies of her wrinkled gray matter. Soaking into her skull.

You were at the stream.

"Stop it." The words didn't hurt this time. Not really. They brought her back to herself a little. But not quite enough.

She told you not to go out that far but you did. You always did.

With nothing but the dark to cradle her thoughts, there was nothing left to anchor them. Nothing to keep them solid and safe. Nothing to protect her mind from itself.

It's your fault he never made it back.

And this is it, Sash realized.

This was the punishment.

It wasn't the darkness. Or the cramped quarters. Or the

silence. It was all three, working in perfect, harmonious tandem, to ensure that she would be purely and perfectly alone with her thoughts.

And sometimes, Sash realized as hot tears tracked down her cheeks, there was nothing more horrifying than that.

Your father is dead and you're the one who made it happen.

"No." But it was such a weak word. So small. So easily devoured by the blessed dark.

Tell me.

The voice changed timbre. It fell deeper. Got rounder.

Are you proud of yourself, Alexandra?

"No."

Are you proud?

And then, no words. Not even that one. Not even no. Just a single wordless cry as Sash clapped her battered hands against her ears and screamed.

CHAPTER 33

YUNA

Darkness, Yuna had begun to appreciate in a way she never had before, was a blessing. Truly. Undeniably so.

It was also a curse.

Hidden in the alcove beneath a set of winding stairs, Yuna held her breath as long as she dared. And when that proved to be an unsustainable tactic, she fought to keep it as quiet as possible. In and out through her nose, a noiseless rush of air through her aching lungs.

Ensconced in the darkness, she waited for the thing to pass her by. The thing she'd heard upstairs. The thing that stalked the night.

The thing that she knew, deep in her heart, was not human. Maybe it had been, once upon a time. But whatever it was had shed any trace of humanity long ago. Now, it was a beast, twisted and unrecognizable. Hungry. Ravenous.

From her hiding spot, Yuna could see the shadows writhe.

Click.

Skkritch.

It was closer now than it had been five minutes prior. How long had she been curled up under the stairs? Hiding like a rabbit in a thicket from a big bad wolf?

You can't stay here.

The thought blazed across her mind like a bolt of lightning.

She couldn't. It was true. She couldn't just sit here and wait to die. People were depending on her, even if they didn't know it.

Seven years.

Sash was depending on her.

They need you.

It wasn't her voice now. It was Junsu's, clearer than it had ever been.

Yuna unfolded her legs out from under her—quietly, so painstakingly quietly—and rose, peeking out first left, then right. Not that it made much of a difference. She was completely in the dark.

She tiptoed through the hallway, back toward what she was fairly certain was the ballroom. The moonlight that had been so generous with them before was all but shrouded behind a thick veil of clouds, its illumination feeble. Pointless. She navigated her way down the corridor by memory and by touch, her hand trailing along the flocked velvet wallpaper, which had gone uncomfortably moist from the evening dew. Yuna could feel the hairs at the nape of her neck beginning to curl, the way they did when she worked up a good sweat in dance class. Her skin was too hot, too clammy. Every breath sounded like a gunshot in the silence.

Click. Click, click, click.

Yuna froze, her hand on the wall.

It was closer now. Moving faster.

And it paused when she did.

Run, said a voice not her own. *Run. Now.*

She ran.

The clicking picked up pace behind her, like whatever that thing was was working its way up from a slow jog to an outright gallop.

Yuna pumped her legs as hard as she dared, ignoring the burn from having crouched so long behind the stairwell. She was stiff, aching all over, but none of that mattered now. Not when she could hear the pounding drumbeat of its uneven gait behind her, when she could hear it make that horrible rasping sound.

And then she heard that rasping sound repeated. A different tone. A different pitch.

Like wolves howling at each other in the night, telegraphing their distance, their location. The trajectory of their prey.

You won't make it.

Something lunged behind her. The carpet runner beneath her feet slid backward as something grappled for purchase. She heard the whoosh of it launching itself into the air. Yuna stumbled, slamming her left knee onto the wooden floor. The thing—a thing, not an animal, not a person, a thing—sailed over her head. Its claws—that's what they were, talons, nails maybe, deformed, sharp, broken—snagged at her hair, dislodging half of her bun.

The thing hit the floor in front of her. Hard. In the darkness, Yuna couldn't discern its specific shape. It was black against black. Its breath rattled and rasped, wet and loud in the silence.

Yuna went still.

Overhead, a caved-in section of roof allowed a brisk autumn chill into the house. Yuna held her breath, waiting. Watching. The thing sounded as though it was picking itself up off the floor. Its nails scratched at the threadbare runner, finding its footing.

In the distance, another sound emerged, low and thrumming. Like the quiet hum of the generators in the bunker. They were always there. Ever present. Ever on.

But this sound was new.

It grew louder as it approached. The thing in the shadows made a snuffling noise, as if confused.

The sound grew and grew, pulsating. Rhythmic.

Mechanical.

You can run now. It can't hear you.

Yuna drew her legs in close, getting into position to sprint away from the thing on the floor. She was almost ready. She could make it. She could—

A light, sudden and searing, glared through the opening in the roof, capturing both Yuna and the thing in horrid, stark relief.

Her eyes didn't know where to settle. Up, where the light was strongest, to see what it was. What made the noise accompanying it. Or straight ahead, on the abomination before her.

Run.

The thing defied description. Yuna's mind tried to twist it apart, to fit it into a box, a shape, a form that made sense, and she couldn't. There were legs. A twisted torso. Red, raw skin that reminded her of so much hamburger meat.

Run.

The thing looked back at her, craning what looked like a neck—the angle was wrong, it shouldn't bend that way—downward, toward Yuna, away from the other thing overhead.

For one breathless moment, Yuna and the thing locked gazes.

(Its eyes. Where were its eyes?)

Click. Click, click, click.

There. A hole in the thing's cheek. Open. Gaping. Through it, Yuna could see a flap of what looked like muscle tapping against something shiny and white.

(Bone.)

From another part of the house came another round of clicks. From the rooms above, another. And another.

(Everywhere. They're everywhere.)

Run.

The thing reared back on its mangled legs, as if ready to leap. To pounce. To tear.

Yuna ran.

Not fast enough.

She was going to die here. Torn apart and mangled on the floor of this hideous, opulent house, her body left to decay amid the ruins.

You can fight.

That voice was hers. Not a ghost's. Just hers. As she ran through the hallways, knocking into busts on their pedestals and cracked benches and fallen wood, a series of thoughts also slammed into her, one by one.

The library.

The armor.

The sword.

Yuna pivoted, her bruised knee screaming in protest at the sudden change of direction. Bracing herself for impact, she threw her shoulder against the library door, all but falling through it when it opened with far more ease than it had the last time. Her head jerked up wildly, looking for the thing she sought, the thing that could stand between her and the things behind her—

There.

Yuna kicked the door shut behind her and pushed herself up, scrambling for the coat of arms set against the wall.

And the sword in the glass display case beside it.

Yuna went to the case, fingers seeking a handle, a knob, a clasp, anything. What they found was a lock.

Locked. The word ricocheted inside her skull, taunting her. Mocking her.

But wait.

She looked at the desk, overly large. Ostentatious. On it sat a coat of dust. An empty pen holder. A blotter with stains on it, the provenance of which Yuna didn't want to know.

And a globe. Small and marble and heavy.

It was too large for one hand. She had to cradle it in two.

Click, click. Click.

Closer now. Right outside the door.

Yuna heaved the globe up and threw it as hard as she could at the display case. The glass shattered, earsplitting. Cacophonous.

The things in the hallway screamed.

Heedless of the jagged bits of glass protruding from the case, Yuna reached in and grabbed the sword.

Right as the door fell open, knocked clear off its hinges by one of those things.

(What are they? Who are they?)

No time to wonder.

The one in front leaped toward Yuna. The knife—sword?—came up in her hands, hilt clutched in a white-knuckled grip, blood roaring in her ears louder even than the thing in the sky. The thing with the light that marked her as a target. The thing that stole her only protection from *these* things, the darkness. She could still hear it outside, churning the air above, its awful light filtering in through the library's windows.

The smell hit her before the creature did. Pungent and thick. Like spoiled meat left outside to rot on a hot summer's day. Something hot and wet landed on Yuna's cheek. Spit?

The blade cleaved through its skull—oddly soft, Yuna realized in a distant, detached way.

Something even hotter and wetter sprayed across the side of her face.

Blood.

Tightening her hold on the sword—slippery now, wet—Yuna pressed one foot into the thing's chest and pushed.

It slid back, clear off the sword.

The thing outside the building seemed to pull back. The noise—that thrumming whir—faded, as did the light. The library was plunged once more into a darkness even more complete, now that Yuna's eyes had been burned by its illumination.

Praise be the blessed dark.

The words were Moran's, but the thought was Yuna's.

As quietly as she dared, she pressed her back against the bookshelves. Inch by painstaking inch, she followed her way along the wall as the clicking things grew closer.

But not to her.

From the sound of their movements against the floor, nails scraping against hard wood, it seemed as though they were clustering around their fallen brethren.

Good. Mourn him. It.

Yuna slipped through the door, the sound of her sneakers against the wood muffled by the shriek from one of the things in the library.

Elation? Ecstasy? Grief?

The sound was both human and not. Foreign and familiar.

Yuna ran.

She ran and ran and ran, all the way to the ballroom and the hatch she prayed was still open, bloodied sword still grasped tightly in her hands, notebook still digging painfully into the knobs of her lower spine.

Her breath burned hot in her lungs as she kicked the piece of wood still holding the hatch ajar. She fell into the ventilation pit, her shins quaking with the impact. She spared only the quickest of glances up to make sure the hatch had fallen shut behind her. It had.

Even then, she didn't stop running.

She was halfway through the air ducts when she heard it.

No.

No.

It's in your head.

It's not real.

Run.

She pushed herself harder and faster, her knuckles scraping against the uneven metal of the ventilation shafts.

But the noise came again, the same one she'd heard in the

manor. An uneven clicking, like something hard and sharp beating out a broken staccato rhythm against exposed bone.

Whatever was on the surface wasn't on the surface anymore.

It was inside. With them.

The bunker—the place they'd believed for ten long years was their impenetrable fortress—had been breached.

There was nowhere left to hide. Nowhere to run. The hatch was sealed. And the monsters were here.

CHAPTER 34

GABE

Not three hours had passed since they'd come out of hiding, and Moran was already calling another bunker meeting unlike any other. Gabe'd had quite enough of those. The last one had nearly broken him. Now he was sitting on even more information, and far worse than the book. Than Olga. Than the man with the rat. Than anything else.

The exclusion zone.

The words tasted illicit in his mouth. Delicious, even.

A zone of exclusion, which naturally would imply inclusion somewhere else. Just somewhere not here.

But whether he would have the chance to share this information seemed to be out of his hands. It was in theirs, the people who had betrayed Sash, one of their own, so readily. What would they do to him, he wondered, if they knew what he had done to earn that knowledge?

The exclusion zone.

They sat in a half circle. A crescent of familiar (overly familiar) faces stared at Gabe, their expressions ranging from confusion (Lucas) to disappointment (his mother) to oddly ghoulish glee (Misha).

At the open end of the circle sat Gabe. Alone. Sash was still in confinement, and Yuna was . . . Gabe didn't know where Yuna was, but he could only assume she was off somewhere trying to help Sash. He hoped that she did. Because right now, he was feeling distinctly beyond help.

His mother's hands were in her lap. She was rubbing them together, end over end. Every now and then her eyes would find Gabe's and something would pass through them. Then, she'd look away, sometimes at the wall, sometimes down at her fidgeting hands. Either way, it was like she couldn't stand the sight of him. Like looking at Gabe was too much for her to bear. His father stood by her side, a protective arm slung across her back, his gloved hand grasping her shoulder. It looked like a grip that must have hurt, but maybe it was grounding them both. His father's other hand rested on Lucas's shoulder. It was sort of like he was the only thing holding the fragments of their family apart in that moment.

And he probably was, considering how royally Gabe had screwed up.

Dr. Moran loomed over where he sat, her face arranged in a semblance of impartial civility.

"Do you know why we're gathered here today, Gabriel?"

"It's Gabe."

The doctor's eyes twitched. It was almost imperceptible, right at the corners where her crow's-feet started to gather, but it was a thrilling little tic all the same. It was such a Sash thing to say, it probably drove Moran absolutely mad.

"Insolence won't help you now, I'm afraid." Moran strode around Gabe's chair—a singularly uncomfortable seat of the folding metal variety—seemingly for no good reason. She went around the back, as if seeking to unnerve him. Successful on that front, considering the way the skin at the nape of his neck puckered into gooseflesh.

Her hand settled on his shoulder, fingers curling around the slope of bone, nails digging into his flesh—even through her gloves. He tried not to tense, but it was a losing battle. She knew what she was doing.

When she spoke, her voice was louder, more resonant. It projected through the room, washing over every soul with its authority.

"We are here today because one of our own has violated our most sacred tenet."

Gabe fought to give nothing away. But his eyes darted toward Moran, entirely of their own volition.

Deny it, whispered one part of his brain. *Defend yourself.*

Keep your idiot mouth shut, whispered another, probably wiser part.

He kept his mouth shut.

The hand on his shoulder tightened.

"Gabriel Correa made contact with the surface."

A wave of whispers rose from the gathered crowd, like the susurration of wind through the trees.

It was an odd memory, floating up from the deepest recesses

of Gabe's subconscious. He hadn't heard that sound in years. Wind through the trees. What a thought.

"Gabriel Correa . . ." Moran luxuriated in the vocalization of his name, as though she were savoring the hard edge of every consonant. The soft curve of every vowel. "Went outside."

The words were a lit match thrown on a pile of kindling.

"He wouldn't!" Lucas shouted, surging forward through the crowd, nearly knocking Yuna's mother down as he did.

His father tugged Lucas back, wrapping an arm securely around the boy's chest. "What proof do you have?" He shook his head without waiting for an answer. "My son wouldn't do that."

Moran made a quiet tsking sound. "Oh, but I'm afraid he did, Mr. Correa."

"How do you know?" Gabe's mother asked, her voice the thinnest octave above a tremulous whisper.

"In my office," Dr. Moran said, stretching out the words again, knowing she had a rapt audience, "I have a radio."

And then, Gabe's blood seemed to still in his veins. It wasn't cold. It was ice. A roar sounded in his ears, like a train barreling down train tracks. Train tracks Gabe was strapped to.

"I keep it because I have never lost hope. I have never once given up listening for word from the outside. From other survivors."

It wasn't true. She had told them again and again that they were alone, that they were all that was left, that there was no one else out there coming to rescue them. That they were all they had.

"I kept this to myself for I did not want to gift you with the curse of false hope."

"That's bull and you know it." Gabe clapped his jaw shut so

quickly it hurt. What had possessed him to say that? That was a Sash thing to say, not a Gabe thing. And yet he *had* said it. And he couldn't unsay it.

"You'll have your time to speak, Gabriel." Moran walked around the chair again, coming to a stop in front of him. "On that radio, I heard something I hadn't heard in many years." She turned to him so the full weight of that dark gaze was on him.

"An incoming transmission." She let the words lie there, stinking between them. Odiferous in their damnation.

"How is that possible?" Gabe's father asked. It was such a Dad thing to do. *Question everything.* That's what he always said.

Well, Gabe had. And look where it had landed him.

"An outgoing transmission, naturally." Moran paced in front of Gabe, hiding him from the group and then revealing him in turns. "But what shocked me even more than receiving it was the voice I heard on the other end."

She paused, standing just stage left of Gabe.

How very dramatic.

Inclining her head in his direction, she said, "A familiar voice. Gabriel's voice."

His father shook his head. "No. That's not possible. How would Gabe even—?"

"He went outside." Moran bit out each poisonous word. "He went outside and he found a radio. And he used that radio to broadcast a message to whoever was listening." She angled her face back toward Gabe. "But the only person to hear it was me."

No.

He wanted to scream the word at her. He wanted to fling it into her face like acid.

But he couldn't. Not without confessing to the very thing she was accusing him of, the thing that he did but had promised to never speak of. Not for his sake, but for Yuna's. For Sash's.

"And for that," Moran said, turning back to the small gathering, "he must pay."

"Pay with what?" Gabe asked. His tone was a hair shriller than he would have liked.

"Nothing comes without a cost, Gabriel. And this one shall be fitting of the crime."

"I haven't committed a crime," Gabe said. It was stupid and futile, but he had to try. He had to.

"Shall we put it to a vote?" Moran turned to the audience—her captive audience—and spread her arms wide. A beseeching gesture. A move that said, *This troublesome boy is making this hard when it doesn't have to be.*

"All those who think Gabriel should be punished for his transgressions . . ." Moran's eyes raked over the residents of the bunker, pausing long enough to make each of them feel seen. "Raise your hands."

Misha's hand went up without the thinnest sliver of hesitation.

Of course.

That wasn't surprising. Not in the least.

Also not surprising: Mrs. Eremenko. Yuna's mother. Slightly slower, but still, Yuna's father.

Nastia, at least, kept her hand down. Her brows pinched together as a realization began dawning on her face. This—all of this—was madness. And too many of them were okay with it.

Lucas turned his gaze up to his parents, his two hands clutching his mother's forearm. He looked so young in that moment.

So small. Not like the boy who was already perilously tall for his age, who would probably one day tower over Gabe and their father alike.

"Mama?" Lucas asked, voice soft. Scared.

She didn't answer. Her eyes were locked on Gabe's. Her mouth twitched at the corner, as if she were holding something back. Tears. A scream. He didn't know.

What he did know was the way his heart sputtered and stalled when her free hand—the one not holding Lucas—inched upward. She squeezed her eyes shut, hard enough to send a tear sliding down her cheek.

"Mom?"

She couldn't have. She didn't.

She did.

His father stared at her as if he had never seen her before.

"Linda, what are you—put your hand down!"

He reached for her but she shrugged out of his grasp, crying now. But she said nothing. Nothing to explain herself. Nothing in her son's defense. Nothing.

Gabe's chest cavity felt weirdly hollow, as if someone had taken a spoon and scooped out all the important bits.

He watched in a silent stupor as Moran unearthed what looked like a ceremonial dagger. It was long and shiny and had a slight curve to the end of it.

"What do you think you're doing?" Gabe's father tried to surge forward, but his mother—no, she had become something else, someone Gabe didn't recognize—grabbed his arms and tugged him back.

"There must be rules, Gabriel." Moran smiled at him sweetly. "Surely you understand."

What he understood was this: A psychotic charlatan was about to exact her pound of flesh. What would she do? Cut him? Carve some symbol of shame into his chest? Maybe more, if she liked the way it made her feel. Gabe strongly suspected that she already did. There was an eager gleam in her eyes that made him want to cry and scream and maybe wet himself a little.

"Misha. If you will."

Oh, he would. Misha broke away from the rest, tugging a table closer to where Gabe sat as he did so.

Gabe tried to stand, but Misha was too fast. He pressed down on Gabe's shoulders, rooting him in place.

The knife caught the light as Moran drew it, again and again, across a whetstone. Where had she gotten a whetstone? And when? He'd been eyeing Misha and now there was a whetstone. The blade hissed as she pulled it over the stone, her movement slow and deliberate, calculated to give him plenty of time for his dread to build.

"We can end this now," Moran said. "No one has to get hurt. Just tell me where you found the radio."

Sash's voice flitted through his head as Gabe met Moran's eyes. In that moment, he knew the truth, as bare and hideous as it was.

She's lying.

She's been lying the whole time.

Twice he had to swallow past the cloying lump of fear in his throat. It was sour, like bile. He rolled his eyes upward to meet Moran's. She peered down at him, her face the same placid benevolent one she wore during their one-on-one sessions. He made sure to hold that gaze when he spoke:

"What radio?"

The knife froze, scraping against the stone. The sound made Gabe's body seize, the way it did when he heard nails on a chalkboard or metal utensils scraping against a plate.

"You know what radio." Moran's voice had lost the sheen of benevolence. Her consonants were hard, clipped. Impatient.

"This is ridiculous!" his father shouted, barging through the others, or at least attempting to. But his progress was stalled by Yuna's mother and father. And Sash's mom, even after what they had done to her own daughter. The three of them held him back while Gabe's mother wrapped both her arms around Lucas, turning his face away to hide his gaze against her collarbone. As if not seeing what was about to happen would scar him any less.

"He's just a child!" Gabe's father shouted.

"There are no children here," Moran intoned. "Only survivors. And we all must do our part."

"I don't know what you're talking about." Gabe shook his head, even though he knew it was futile. It was all futile. This interrogation. This mockery of a trial. His father's protests as Yuna's parents held him back. "I didn't do anything."

A lie. And they both knew it.

Moran smiled at Gabe, satisfied. She *knew* she had him. She *knew* she had won.

"Misha, hold him still."

Gabe thrashed in Misha's arms, but the young man was strong. His arms pinned Gabe to the spot with the surety of iron bands.

"No!" Gabe cried.

Then Misha held his entire body down with one hand, while the other slammed his wrist onto the table. The force of it sent shockwaves of pain up Gabe's arm, but he knew it was nothing compared to what would come. Futile. Futile, futile, futile.

Moran placed one hand on his outstretched fingers. He tried to curl them in, to do something, anything, to make this not happen, but Moran leaned her weight against his hand, flattening it.

Futile.

"Please." Gabe's voice cracked over the word. He was too scared to hate how awful it sounded. "Please don't."

Not his hands! They fixed things. They were useful. They were *his*.

Moran's own fingers—thin and wiry but strong—pried two of his apart from the rest. The littlest finger and his ring finger. His left hand. Not the one he used the most. She wasn't stupid. She was smart and she was cruel and that was the worst combination of all.

Gabe's eyes rolled upward as she drew in a steady, calm breath. When she looked down at him, there was a fire in her own eyes that made him colder somehow.

"With this blade," Moran said, lifting the knife high enough to catch the recessed light bleeding from the corners of the room, "I cleanse you."

With that, she brought the knife down, hard and swift and merciless.

CHAPTER 35

SASH

"Sash?"

Something rapped softly on the door, or at least what Sash *thought* was the door. It was too dark to tell. Left had become right. Up had become down. Silence was deafening, and noise was a far-off dream.

Sash squeezed her eyes shut.

It's not real.

You're hearing things.

No one is coming for you.

You're going to die here.

In the dark.

Alone.

But then, the knocking came again, more insistent this time.

"Sash, are you in there?"

It was the inanity of the question that drew Sash to the surface of her tormented solitude.

"Of course I'm here." Her voice cracked, hoarse from disuse. "Where else would I be?"

"Why are you always such a b—"

Sash scrambled toward the door, banging her knees into it in her haste. "Nastia?" She pressed her forehead to the door, her palms flattening against the metal. "Is that you?"

"She hurt him, Sash." Nastia's voice didn't sound like her. It was thin and reedy. Not self-assured and petulant. Not like Nastia at all.

Maybe you are hearing things. Maybe none of this is real. Maybe—

"Wait," Sash said, stopping her own poisonous thoughts in their tracks. "Who hurt who?"

She rose up on her knees, feeling at the door, cursing its seamless construction. There was no handle on this side. No lock. No hinges to take apart, even if she had tools to do it. No way out.

"Gabe." The girl who only vaguely sounded like Nastia sniffled. (Or at least Sash thought she did. It was hard to tell through a thick layer of metal.) "His fingers. Misha held him down, and she . . ."

Nastia fell quiet, her words trailing off into nothingness. It was possible she said something, finished the thought, completed the horrid sentence she didn't really need to complete, but Sash couldn't hear it.

Her fists were raw and bloody and bruised. Her skin was abraded. Torn. Her voice hoarse from screaming into the void, but still she began hammering at the door. Nastia was quiet for too long. It could have been seconds, it could have been minutes, Sash was well past the point of following time with nothing—no light, no sound, nothing—to track it. All she knew was that the silence was even more maddening than it had been before that wretched, aborted sentence hung around her like a noxious cloud.

"Nastia!"

"I'm sorry." A choked sob. "I'm sorry. I never should have . . . I'm sorry."

Something on the other side of the door jingled.

Metal against metal.

Something small, something Nastia could carry without being caught.

(Keys.)

Sash scrambled back, away from the door. The tumblers rattled against one another as the door was unlocked. Then the groan of a rusted handwheel creaking, creaking, creaking, and then—

Light.

Sash squeezed her eyes shut, clumsily raised her hands to cover them.

"Get up." Now, Nastia was beginning to sound like herself. Horrible child. A brat. A savior. An angel. "Misha will be back any minute. I told him I'd watch you so he could go wash up and get something to eat."

Sash blinked, her vision blurry. The light burned after having been in the dark so long.

"Come on." Nastia wrapped her hands around Sash's bicep and pulled, but Sash collapsed against her sister. Her equilibrium was shattered from the isolation, the darkness, the absolute bone-crushing despair.

"How long was I in here?" Sash's mouth felt somehow both dry and sticky.

(Gummy bears sizzling on the hot roof of a car. A man laughing—her father—as she squished a handful between her palms. Her mother in the front seat, aggravated, angry.)

"Half a day, maybe." Nastia poked her head out of the small room. It looked so much smaller now with the low, red light from the hallway dripping in, filling up its empty spaces. Not much space to fill.

Half a day. Twelve hours, give or take. It felt like longer. So very much longer.

"Wait." Sash paused the moment both her feet were over the threshold. She was out of that room. Out of it. Never going back in. Never, not ever. "What did you say happened to Gabe?"

Nastia tried pulling Sash along, but she remained stubbornly rooted to the spot. "Sash. Come on!"

"I'm not going anywhere until you tell me what happened to Gabe. Where is he? Is he okay?"

"He's alive."

"That isn't as reassuring as you think it is."

Nastia rolled her eyes but the gesture was a shadow of its former self. "It was only two fingers."

Sash's hand tightened around Nastia's forearm. The other girl tried to pull back, but Sash's grip was iron. Solid. Unyielding. "What do you mean 'two fingers'?"

"Sash, you're hurting me."

"Nastia."

"She found out about his radio."

Something clicked in Sash's jaw. Her skull ached from how

hard she ground her teeth together. "How? Did you tell her?"

The hurt that shot across Nastia's face was unjustified. Like she hadn't done the things she did. Hadn't sold her own flesh and blood out for a pat on the head from a madwoman. "No. I didn't."

"I don't believe you," Sash bit out. Radical honesty. If not now, when?

"I don't care if you believe me," Nastia said. "Let's just get out of here before we get caught. Be mad at me later, or at least somewhere else."

She was right. Of course she was right. Now wasn't the time or place for vengeance. (Is that what she wanted? No. No, not really. Not at all.) Now was the time to rally. To escape. To plan. To find Gabe and Yuna and—

As if summoned, the girl in question rounded the corner, her sneakers skidding over the metal tiling with such alacrity their rubber soles squealed.

"Sash!" Yuna called out upon sighting her. Those long, nimble legs ate up the distance between them. Nastia tensed at Sash's side.

Yuna's hair was in complete and utter disarray. It was so wildly unlike Yuna that it took Sash out of her body for a second. Made it harder to notice what other things were wildly wrong.

"Why are you covered in blood?" Sash reached for Yuna, her hand smearing red across the other girl's cheek. "What happened to you?" And then, when she saw what Yuna was holding in her hand, she added, "Is that a sword?"

Yuna nodded once, then shook her head. "I went up. To the surface. Had to see"—her breath broke over the words as she gasped for air—"if I could find something to prove Moran wrong. Prove you right. It was worse than we thought. So much worse." Another shake of the head. "You don't know."

She reached behind her to retrieve something tucked into the waistband of her pants.

A notebook. Leather-bound. Old. Sash took it from Yuna's trembling hands.

"What is this?" She squinted as she flipped through the pages. Numbers, numbers, more numbers, all arranged in orderly rows, like soldiers lined up for inspection.

"Experiments," Yuna gasped out. "Moran. That's what we are. That's what this is. The bunker. The Cataclysm. All of it. It was her. Lumnezia."

Sash mouthed the word *Lumnezia* silently. The scrapbook. The photo. The newspaper clipping. The mysterious illness cutting a path through a boarding school in the Swiss Alps.

Experiments. That was what they were. That was *all* they were.

Yuna heaved herself upright, sword trembling slightly in her hand as she tightened her grip on it. "The air outside . . . it's been safe for seven years. It's all there."

Seven years?

Seven years?

Nastia yanked the book out of Sash's hands. Sash didn't put up a fight. Her fingers tingled, her skin oddly numb.

"That's ridiculous. Let me see."

Seven. Years.

"There's no time!" Yuna shouted, snatching it out of the younger girl's hand.

"Hey!"

"Yuna—"

"They're here!" Yuna's voice was shrill. High and scared,

but controlled somehow. "In the bunker!"

Sash's throat seized like it might close. She thought she understood. But—no. It couldn't be.

"What's in here?" Her voice sounded distant to her own ears, like someone else's words were coming out of her mouth.

She knew. But she didn't *know*. She had to *know*.

"The monsters. From outside. They're in here. With us."

"There's no such thing as monsters," Nastia said, but her tone was soft and unsure. Her eyes locked on the blood splattered across Yuna's fair skin.

A sound from the other end of the hallway cut off any clever retort Sash's brain was attempting to brew.

Misha stood at the far end of the corridor, his shirt darkened at the sleeves by something that Sash did not want to think was blood. (It was definitely blood.)

Only two fingers. And yet. All that blood.

"I knew I couldn't trust you." Misha spit on the floor in front of him, something like revulsion clouding his eyes. "Can't trust any of you."

"Yuna, Nastia." Sash didn't take her eyes off her brother. He was big and he was dumb, but he was fast. "Gather the others. Get them to safety. Tell them what you told me. I'll handle him."

"What do you mean 'handle him'?" Nastia asked, voice an octave higher than it should have been. "How are you going to—?"

But Yuna was already tugging the other girl down the hallway. She paused only a few feet away. Her brow hardened. She looked so determined.

Yuna grabbed Sash by the arm and spun her around.

"Yuna, what are you—?"

The question ended with a collision of lips.

Sash froze, her eyes going wide. Yuna's mouth moved under hers, just the tiniest increment of an inch, but it was enough to spur Sash to action.

Yuna pulled back, her lips shiny and swollen, her eyes wild. "Don't die."

"I won't." It was a ridiculous promise to make, but in that moment, Yuna could have asked for every star in the sky strung together like pearls and Sash would have promised to have it done by morning.

Misha spat again. "Disgusting."

"Screw you, Misha," Yuna said. She flipped the blade in her hand, offering the hilt to Sash.

That, at least, was enough to give Misha pause. He stopped, brow furrowed, face pinched, waiting.

"What?" Nastia's eyes bounced from Yuna to the sword to Sash to her brother and back again. "You can't use that on our brother."

Sash's fingers brushed Yuna's as she wrapped them around the sword's handle. Their eyes met for the slimmest of moments, but it was enough.

"Protect my sister," Sash said.

Yuna nodded, just once. "I will."

A smile, entirely out of place. The world they knew was a lie. And even that falsehood was falling down around them, threatening to leave nothing but rubble in its wake.

With a grin, Sash called out her fighting words: "Catch me if you can, Misha."

And then, in the opposite direction of Yuna and her family and her friends, she ran. Toward the monsters and not away.

CHAPTER 36

YUNA

Yuna ran through the corridors of the bunker with Nastia at her side, trying desperately not to think of Sash facing down her own brother. Sash, armed with a sword she didn't know how to use. (Yuna hadn't either, but as it so happened, sticking the monster with the pointy end worked just fine.) Sash, confronting someone nearly twice her size.

If anyone can, it's Sash. The thought was almost a comfort. Almost. *Repeat that until you believe it.*

"They're in the common area," Nastia said, her words labored. Her breathing harsh. She shouldn't have been out of breath; she was in good shape like Yuna, almost as dedicated to learning ballet from Mrs. Eremenko as she was.

(Years of malnutrition. Not enough food. No sunlight. Nothing good. The body withering away.)

Yuna pushed the thoughts aside. They served no purpose now. They would only weigh her down.

"Is Moran with them?" The question burned Yuna's throat. Too much running. Too much fear. Too much everything.

What she wouldn't give for a dull moment when all of this was done.

"No," Nastia replied breathlessly. "I don't know where she went, but she wasn't with us. I haven't seen her since the meeting."

Well, that can't possibly be good.

But one problem at a time. That was the only way through anything.

They barreled into the common area like two bats straight out of the bad place Yuna's mother prayed so fervently to avoid.

Several heads jerked up at their arrival. The folding chairs had been arranged in a loose circle. The crucifix pendant dangling from the thin gold chain around her neck was still clasped firmly in Yuna's mother hands.

They were praying. For what? Yuna? Sash? A salvation that would never come?

"Where have you been?" The question was sharp. Full of recrimination. Suspicion. Unconcealed anger.

"Outside."

The bald honesty with which she answered surprised even herself.

Her parents shot to their feet. Her father's eyebrows twitched up and down, the way they did when anger wasn't strong enough a word to describe his current condition. Furious. Enraged, even. "Again? After all that, you—"

"Moran's been lying to us for years. Sash was right." She pulled the journal out of her waistband, holding it up like the smoking gun it was. "And if you don't believe me, I have Moran's own words to prove it."

Yuna's mother sputtered, incandescent. "You write a silly story and you expect me—expect us—to just—"

Yuna cut her off with the most powerful thing she could possibly say. "The air was clean enough to breath seven years ago."

A silence fell among the group. They were each as still as mannequins, except for Gabe, who swayed a little where he sat. Only then did Yuna notice the bandage around his hand.

"What happened?" There were too many thoughts in Yuna's head to keep them straight.

Monsters in the bunker. Moran a captor, not a savior. Sash with a sword. Gabe bleeding?

"Got eight fingers now instead of ten." Gabe's speech was slightly slurred, from pain or something else meant to dull it. Administered perhaps by Moran from the stash of medications she used so sparingly she might as well have not used it at all. "Long story."

"You had to be punished," Mrs. Correa said, shaking her head. "I'm sorry, mijo, but—" She reached for him, but Gabe flinched away from her.

"Don't." Gabe's voice was thick, but firm. "You let her do this to me. You don't get to say anything about it."

She reared back, stricken. "Gabriel, it was for your own good. She had to show you—"

"Linda." Gabe's father placed a hand on his wife's arm. She fell silent, her eyes dropping to the floor.

Mr. Correa turned back to Yuna. "What do you mean the air was clean seven years ago?"

"Moran wrote it all down. Everything. The readings she took every time she went outside at night. The atmosphere, the environment. It was livable three years after the Cataclysm. It's all here. In her journal. There was something about a radius or a distance or—"

"An exclusion zone," Gabe muttered. "The radio. The transmission. They said something about an exclusion zone."

"I think that's what we've been living under this whole time."

"But why?" Nastia asked. "Why would anyone do that?"

"For fun?" Yuna ventured. "I don't know. All I know is that this reads like some lab journal. *We* were the experiment. But I don't think it worked out the way she wanted to, and now she's scrapping the whole thing."

Yuna slammed the book on the table. Mrs. Eremenko jumped, her normally stoic composure just beginning to crack. It had taken the loss of a husband, a mother, maybe even a daughter to cause those discernible fissures. How much more could she take before she shattered completely? Even after everything, even after she'd betrayed her own daughter—the one person on this planet she should have loved without condition—Yuna didn't want to find out. She wouldn't wish that on anyone. Not even a mother who would leave her own daughter at the mercy of a madwoman.

But Gabe's own mother had. This bunker had changed them. Mrs. Correa. Mrs. Eremenko. Misha. Made them malleable. And Moran had molded them into what she wanted them to be:

obedient. Unquestioning. The ones she couldn't mold, she did her best to silence. Sash. Olga.

But not anymore.

"It's all in here. The trips outside. The measurements she took. Air quality. Water contamination. Soil viability. It's there. You just have to read it."

Shaking her head, Mrs. Correa tightened the shawl across her shoulders. It was ratty and threadbare after years and years and years of use. (Seven years too many.) "This can't be true."

Mr. Correa broke—very gently—out of his wife's one-armed grasp. He reached for the book slowly, as if expecting it to scorch his flesh upon contact.

(Like the sun did once. But not now.)

(Not for seven years.)

With trepidation shivering up from his fingers, through his wrists, twining its way up his arms, he opened the journal. The wrinkles on his face—shallow as they were—began to deepen with every page turned, every number read, every word digested. When he looked back up to meet Yuna's gaze, he was a different man than he had been minutes before.

"It is true."

Yuna nodded.

His wife shook her head more vehemently this time. "No. It's not. She wouldn't have lied to us. It wasn't safe."

"Linda—"

"No!"

Yuna had never heard Gabe's mother raise her voice like that. Sash's, all the time. Her own mother, occasionally. But Mrs. Correa was soft-spoken. Stalwart. Not frantic. Not like this.

She was shaking her head in short, sharp bursts now, repeating the same word over and over and over. "No. No, no, no."

Her husband laid his hands on her shoulders—large, with knobby knuckles visible even through his gloves, so like Gabe's—and squeezed, anchoring her. "Linda, it's true."

"How do you know?" Lucas asked, voice quiet. Tremulous, like small rocks skipping down the side of a mountain.

"*What* do you know?" Gabe asked, more incisively.

Two different questions, Yuna realized. Two different questions with two different answers. Both which might lead them to the same place.

Gabe's father turned to look at his sons, eyes laden with something Yuna thought might be shame. "You know I worked at the plant."

Gabe nodded, shoulders tight. Mouth pressed into a thin, hard line. The bandage around his left hand was beginning to turn pink with blood. The gauze, Yuna thought distantly, wasn't thick enough.

"The factory was segmented. Rigidly. One department didn't know what the next was doing. What the component parts were, how they fit together, what they were being used for."

"But you knew," Yuna said. It wasn't a question. There was something about the tone of his voice, the self-loathing laced throughout that spoke louder than all the words he didn't say.

He held his son's gaze but nodded at Yuna's remark. "It was my job to make sure some of the segments were coordinated. Timing was . . . a delicate thing with our work."

"What was your work?" Yuna asked.

"You were an engineer," Gabe said. His voice was hollow in a way she didn't like. It was as if someone had taken all the things that made him Gabe and carved them out from the inside.

"I was." A short, slow nod from Mr. Correa. "A biochemical engineer."

"What does that mean?" Lucas asked, sounding even younger than he was.

(The youngest of them all. What did he remember about the world Before? Nothing?)

Deep inside Yuna's chest, her heart felt like it was twisting.

They had no time for this. The bunker had been breached. They weren't alone. And yet, this had to play out. The show had to go on.

"You told me the plant manufactured medicines," Gabe said. "But that wasn't it, was it?"

Mr. Correa snorted. It was not an amused sound. It was too full of years of hatred and disappointment and other things Yuna couldn't name. "Medicines aren't half as lucrative as the alternative."

"What was the alternative?" Yuna asked, even though she already knew. Deep down, she knew.

"Weapons," Gabe said before his father could. "You made biological weapons, didn't you?"

His father didn't answer. He didn't have to. The way his eyes slid away from his son's, the sagging of his broad shoulders, the shaking exhalation of his breath—all told them the truth.

Mr. Correa shook his head. "Part of my job was setting up safety measures. What happened should have been impossible. It never should have—"

"Unless someone made it happen," Yuna interjected.

Gabe's gaze found hers. They were wet, his eyes. Tears clung to his lashes, threatening to fall but not quite doing so.

"Moran," Gabe said.

Yuna nodded. "Yeah. But look, we have to go."

"We can't," her father said. Her parents were as deeply entrenched in their denial as Gabe's mother. "There's nowhere to go. Nowhere safe."

"She lied to you, Appa!" Yuna had never raised her voice with her father before. Never would she have dared. "She lied to all of us. She's been lying this whole time. And if we don't leave now, we're going to die down here."

Her mother looked at her father. Her hand was wound tightly with his. Touching. Through gloves, but still. They hadn't touched each other in years. "Yobo . . ."

"Appa," Yuna begged. "Please. Listen to me. For once in your lives, listen to me." She handed the book to Nastia. An odd moment of trust between them. But life was not what it had been the day before. It wasn't what it had been an hour before. They were in uncharted waters, flailing their limbs, trying against all odds to stay afloat. "There are monsters outside. Maybe they were people, or dogs, or I don't even know. But they're not just *outside* anymore."

"Did you let them in?" Mrs. Eremenko's eyes bore into Yuna like daggers made of ice. "Did my daughter?"

Yuna shook her head. "I closed the hatch behind me. They were already here."

"Rats," Gabe said, swaying even more precariously as she tried to stand. "I found rats in the water tank. Bunker breach."

"Scrapping the experiment," Mr. Correa said softly. To himself more than anyone else. He shook his head, snapping out of the poisonous reverie in which he'd found himself. "You went up? Outside? To the surface?"

Yuna nodded. "Twice now. And I'm not dead yet."

"It's not possible," her mother whispered. But there was no conviction in her tone. No fire. No steel.

"It is. And that's where we have to go if we have any hope of surviving."

"Where's Sash?" Gabe asked. Gabe, not Sash's own mother.

"Buying us time." Yuna went to the kitchen area and grabbed the meanest-looking knife she could find. "Follow me if you want to live."

She made her way to the door, trusting that they would, in fact, follow. Chair legs screeched against the floor as they got up. Fell in line. Waited for Yuna to make the first move.

And so she did, peering through the doorway to see if anyone—or anything—was waiting outside. The hallway was empty, lit with naught but low red lights. "Come on."

Her voice sounded like a stranger's. Confident. Self-assured.

It felt like a lie.

Maybe not all lies were bad. Maybe some saved your life when the truth would have been too much to bear.

Yuna pressed a finger to her lips, gesturing for silence. Behind her, Mrs. Correa nodded. A fine tremor had taken hold of Lucas's entire body, and it seemed as though his mother's arm around his shoulders was the only thing holding the boy together. Gabe caught Yuna's eye as he brought up the rear. In his uninjured hand was another knife plucked from the kitchen stores. He nodded at Yuna. She nodded back.

You can do this, she told herself as she stepped outside of the dining area, into the unknown. *You can be brave.*

You have no other choice.

CHAPTER 37

GABE

They were nearly at the far end of the hallway, the one that would lead them to the hatch. The main one, not the secret one. The one through which Moran left in her hazmat suit with her oxygen tank. The one that led her to the surface.

There was no need for the secret door. They weren't hiding. They were fleeing. Escaping.

Into the exclusion zone.

A newspaper headline Gabe recalled seeing, many moons ago, flitted through his mind. There were stacks of newspapers in the bunker. Some were to line boxes of supplies, some were just there, gathering dust, slowly being converting into recycled paper (newsprint never recycled as nicely, but they had more of it).

Exclusion Zone Declared Around Chernobyl.

The newspapers in the bunker had a similar theme running

through them. Disasters, both natural and man-made, screamed at the reader from the front page. Cornelius Moran had built this place in fear, and, judging from the headlines, the world had provided ample fuel to stoke that fire.

Chernobyl. 1986. April, if Gabe recalled correctly.

Facts were good. They were solid. They were unchanging. They kept you sane when the rest of the world insisted on going mad.

A nuclear reactor exploded, pitching the surrounding town of Pripyat into chaos. And eventually abandonment.

His hand throbbed. Pain radiated up from bloodied stubs where two of his fingers had once been. He couldn't feel their absence—intellectually, he knew they were gone—beyond the utter, complete, all-encompassing pain that coursed up his arm and into the rest of his body. It was like his blood had been infected with it. It was all there was. Pain and nothing else. No fear. No horror. No doubt.

Just pain.

Which, as it turns out, could be a good thing when your other options were all as terrible or worse.

Yuna was a speck in the distance.

The hatch loomed beyond her, shiny and red. Redder still in the crimson glow of the safety lights. The only door of that color in the bunker.

Almost there. Almost outside. Almost free.

The lights went out.

CHAPTER 38

SASH

I don't want to kill him.

That was the thought that ran through Sash's head as she barreled straight toward her brother, sword in hand.

But if I have to . . .

She wouldn't let herself complete that thought.

She didn't even know what was true. You never knew what you were capable of until you found yourself in a position to make that discovery. Usually, the hard way.

Misha blocked the hallway, his absurdly broad shoulders filling up more space than they had any right to.

"Get out of my way, Misha."

He cocked his head to the side. "Why would I do that?"

Sash skid to a halt and held up the blade, wiggling it menacingly. Or at least she hoped it was menacing. "Because I have this and you don't."

Misha shook his head, his lip curling into a sneer. "You're just the same as you've always been. A stupid little girl."

"I know you are, but what am I?"

"I won't let you get my family killed," Misha said, his arms spreading as if he was some kind of goalie defending a net. "Not again."

Sword aloft, Sash paused. "What do you mean 'again'?"

The little laugh that escaped Misha was worse even than the silence that had dogged her so in the punishment room.

He clenched his fists so tightly his knuckles cracked. The sound bounced off the walls, louder than it ought to. Sash tightened her hold on the sword hilt. It felt expensive, well-balanced. That wouldn't help her wield it with finesse, but it was something.

Misha barked out a second harsh laugh. "Are you going to kill me like you killed Dad?"

It was enough to loosen her hold on the sword. She managed to catch it—thankfully, not by the blade—before it could hit the floor. "What?"

"Don't do that." Misha's nostrils flared. "Don't act like you don't know."

(Light, blinding her. Squeezing her eyelids shut against it.)

Her scars itched like the wounds were fresh.

"He didn't have to die." Misha's voice cracked over the last word. A roadblock to trip him up.

(Pressing her body against her father's chest. The buttons of his shirt digging into her cheek.)

"He could've been in here with us."

(Her exposed arm burning, skin melting, acid raining down from above.)

"Misha—I—"

(Her father's body arcing over hers. Shielding her.)

"Don't."

(The smell of his skin burning, burning, burning under the cursed sun above.)

"I didn't—"

(The long silence. Cowering. The dying light. The weight of a body—not a father—crushing her. Saving her.)

"Stupid. Stupid girl."

Sash lowered the blade.

That was all the opening Misha needed. He lunged at her.

Her response time was too slow. Part of her was here, in the bunker, gazing headlong into those crimson lights, but another part, a bigger part, was somewhere else entirely.

"I pulled his body off of you!"

A body, larger than the one in her memory, slammed into her.

"Mom told me to bring him back!"

Together, they fell back against the cold, hard floor.

"And all I got was you!"

The shock of impact brought Sash back to herself. Misha was kneeling above her, his hands closing around her throat.

Misha, stop, she wanted to say but couldn't. Already, the words were stolen from her.

"It was your fault."

Her hand spasmed, fingers twitching open. The blade clattered to the floor, metal against metal.

"He died because of you."

One hand slapped at Misha's wrist. Beat against the side of his forearm.

"He died protecting you."

Nails digging into the skin of his arm, his wrist, his hand. Anything she could reach. Tearing into flesh. Making him bleed.

"You were too stupid to run. Too stupid to do what you were told."

Her legs kicked out uselessly, heels beating against the floor.

"It should have been you."

His hands tightened around her throat, bruising. Squeezing. Crushing.

The world went dark around the edges. The red light narrowed to a circle, shrinking smaller and smaller until the only thing she could see was her brother's face, drenched in a scarlet glow.

Sash's fingers clawed at his hands but it wasn't enough. Her fingers were numb. Weak. Limbs refused to listen to the commands her oxygen-starved brain was sending them.

This is it.

The words were sharp in a way nothing else was.

This is how I die.

The lights went out. The last thing Sash saw was Misha, but he wasn't looking down at her. Not anymore. He was looking up, eyes going wide, mouth opening in a scream.

And then, nothing.

CHAPTER 39

YUNA

The darkness is good.

The darkness will protect us.

These words repeated themselves over and over in Yuna's head as she cowered in that very darkness, surrounded by the soft sounds of other people cowering.

Everything was louder in the dark.

Her own breathing was riotously loud in her ears. Her heart a violent drumbeat against her rib cage. Every movement, no matter how minor, had a resonance to it. Under the light of day it might pass unnoticed, but now, in the cloying blackness, it felt like a blaring alarm.

Beside her, someone—her mother perhaps, or maybe her father—shifted their weight, leaning into Yuna's arm. The one carrying the knife. Cotton rustled against skin, the whisper of it so abrasive it made her skin itch.

Be quiet, she wanted to scream. Be still.

They can't hurt us if they can't see us.

She angled the knife away from whoever was pressing against her side. It wouldn't do to stab someone in the dark. They might shout or yelp or do something else to draw attention.

And if attention was drawn, she would need that knife free and mobile.

Click.

Click.

Click.

Nail on metal. A different quality to the sound than when she'd heard it in the manor. There had been open spaces up there. Rotting wood under foot. Mildewed carpets to eat the sound.

Now there was nothing to absorb the noise. Only cold, hard metal to reflect it, to bounce it back toward them over and over, around and around until it was hard—no, impossible—to pick out its origin in the silent dark.

Skkkritch.

Something dragging itself over the floor paneling.

Criiiiiiick.

A new sound then.

Metal, rending, tearing, opening, exposing—

Swallowing, Yuna leaned forward. (The saliva in her mouth was loud, so very loud. Had it always been that loud?) Gingerly testing the space in front of her, she moved forward, inch by terrible inch. The darkness was so complete, she couldn't see her own hand in front of her face, a blessing, a curse.

The hatch was close. They'd been *so close.*

But maybe they could make it still. Maybe if they were slow

and quiet and deliberate, they could make it to the door.

With her free hand, Yuna softly touched the arm of the person beside her. They started, a tiny yelp escaping the confines of their lips.

Skrriii—

A pause.

Listening.

Waiting.

All of them.

Monster and man.

Yuna's hand flew up, as fast as she dared, to softly touch the mouth of the person in question. The narrowness of the jaw. The sharpness of the chin. Pointed, like the bottom half of a heart.

Her mother.

The woman trembled under Yuna's touch.

Click, click. Click.

Yuna placed one finger on her mother's cheek. With a light touch, she spelled out two letters, right on the woman's skin.

G. O.

Go.

A frantic shake of the head dislodged Yuna's hand.

Groping blindly in the dark, she sought out her mother's hand. Yuna squeezed.

Take Appa's hand. She thought the words as loudly as she could, screaming them in her mind. Prayed to every god—dead gods, forgotten gods, vengeful gods, and merciful gods—that her mother understood.

They could not afford to lose one another in the dark.

Connection was all they had. Connection was how they would survive.

Yuna's mother squeezed back.

(Not enough.)

Careful of the knife, Yuna pulled her hand back from her mother's iron grip and let her newly freed hand explore the immediate vicinity until it landed upon someone else. A woolen sweater, the weave recognizable under her touch.

Appa.

She took his hand, wasting no time, and joined it with her mother's. Then she took her mother's other hand and squeezed, not gently this time but hard.

Understand.

Touch would save them.

Fear would doom them all.

Down the line, Yuna could hear the soft sound of people moving, trying desperately to make as little sound as possible.

They were doing it. They were joining hands.

At the beginning of the chain, Yuna moved forward, tugging her mother along behind her, each footfall deliberate, every impact of toe to floor as measured and careful as possible.

Yuna's understanding of the world narrowed to one foot in front of the other, leading their procession perilously through the dark.

This blessed dark.

This cursed place.

She felt her way along the wall with the back side of the hand holding the knife. The wall was her anchor, her guiding constant.

Follow it straight and the hatch will be there.

The moment her knuckles brushed against the rivets that surrounded the hatch, she sunk her teeth into her bottom lip. She had to hold back the shout of triumph that wanted to be set free.

They were there.

They had made it.

But then, the only thing worse than the lights going out happened.

The darkness was a blessing.

But the lights . . . the lights turned on.

CHAPTER 40

GABE

Gabe squeezed his eyes shut against the onslaught of light, brighter than any he'd ever experienced inside the bunker. Vivid. White. Searing. Tears pricked at the corners of his eyes, falling freely over his cheeks.

It was too much. Entirely too much.

They didn't know how to handle that much illumination. How to filter it into a form that could be digested, processed, understood.

But closing his eyes was the biggest mistake he could have made.

Something slammed into Gabe's shins, knocking him down. The knife fell from his hand, the sound of it clattering to the floor paneling swallowed by the chaos erupting in the narrow corridor.

Screaming. Only some of it human.

"Get out! Go, go, go!" Yuna's voice arched above the madness, coming from the direction of the hatch. He'd seen it in the distance. Close and far, all at once. Yuna had gotten them there. She was shepherding people through it. She was—

Gabe's own pained shout rose above all the rest as something dug into the thick denim of his jeans.

He opened his eyes, knowing he had to and wishing he didn't.

The thing on him defied description.

Open sores, like the man with the rat. But more, so many more. The surface of the thing's skin was covered in them, like a pelt of blistered flesh.

A skull, mishappen. Half-smashed. A face so completely covered in scars its features were subsumed. The other eye, wild and lolling, the whites shot through with angry red and sickly yellow.

A mouth brimming with irregular rotting teeth, broken, jagged, sharp.

Blackened nails, scrabbling at Gabe's legs as it tried to find purchase on his jeans.

He kicked wildly. Kicked the thing in the cheek, the jaw, the nose, the forehead. It reared back as blood—dark and thick in a way blood shouldn't ever be, like tar—spurted forth. Gabe backed away in a sort of crab walk.

Backed into a wall—no, not a wall. A door.

He tore his eyes away from the writhing thing in front of him, to glance up.

An auxiliary electrical closet. There were two of them at either end of the bunker. Each was connected to the central generator room, the tiny closet with the tangled wires.

The tangled wires Gabe knew were a hazard.

A bomb waiting to go off.

He grabbed at the door handle, ignoring the lance of pain shooting up his arm when his bloodied, bandaged stumps hit metal, and wrenching the door open.

The darkness would save them.

Through the mass of bodies—human and otherwise—Gabe saw Yuna hacking away at the things, monsters, creatures. At least half a dozen. Maybe more. Maybe less. His own father was by her side, swinging what looked like a heavy wrench. Between the two of them, they made a hole for the others to scramble toward the hatch. To escape.

"Gabe!"

His father spotted him at the same instant.

Between them, three of those things reared up. They jostled one another, spittle and blood flying from their maws.

"Get Lucas out of here!" Gabe shouted. "Go!"

Whatever his father said was lost. Gabe threw himself into the electrical closet just as one of the things leaped for him.

Its body slammed into the door as Gabe shut it behind him with a well-placed kick.

The sounds raging from the hallway outside were dulled by the heavy metal door. The light in this room was far dimmer, emanating from a single exposed bulb overhead.

Just enough to see the mess of wires in front of him. And the small toolbox at his feet, stamped with the following words:

FOR EMERGENCIES ONLY

He thought that maybe this situation qualified. Gabe flicked open the locks on the box and grabbed something sitting at the top, something that would help the others escape. Buy them time enough to get free.

A flare.

With his injured hand—now bleeding freely through the bandages his mother had wrapped around his severed fingers—he grabbed a fistful of wires. Then he yanked them out of the wall with all his might.

The small, pathetic bulb overhead went out.

He could do this. Once they were outside, they would be safe. They just needed time. And the things locked in the bunker needed to not get out. Not now. Not ever.

Without giving himself time to stop, to breathe, to think about the absolute madness of what he was about to do, he opened the door and lit the flare.

Orange light pierced the shroud of darkness.

"You want me?" Gabe shouted. A series of clicks and barks and purely animal screams answered. "Come and get me."

And then, flare in hand, he ran.

CHAPTER 41

SASH

It happened too fast for Sash to be able to stop it.

Misha's mouth opening in a scream.

The sound cut short by something heavy slamming into him.

The lights going out. Completely. Not even the red half-light they'd been told for years and years and years would always be there. No, this darkness was complete. Thick and impenetrable.

All Sash had left was sound and smell and touch.

Weight, heavy on her legs. Misha's knees digging into the meat of her thighs as he tussled with someone—something?—above her.

A fetid smell. Rancid. Like rotten meat.

Another scream this time. Not Misha's voice. Something else. Something that didn't sound like a person.

The sound of fabric ripping.

A gurgle cut short.

The snap of bone.

The drip, drip, drip of something hot and wet on her face.

Then, a single point of light flashing in the darkness. A shot echoed through the black.

Sash experienced a slivered moment of illumination, just enough to see the source of the sound. A woman's hand—long-fingered, bony—holding a gun.

Misha's weight slumped against her. But it was too heavy for even Misha's considerable stature. It was Misha and something else. Misha and more.

Sash pushed at Misha's shoulders with all her might. He was heavy, so heavy. And there was something leaking on to her chest, soaking through her shirt.

Blood.

With a wail, she pushed, scrambling away from her brother—the body—and whatever that thing was.

Blood.

Her hand swiped at the mess on her shirt, coming away tacky and hot.

Misha's blood.

A tremor worked its way through her whole body, starting with her hand and expanding outward until every bone, every muscle, every sinew was shaking, hard enough to tear her apart at the seams.

Then the lights flared on.

Sash's eyes closed reflexively against the glare—unbearable, white, hot—but not fast enough. She saw it. She saw everything.

Her brother prostrate on the floor. Facedown in a sluggishly expanding pool of his own blood. The track her own body had made as she'd pushed herself through it. A thing wrapped around his shoulders and back like some kind of horrible limpet.

And at the other end of the hallway, Dr. Moran held a silver revolver in her hand. The pearl handle gleamed iridescent in the light.

Moran lowered the gun—just a few inches, not entirely—and made a disappointed noise in the back of her throat.

"What a shame," said the doctor. "He was such a fine lieutenant." Then she sighed. "But better him than me."

Sash opened her mouth, but no sound came out. Closed it again. She didn't know what she was trying to say. What she *should* try to say.

Moran studied her for a moment. "I'd run if I were you. My pets do so love the light." She tapped the side of her nose. "And the smell of blood drives them absolutely wild."

Looking at the doctor was terrible, but so much less terrible than looking at the table before her. The two figures locked together. Joined by the single bullet that had ripped through one and entered the other.

With a swirl of her red skirt, Moran turned and left, footfalls echoing through the hallway as she departed. She turned a corner—toward the hatch, Sash's mind supplied. Not the main one. Not the one through which she left every night to take her readings, wrapped up in a suit of armor she didn't need. The suit had been for *their* benefit. For her lie.

Sash placed one bloody hand on the wall and pulled herself up, leaving a crimson smear against the textured metal. Her legs weighed a hundred, a thousand, a million pounds each, but still, she put one in front of the other. Again and again.

Don't look back.

She forced herself forward, moving in the direction of the doctor and the gun.

Whatever you do, don't look back.

CHAPTER 42

YUNA

She was the last through the door.

Mr. Correa had tried to stay behind, to go after Gabe, to protect his son, but Yuna stopped him. With one hand on the back of his shirt—and strength she hadn't known she possessed—she'd shoved so hard the cotton tore, but it was enough.

Enough to throw him through the door.

Enough to swipe at the things trying to flood past her.

Enough to dig the knife into the chest cavity of one that lunged at her.

Enough to fall backward through the hatch.

Enough to slam it shut, to kick the snapping jaws trying to squeeze through, to slice at the fingers prying at the open door.

Enough to fling her weight against it, to hold it shut, to spin the hand wheel.

Enough to push them to the surface, up the ladder Moran had scaled how many times? Hundreds? Thousands?

Enough to suck in a lungful of air—fresh, clean, pure—when she reached the surface.

Enough to save a few.

But not enough to save them all.

CHAPTER 43
GABE

An accident waiting to happen.

That's what Gabe's father had called the generator room with its tangled wires, its exposed power sources, its flimsy, haphazard construction. Its illogical design, brought to life by a madman driven by fear and paranoia.

An accident waiting to happen.

Waiting for the right combination of elements. A dropped tool here. A forgotten safety cap there.

"If this thing blows . . . ," his father had said, many nights ago. He'd been walking his son through the machines' idiosyncrasies, guiding him to take care of them, like a gardener with a particularly poisonous patch of exotic plants. "Then we're all dead. Boom. Kablooey. That's a wrap, folks." A mournful shake of his head, the one he used whenever he was forced to bear witness to subpar craftsmanship.

"An accident," his father had said, "waiting to happen."

As it turns out, Gabe thought, yanking wires out of the wall, rerouting power, exposing delicate copper, fastening things together that absolutely should not touch, *the accident this place has been waiting for is me.*

CHAPTER 44

SASH

It was incredible that Sash was able to find her way to the hatch by memory and touch alone. Their secret hatch, the one that symbolized so much to them. Freedom. Defiance. Hope.

Though perhaps *incredible* wasn't the right word. Not at all.

Her navigation was the most credible thing of all.

She'd lived a whole life in this bunker. It had felt large once, when she'd been small. But now, even in the dark, she saw it for what it was. A cage. A tank. A cell.

One whose corners and curves she knew well.

It was harder once she'd crawled through the air vents, through the hatch, out of the opening in the ballroom floor.

She didn't know the manor.

Not the way a woman who'd spent her childhood in it would. How many years had Moran lived within these gilded walls before she was sent away? How many hours had she spent committing every nook and cranny, every closet and stairwell, every window and door to memory?

Sash had no advantage here.

What she did have was her rage.

The night was dark, darker than it had been the last time she'd been up here. There was no moonlight overhead to illuminate her path, no crisp starlight to guide her.

In the shadows, something moved.

Sash paused. Strained her ears. Listened.

Not something. Several things. Clicking and skkkritching and sniffing and snapping.

"Followed me all the way up here, did you?"

Moran's voice came out of the dark, from everywhere and nowhere.

The creatures in the shadows brayed at the sound of it. Their frenzy made the hair on Sash's arms stand on end. But so far, they hadn't noticed her.

"I'd say I'm surprised to see you make it this far, but that would be a lie."

Where was she? How could she see Sash?

"You always were my favorite, you know."

Sash put one foot in front of the other, taking short, cautious steps. Something brushed against her leg, and she bit her lower lip so hard, holding back a scream, she drew blood.

The smell of blood drives them wild.

How much of what Moran said was truth? How much was false? More lies, more and more, to make them—to make Sash—afraid. To make her doubt.

Sash held her breath.

The thing sniffed at her. A hand—too human, the fingers too long, too nimble to be anything but—wrapped around her calf.

Frozen, Sash waited.

"I always did like your fighting spirit."

Moran's voice distracted the thing. Person? It peeled away from Sash, seeking, it seemed, the source of that sound.

Click, click.

Skkkritch.

The beasts—best to think of them like that, anything else was too unbearable—followed the voice calling to Sash as if summoned.

Bodies, warm and wet and pungent, flowed past her in the dark. She remained rooted to the spot. An obstruction, nothing more.

When the last of them passed her by—she could hear them walking, crawling, dragging themselves ahead of her—she followed.

"It's a shame things ended as they did."

Moran's voice led Sash through the manor. Some hallways she'd seen before, what felt like a lifetime ago, with Gabe and Yuna. Most of the path she treaded was new. It led her toward what she thought might be the rear of the building. Through a room crowded with what looked like boots in the limited moonlight. The Moran family's forgotten shoes. Some were large, but others heartbreakingly small.

What had happened to them? Had they been left to die by a member of their own family, exposed to a sun that betrayed them?

"The initial experiment was a success. More so than I could have dreamed."

Against the wall, a rack of what looked like very large hammers rested above small U-shaped objects with sharp ends. Sash vaguely recalled that they were meant to be thrust through dirt.

Above the objects, a black-and-white sign was just barely legible.

THE FAMILY THAT CROQUETS TOGETHER, STAYS TOGETHER.

"It was the sun, you see. I knew what the chemicals would do when exposed to fresh air outside the lab, but I hadn't accounted for the sun. Such a powerful thing. A giver of life. Isn't that just poetic, Alexandra?"

My name is Sash. The thought was reflexive, like a leg twitching into a kick when the knee was struck just right.

Knees.

Struck.

She had an idea. And she found she rather liked it.

As quietly as she possibly could, Sash toed off her sneakers. One of them hit the ground with a soft, barely perceptible thud, but it seemed impossibly loud to her ears. She went still, listening.

A moment passed. Then another. Nothing.

She'd need to be quiet for this to work. Quiet as a mouse. Quiet as a shadow.

Her hand closed around the shaft of the mallet, the polished wood cold and hard against her skin.

This would do, she thought. *This would do just fine.*

Sash followed the creatures through the house, up a flight of stairs, always staying far enough behind that she could run if she had to.

But the farther she traversed the stairs, the more that felt like a lie.

The last step opened up into a hallway she recognized. Sash could barely make out its outlines in the dark, and she could definitely hear it. Could hear how close the walls were, how expansive the ceiling was. How loud the beasts were. How numerous.

Her labored breathing cut through the darkness, each harsh pant sending a fresh stab of fear through her heart.

There were too many of them.

She couldn't fight them all, not with any hope of surviving. And she had to survive. Yuna and Gabe and Nastia and Lucas and all the rest—they were depending on her. If she died, so would they.

And so, Sash did the only thing she could think of. She knew where to find what she needed. She'd been in this room before. She and Yuna had plundered its wardrobe. Had unearthed its secrets.

She'd ignored the light switch the first time she saw it. There was no electricity left. Not in a world that had collapsed, had ceased to exist.

But Moran lied. For years, she had piled lie upon lie, burying them beneath a mountain of falsehoods. Those lies had held them captive for a decade. But now, Sash was counting on one to save them.

There was no secret underwater spring feeding their generators.

There was *power* flowing through this house. Into the micro-cosmic world beneath it.

Sash flipped the light switch, heaving the mallet up for a charge. One good blow. That was all it would take to put an end to Moran once and for all. Just one good swing, aimed straight for the head.

She had the barest second to see Moran standing in front of her desk, frowning into an open drawer, surrounded by what she called her pets.

"What happened to my notes?" Moran asked.

And then the ground erupted.

◎ ◎ ◎

You think you know what an explosion will feel like.

You've read enough comic books, ingested enough science fiction, enough adventure, enough fantasy.

You think you know what the concussive force will feel like.

You think you know how hot it'll be.

How loud.

How terrifying.

You are wrong.

◎ ◎ ◎

Sash's back slammed into the far wall, her head following a fraction of a second later. Her vision sparked with lights only she could see. She slumped to the ground, stunned. The world passed by in slow motion.

How long did she lie there? It could have been seconds. It could have been hours. Her limbs refused to function the way they should.

Dust clouded her vision, but as it fell, she could see the hole torn open in the floor.

Moran was gone.

The room was collapsing around her.

The velvet curtains on the four-poster bed had caught fire. Even now, with the frame of the manor house groaning under the weight of its own fall, she could see them.

Beasts. People. Animals. Twisted by the whims of a cruel and pernicious woman more monstrous than they could ever be. Hurtling themselves toward the fire.

Like lemmings off a cliff.

A woman's scream brought Sash back to herself. With all the strength she could gather, she pushed herself away from the wall.

The scream had come from the crater in the floor.

She inched forward, peering over the edge.

Hands, bloodied and dirty, clung to a piece of fragmented wood flooring.

From below, Dr. Moran's face stared up at Sash, eyes wide and fearful.

"Help me."

Sash couldn't help it. Her throat—sore, raw, aching—burned with each hiccupped laugh. This hadn't been her plan at all. But she would certainly take it.

Moran grabbed at one of Sash's hands, her fingers digging into the flesh of her wrist.

Sash stopped laughing.

Past the doctor's swinging body, Sash could see them. Moran's pets. Driven wild by blood and fire and terror. Clustered on the debris below, snapping at the woman's heels.

Even a beast will turn on its master when the pain is bad enough.

The fire around her burned brightly, heat beating down on

the back of Sash's neck. Moran's hands clasped her wrists, dangling just above the pit.

"You wanted us to believe you were a god." Sash's voice sounded both clear and distant to her own ears, like it was coming from someone else. Or maybe someone she was becoming, whoever that might be.

Moran's fingers tightened on Sash's arm in twitching desperation. Her eyes were wild, desperate. If even a single shred of pity had survived all those years in the bunker, Sash might have been tempted to pull the wretched woman up. She wouldn't have. But the temptation would have been there nonetheless.

Sash leaned in closer, so her next words could be heard over the clatter of metal tables toppling into the crater. The creatures below clambered atop them, their twisted limbs reaching up, craning for Moran's feet. "But you're not a god. You're not a savior. You're not a hero. You're nothing."

"You can't do this, Alexandra." Moran's eyes darkened, her head jerking side to side as her lips curled into a sneer. "You don't have it in you."

Sash spoke her next words right into the doctor's face, close enough that she could count her eyelashes. "My name is Sash."

With that, she let go.

EPILOGUE

DAYBREAK

Gabe's legs burned as he took the stairs by twos. Up and up, past the emptied picture frames, past the emptied rooms, past the places where people used to be.

She was here. He knew it. She had to be.

He had set the timer, checked the rooms. Scoured the bunker with the precious minutes he had left. Tripped over Misha's body. Felt not the slightest ounce of remorse for it.

Sash was nowhere to be found.

In the manor, his mind hollered. *She's in the manor.*

The manor, which was directly above the bunker.

The bunker he had rigged to explode.

He'd almost made it to the top of the stairs when it did just that.

◉ ◉ ◉

Hands held Yuna back as she watched the manor burn.

"We're here to help! Stop it!"

The hands did not belong to her family or her friends.

They belonged to strangers. People who shouldn't exist. People who should have perished in the Cataclysm that had stolen an entire world from them. From her.

But of course, the Cataclysm hadn't stolen anything.

Moran had.

◎ ◎ ◎

Something closed around the back of Sash's shirt.

"Sash, come on! We gotta go!"

A voice she knew.

A voice she loved.

"Gabe?" Her own voice croaked, burned and weary.

Whoever that voice belonged to pulled her along, dodging falling beams and crashing statues as the manor collapsed.

◎ ◎ ◎

"They're in there!" Yuna could hear herself screaming, but her voice was distant to her own ears. "My friends are in there."

Another voice, obscured by a mask of some sort, a voice she'd never heard before. A voice that had, with so many other voices, come tumbling out of a green jeep with the words US ARMY emblazoned on the side.

"Nobody's surviving that, kid."

◎ ◎ ◎

But of course, somebody had.

Two somebodies, as a matter of fact.

◎ ◎ ◎

Gabe half carried Sash up the hill, toward the line of lights in the distance.

Headlights, his mind supplied, plucking the knowledge from a disused recess of his memory.

Cars?

Something clogged his throat as his exhausted mind put the pieces together.

He'd called for help, and someone had listened.

◎ ◎ ◎

Sash laughed. She couldn't help it. They were outside. There was light.

And they were alive.

They were alive.

◎ ◎ ◎

When Yuna saw two figures crest the ridge behind the manor, not even the US Army could hold her back.

◎ ◎ ◎

Three bodies slammed together, not from an explosion or an act of violence, but sheer, stupid, unadulterated joy.

They fell in a heap as boots surrounded them, heavy treads sinking into the mud. Gloved hands pulled them to safety, past the line of lights, into the waiting arms of their families, bundled into the back seats of jeeps.

◎ ◎ ◎

They drove away from the manor and into the world beyond.

They drove past high fences and barbed wire and floodlights pointed inward.

"The exclusion zone," Gabe whispered, one hand holding Sash's. A medic worked on the other, peeling away his soiled bandages.

◎ ◎ ◎

Yuna chucked off her gloves.

"Keep those on," one of the masked soldiers said.

Smiling, Yuna wrapped her bare hand around Sash's. The other girl met her eyes. That gaze held multitudes.

"No."

◎ ◎ ◎

◎

325

◎

For the first time since the bunker, Sash looked back. Through the rear window, she saw it.

A lie, destroyed.

A truth revealed.

A corona of light crested over the ruined bulk of the manor. It stung Sash's eyes, it was so bright. But she didn't close them. She wanted to see. She needed to see.

Her first sunrise in ten years.

The first sunrise any of them had seen in ten whole years.

Her vision blurred as tears clustered on her lashes.

"We did it," Yuna whispered to Sash, her lips brushing against the shell of her ear.

Gabe tightened his hand in Sash's, shaking so viciously she knew that the three of them touching, holding one another without gloves or lies or fear to separate them, was the only thing holding him together.

Sash nodded, watching the lie they'd lived for ten long years burn. "We're free."

ACKNOWLEDGMENTS

When I started writing the first draft of *The Buried* in 2019, I had no idea that a global pandemic would soon fundamentally shift the way we interact with one another and the world. If I had known, perhaps I would have written a different book. A happier one. One not about people trapped behind closed doors, unable to reach out and touch the ones they love.

That was the reality of so many in 2020, and I was no different. Those circumstances made *The Buried* one of the most difficult things I've ever written. And I could not have written it alone.

I want to acknowledge the people who helped me keep it (somewhat) together. Gregor Mackenzie Chalmers, you fed me well and made me take breaks when I needed them. Catherine Drayton, you were always kind when I finally admitted I needed time and space to write. Zack Clark, you were patient when I desperately needed it. My family, who found ways to support me even from an ocean away.

What the world needed most in 2020 (and beyond) was kindness, and I was fortunate enough to receive it from so many, near and far. So for that, thank you.

ABOUT THE AUTHOR

Melissa Grey is the author of *Rated*, *The Buried*, and the Girl at Midnight trilogy. When she isn't writing books, she's designing video game narratives. She currently lives and works in Iceland.